"I want you to kiss me," Lord Wolverton urged. "Just once."

"Just once," Emma whispered, her voice skeptical, unsteady.

He drew her tightly into his arms, ignoring her whispered protests. Emma's lips tingled in expectation as his lips brushed her mouth. Pleasure lanced like sunlight through her senses, her confusion.

"Lord Wolverton," she said, unable to subdue another shiver, "this cannot be good for your health."

His tongue encircled hers, a slow tease of sensation that intensified her breathless pleasure. "Believe me, it is."

Also by Jillian Hunter
(Published by Ballantine Books)

THE SEDUCTION OF AN ENGLISH SCOUNDREL
THE LOVE AFFAIR OF AN ENGLISH LORD
THE WEDDING NIGHT OF AN ENGLISH SCOUNDREL
THE WICKED GAMES OF A GENTLEMAN
THE SINFUL NIGHTS OF A NOBLEMAN

The Devilish Pleasures of a Duke

A Novel

Jillian Hunter

BALLANTINE BOOKS • NEW YORK

A Ballantine Books Mass Market Original

Copyright © 2007 by Maria Hoag

All rights reserved.

Published in the United States by Ballantine Books, an imprint of The Random House Publishing Group, a division of Random House, Inc., New York.

BALLANTINE BOOKS and colophon are trademarks of Random House, Inc.

ISBN 978-0-345-48762-9

Cover illustration: Iskra Design, Inc.

Printed in the United States of America

www.ballantinebooks.com

OPM   9 8 7 6 5 4 3 2 1

For Jennifer,
with all my love

Chapter One

There was a wolf at the wedding.

Emma Boscastle, the widowed Viscountess Lyons, was not sure whether it had been a guest or one of the maidservants who had whispered the unsettling observation in passing during the wedding reception. At first she thought nothing of it. The remark could have referred to one of their host's large hunting dogs or merely to a ravenous guest.

A lady did not lessen herself by a listening to idle gossip. By profession she was obligated to set an example to others and not to indulge her prurient curiosities. This was, after all, the wedding of one of her former students, held in the Portman Square home of the bride's in-laws, not a common countryside assembly.

Several minutes into the nuptial breakfast, however, the remark took on a more intriguing design. She'd just decided that the handsome gentleman standing across the room had an appealing air of

the disreputable about him. Which would explain
why she could not resist staring at him and why she
ought to stop. Sadly enough, the fact that he was
accompanied by three of her own brothers, Lords
Heath, Drake, and Devon Boscastle, only enhanced
his dangerous aura. He was probably a person to be
avoided. Heaven knows she would have avoided
her own family if she were not related and therefore
obligated to offer them guidance.

Her suspicions about the attractive stranger were
only confirmed after the champagne toast when he
turned suddenly and smiled at her over the top of
the wedding cake. She returned his roguish smile
before she knew what she was doing. His perceptive hazel eyes positively twinkled with mischief.

Did she know him? Surely she'd remember a man
with his commanding presence unless he had never
been presented to her in polite company. One had
to admit he pleased the eye with his dark, wheat-
blond hair, chiseled features, and broad-shouldered
frame.

She hazarded another thoughtful glance at his
angular profile. He exuded the restless energy of a
wolf in gentleman's attire—A shock of realization
went down her arms. It couldn't be. Her brothers had
not brought the notorious Adrian Ruxley, Viscount
Wolverton, to Miss Marshall's wedding.

A wolf at the wedding. The scandalmongers referred to him as a professional mercenary. If one believed the worst, he was a soldier of fortune who'd

turned his back on his aristocratic upbringing to spite his father and had chosen to fight pirates in foreign lands.

Emma's younger sister Chloe, admittedly not the most unbiased of witnesses, claimed that Lord Wolverton was misunderstood, a valiant rogue and loyal friend to his select circle of friends. Emma suspected that the truth lay somewhere in the middle of these differing opinions.

Would her brothers have dared to invite such a disputatious person to a wedding?

Of course they would. The dear scoundrels might be settling into their respective marriages, but they were still possessed of the scandalous Boscastle spirit. Honestly, nothing was sacred in this family. Her siblings picked the most controversial of companions, men and women that proper Society scorned. In fact, Emma had been so afraid that one of her brothers would embarrass her that she'd missed half the ceremony keeping an eye on the three of them.

Still, the wedding had gone off like a dream; despite the bride's repeated avowals of gratitude toward her mentor, Emma had modestly refused to acknowledge the role she had played in making this a memorable event.

She was a woman who cherished tradition. Observance of formality almost enabled one to forget the vulgarities that existed outside the polite world.

More than anything she enjoyed a good wedding.

Another breath of hope gently released into stale humanity. The bonhomie. The beautiful gowns. The dignity of ceremony and commitment.

And then, at the conclusion, came the lyrical clink of bone china as one savored a well-prepared breakfast. She gazed in pleasure at the heirloom silver polished and regally placed upon white damask tablecloths. Detail. Lovely detail. It made one believe that life could and should be marked by order and beauty.

"I shall be attending your nuptials next, Emma," her cousin Charlotte teased, appearing at her side. "The girls are taking bets on when Sir William will offer for you."

"Taking bets? The students of my academy?" Emma laughed reluctantly. "He and I have not even discussed our future." Although Sir William Larkin, a gentleman barrister she'd met only a few months ago, had more than hinted at marriage during the few plays and picnics they had attended together.

"Wagering on my wedding," she murmured in mock disapproval. "I don't know what our school has become."

"The best," Charlotte said with an exuberant voice that made Emma wonder how many glasses of champagne her cousin had imbibed. Charlotte was by nature reserved, but one always sensed a certain rebellion simmering beneath.

Still, Emma appreciated the hard-won praise. As

the foundress of a small ladies' academy that was located in her brother and sister-in-law's London home, she took a personal responsibility for her pupils. Those ladies who graduated proudly referred to themselves as The Lionesses of London. In other words, they had survived Lady Lyons's intense guidance to emerge as perfect young gentlewomen.

If only on the outside.

She could not be expected to extend her influence when they left her, unfortunately, and her current pride of cubs was showing quite a wild bent that absorbed all her energy.

"Speaking of the best, where have the girls gone?" she asked. She'd brought her four oldest students to the wedding in the belief one should put etiquette into practice to perfect it.

"The last time I saw them they had just sighted Lord Wolverton and were begging Heath for an introduction."

Emma blanched. Every conceivable form of social ruin flashed through her mind. "And you allowed this?"

"Well, I didn't—do stop worrying, Emma. Heath would never permit the girls to come to harm."

Emma glanced around the room in alarm. "Dear, dear. It isn't the girls who appear to be in danger. Do you see how they behave the minute they're unleashed?"

"Unleashed?" Charlotte asked, startled. "Is that the word that you used?"

"Just look for yourself."

Lord Wolverton stood rather helplessly in the center of the female circle looking . . . like a man desperate to escape. It was an image one could hardly reconcile with his reputation as a professional mercenary.

At the moment, however, it was not Lord Wolverton whose conduct deserved criticism, no matter what his past. It was the three girls encircling him with all the subtlety of milkmaids on the common green. Erupting into raucous giggles. Fluttering their fans and eyeing his lordship as if they had forgotten every subtle precept Emma had hammered into their young heads.

She swept forward, forcing herself not to look at their gentleman victim. "Girls, may I have a word with you at the table?"

Three pairs of ivory fans snapped to attention. Chastened by the voice of she whom her own family called the Dainty Dictator, they dutifully trudged toward the table before which Emma waited.

"I shall say little." She gazed at their downbent heads. "Until later. For now you should be congratulating the newlywed couple and, one dares to hope, setting your aim on achieving a similar state for yourselves."

"But he's a duke's son—"

"Silence. He is notorious, and—" Emma broke off in consternation.

Girls being girls, she feared she would only whet

their female curiosity by adding details of the man's adventurous history.

It was her opinion that most young women harbored a secret attraction to forbidden gentlemen. Not that Emma had ever been so afflicted in her past. As the sister of five Boscastle brothers, she had observed one too many wicked males at work to harbor any romantic illusions about marrying one.

"There are only three of you," she said suddenly. "Someone is missing. Where is Miss Butterfield?"

"She ate too much lemon syllabub, Lady Lyons. She ran upstairs and said she was going to be sick."

"At a wedding?"

"Disgusting, isn't it?"

Emma grimaced. "I'll give her a few moments to recover. And then we shall all make a quiet departure." She cast a covert glance about the room for Sir William. He seemed like such a decent gentleman, a little dashing but mature and a man of principles. Surely he had not gone without a proper farewell. But then perhaps he'd tried and she had been too distracted to notice—

Distracted.

She looked up hesitantly, into the hooded eyes of the man standing across the elegantly spread table. Normally she would not meet a man's regard long enough to make an assessment. But what a remarkable face he had. In an expert glance she took in his well-tailored cutaway gray silk coat and the black

pantaloons that molded a pair of long, muscular—
she blinked in disappointment.

Was the man wearing riding boots, to a wedding?
And had he just pressed the heel of his hand down
on the table beside the plate of herbed sausages?
That would never do.

She *tsk*ed to herself, turning away before he
could notice her. Too late.

"I beg your pardon," he said over her shoulder.
She had to admit he had a deep, beautiful voice. "If
you just said something to me, I didn't quite hear it."

Much ado about nothing.

A decade had not changed the dreary rituals of
English Society.

Having escaped the voracious debutantes that
Heath had warned him would attend the wedding,
Adrian had wandered over to the table and the
graceful-looking woman who stood on the other
side. Heath's younger sister, he thought.

A safe haven in a sea of insincerity. The Boscastles had committed too many sins themselves to cast
judgment. Adrian felt free in their midst to speak
his mind, to be himself. They poked fun at pretense,
and they were always joking, having one another
on. A man could breathe around the Boscastles.

When the young lady rather shyly smiled back at
him, he put his hands behind his back and pretended to examine the wedding cake. His gaze lit on
the row of candied violets adorning the top tier.

"Comfits," he said. "I haven't had a comfit since I was five. My mother used to sneak them to me at Christmas. Afterward she'd pretend the cook had forgotten them again and she would send back to the kitchen for more."

He glanced around. Then he reached up to pinch one from the cake. A slender white-gloved hand buttoned all the way to the elbow descended upon his wrist like a guillotine.

He grinned playfully. "Sorry. I didn't know they had your name on them."

She stepped around the table to show herself. Not that there was a great deal of her to show, but what Adrian observed seemed more than appealing.

Firm breasts like a pair of apples, a nipped-in waist, and the rest looked promising, or what he could see in her gray-green gown with pleated ribbons and deep flounces at the neck, wrists, and hem. She should have wings, he thought. A garden fairy with fast hands.

"They don't have anyone's name on them," she said under her breath. "They're for decoration."

"Decoration?" he asked in amusement.

"It's in the little touches," she murmured. "The details."

"Is it?" he said, eyeing her covertly again.

"I wouldn't expect you to understand," she said softly, as if comfits were some cryptic code only a certain few could interpret.

He folded his arms across his chest. "I didn't want to understand the damn things, only to eat them."

"This is a wedding," she reminded him, her lips parting in astonishment.

"I know what it is," he said in a mock whisper. "I guessed the instant I spotted the bride and groom. And now I know that the comfits are yours. I wasn't really going to take one, by the way."

"Then why did—oh, never mind."

"Boys," he added, guessing what she was thinking. "We're all the same."

He lowered his hand obediently, noticing her lips twitch in what might have passed for another smile. She looked like a Boscastle, with her compelling blue eyes, but most of her siblings had glossy black hair, and hers was a subtle apricot gold drawn into a figure eight on her graceful nape. Her skin seemed as white, as tempting, as the thick icing on the wedding cake.

He wondered suddenly what she'd look like in the buff with that spun-gold hair twined around her breasts and backside. An angel, perhaps, who incited earthly feelings in this mortal man.

He cleared his throat a little guiltily. "I know what you mean about the details of certain wedding ceremonies," he said. "I've been to jungle kingdoms where human heads are presented as part of the bride's dowry."

She looked at him in chagrin. "That isn't at all what I meant."

He sighed good-naturedly. "I didn't think so."

There was a long pause.

Emma did not react outwardly to his blatant teasing, inured since birth to male provocation. In fact, this gentleman had a long way to go before he could truly unsettle her, although she really shouldn't be talking to him at all. But at least while she did, her students could not make ninnies of themselves over him, and he was in her brothers' company.

"Isn't it fortunate," she asked, challenging him, "that we live in a civilized society?"

"That's a matter of—"

Fortuitously, at that instant, the soft organ music of the small orchestra resumed its soothing recitation. Emma could not guess what he'd been about to say and concluded she was the better for her ignorance. The duke's heir had closed his eyes, singing to himself in a surprisingly pleasant, low-pitched voice. " 'Lord Jesus Christ—' "

"This is no place for profanity, my lord," she reprimanded him gently.

His hazel eyes opened in lazy amusement. " 'Lord Jesus Christ, be present now.' It's the name of the prelude."

"Prelude?"

"Bach. The music. Don't you recognize it?"

"Oh, *Bach*." She caught her breath at the delighted grin he gave her. She thought fleetingly that he didn't look nearly as frightening in person as the accounts of his past exploits would lead one to expect. There was no scimitar between his teeth, at least. "I am sorry," she said at last. "I wasn't paying attention." Not to the music, anyway.

"Think nothing of it."

She nodded, staring across the room. His gaze stole over her. Emma only noticed this secretive infringement because she could see his reflection in the gilt-candelabra mirror that hung above the mantelpiece.

How embarrassing. She *would* have recognized Bach if he had not taken her off her guard with his remark about human heads. Her gaze met his in the mirror. Her cheeks flushed with an unseemly warmth.

He smiled again, with an open candor that rendered it impossible for her to ignore him. It wasn't appropriate, the headmistress of an academy flirting with a soldier of fortune, family friend or not. And at a wedding, mind you. It was a good thing her girls had gone into the small ballroom with Charlotte.

If her students hoped to catch Emma in an indiscretion, she trusted she would disappoint them. She was a widowed viscountess of no great wealth but of a stable, respected place in Society. She accepted her purpose in life, and not only as the founder of an academy for the edification of London's young ladies. As the elder sister of a band of scandal-prone siblings, she had offered herself to serve as the moral compass of the clan.

The fact that none of the free-spirited Boscastles bothered to consult a compass and consequently wandered through life willy-nilly could not be attributed to negligence on her part. Emma had fought to save her sibs. Heaven knew how she'd fought.

She took great pains to preserve the family name whilst her family did everything possible to taint it. Take the tall, recklessly handsome man who kept studying her in the mirror. Heir to a dukedom notwithstanding, he hardly appeared to be a man with whom a lady should share more than a glancing nod.

And yet there was a playful appeal about him that made her wish she could kick up her heels and indulge in that infamous Boscastle behavior. A few moments of dangerous flirtation, she thought wistfully. She'd married at eighteen, a debutante, and she should have settled into sedate widowhood.

You're the good girl, Emma, both her parents had praised her before they died. *You're our dependable young lady.* And her father had dutifully married her off to a dependable Scottish viscount, the cheerful, quiet-spoken Stuart, Lord Lyons, who had never given her a moment of sorrow until his death from blood poisoning several years ago.

"If you'll excuse me," she murmured, reaching around Lord Wolverton to the table, "I have to find one of my students who's feeling unwell. Oh, and here—hold out your hand."

He feigned a look of fright. "Are you going to spank my knuckles with a spoon?"

"As much as you probably deserve it, no. Do as you're told."

He did. And she dropped three pretty marzipan comfits into his gloved palm. "How did you do that?" he asked in surprise, glancing back at the cake.

She arched her brow. "One learns to be sneaky when one has a reputation for propriety."

He broke into a grin. "Truly? I've always operated on the opposite principle."

"Ah."

He popped two comfits into his mouth and offered her the third. "Open your mouth."

"No, I couldn't—" He slipped the sweet between her parted lips, his forefinger lingering on her cheek for a moment. Emma suddenly found it impossible to swallow. Her mouth tingled.

He straightened. "You're Emma, aren't you? I couldn't remember at first. My name is—"

Emma bit her underlip, backing away. Perhaps he was simply lonely and desired conversation. Or shy—no, he wasn't shy at all. "I know who you are, my lord," she said in a parting whisper. "You've made quite a name for yourself in London."

"You've heard of me then?"

She sighed.

"I'm not as bad as everyone says," he called after her.

She laughed, glancing back at him. "I'll wager you're not as good as you should be, either."

She escaped into the hall and headed up the small staircase to the ladies' retiring room, hoping that by now Miss Butterfield's stomach could survive the short ride home back home to her brother's town house. To her surprise she was still smiling from her encounter with Lord Wolverton. She hadn't expected him to be so candidly disarming.

It was preferable to make a discreet and early exit. She was a little miffed that Sir William had vanished without a by-your-leave, but then perhaps he had been waylaid by a political friend. William was a true defender of the undertrodden and donated much of his time to charities.

Waylaid.

She recognized his erudite voice, the voice that could move the conscience of Parliament, drifting from the niche at the end of the hall. The sharp report of a slap and the indignant but elucidating outburst of a chambermaid followed. Emma found herself torn between making a hasty exit and confronting the son of prattlement who had pretended to court her.

"I will *not* do the improper with you, you twiddle poop," the young girl insisted. "And I'll thank you to keep your trinkets in your trousers."

Emma swallowed her distaste and turned swiftly before either party could see her. She'd heard enough. She gripped the iron railing and started back down the stairs.

What a bitter discovery. Sir William had seemed to be such an upstanding gentleman. What a disappointment, she thought wryly, to realize he was willing to stand up for anyone, and at a wedding. She could never look the pretender in the face again.

"Emma!" he said in shock as, apparently, he caught sight of her.

She glanced back unthinkingly, grateful that his trinkets were not in view, although his disheveled state spoke for itself.

The maidservant squeezed around him, her gaze averted.

"She accosted me," he blurted out at the filthy look Emma gave him. "Bold little baggage shoved me into the wall and demanded I surrender my—"

"—trinkets," Emma said in a soft voice. "Yes, I heard. I wish I hadn't."

"It ain't true, ma'am," the maidservant whispered, straightening her crooked white cap. "I was only doin' me work."

"I know." Emma glanced at Sir William with repugnance. His attractive face seemed flushed from drink and suddenly mean-spirited, not at all mature. He defended the downtrodden, which meant he'd earned the right to take advantage of the working class? How had she missed the signs? Good manners did not always go with a good heart.

"Leave quietly," she said to the maid. "The day is not ruined yet. Brush your hair and behave as though nothing has happened."

Sir William reached for Emma's arm. She recoiled. The maidservant hesitated, for another man had just pounded up the service stairs at the end of the hall behind them.

"Do not touch me," Emma warned William in a low voice.

"We can all pretend this never happened, Emma," he said carefully, grasping her hand. "You and I have a future together."

"Get your filthy mitts off her," the maidservant said, slowly moving to Emma's side. "She's a lady."

Sir William's eyes narrowed in annoyance. "This entire affair is a misunderstanding. I wandered into the hall by mistake. You and I are going to be married, Emma."

"We most certainly are not," she said indignantly.

She tugged her hand from his. He caught it again and closed his fingers over hers. "Shall we announce it now? It would be a very romantic way to end a wedding."

"I'll get help," the maidservant whispered, jabbing one last pin in her cap. "Don't you worry about this little weasel."

Chapter Two

Adrian reached the top of the stairs and halted in his tracks. After Emma Boscastle's straightforward comment about his reputation, and her subsequent disappearance before he could defend himself, he hadn't felt like standing alone at the table like a footman. He decided he'd done something wrong and thought he should apologize, although he would probably only end up teasing her again. Besides, there wasn't much to defend about his reputation.

Perhaps—he looked down. Had she noticed he was wearing his old comfortable riding boots? There hadn't been time to change. Her brothers had dragged him from the park, not informing him of their destination.

In fact, he'd have left the wedding if he had been able to find the other Boscastles. And then he remembered Drake mentioning there was a card room upstairs for the gentlemen. But no one was supposed to tell the bride.

He glanced up thoughtfully at the man and woman talking in the hall above. At first, by the low sound of their voices, he thought he'd interrupted an intimate encounter.

A moment later, he realized the exact nature of the situation.

He pursed his lips, sneaking back down a step. He'd assumed he had offended Emma Boscastle by being himself and not putting on airs. Now he wondered if she'd merely had something else on her mind when he'd been talking to her. Another gentleman. He hadn't been away from England for so long that he had forgotten the intrigues and indiscretions of the aristocracy.

For himself, well, he preferred a more forthright approach to a love affair.

Emma Boscastle's soft cultured voice rose in obvious irritation. "Go home and play with your trinkets in private, Sir William."

Adrian glanced up in astonishment. He thought he must have misunderstood what she'd just said. So, apparently, did the gentleman clinging to her gloved hand, for his mouth dropped wide open.

"Emma!" he said in obvious shock. "From *you* of all ladies. Don't you remember why we became friends in the first place? You admired my fight for the lower classes. You—"

Adrian told himself that eavesdropping was impolite, and a true gentleman knew the value of a discreet exit. Furthermore, he did not wish to interfere. Usually when he poked his nose into someone else's affairs, a fight ensued. And yet as he watched the scene before him unfold, he knew it was only a matter of time before he was forced to intervene. Heath's sister thought she could control the dandyprat. Adrian doubted it.

Emma's response underscored the wisdom of following intuition. "Accosting a maidservant is *not* what I call social reform, you—dog." And then she twisted her wrist in another effort to free herself.

"That's going too far," the man in the tightly knotted neckcloth said. "Come, my darling. You're upset. Have a calming glass of champagne—an entire bottle, at my expense—with me, in one of the bedchambers."

She appeared to bend the tight neckcloth's little finger with her free hand until he turned a sickly shade of gray. Adrian grimaced. It didn't look well for their romance. Emma might be small in size, but that bold Boscastle temperament clearly betrayed her in times of duress. He braced one elbow back against the balustrade, resigned to whatever would come.

"That was a blow, Emma," her companion exclaimed. "Both an insult to my manly pride and to my finger. What a cold woman you are, and here I hoped that you would become my wife."

She shook her wrist. "If you do not release my hand this instant, I shall break your pinkie, William, and with an unforgivable amount of pleasure. I'd as soon marry a—a—"

"—barrow pig," Adrian murmured as he began to unbutton his coat. He was glad now he hadn't stolen those comfits.

"Hush, my pet," the man unable to take a hint replied. "There's someone standing on the stairs. We're liable to be overheard."

Emma glanced over her shoulder, releasing an exasperated sigh as Adrian met her gaze and smiled at her. "*Oh.* Not him again."

He shook his head. What could he say? He should have escaped when he had the chance. Now he had no choice but to intervene. She had seen him. He'd seen her.

And typically, when Adrian made an entrance, affairs tended to go from bad to worse. Still, he thought in cheerful resignation, he understood the Boscastle brothers well enough to know they would not tolerate any mistreatment of their sister. Furthermore, they had championed him on more than one occasion since his return to England.

He had an obligation to return the favor.

Emma was not a woman to make idle threats. As distasteful a task as she had pledged, she would carry it through before enduring another moment of the clodpate's touch. "I beg you, William," she whispered, "stop making a fool of yourself. Release my hand."

He thrust out his lower lip. "Not until you agree to marry me."

She was immensely thankful for the inborn breeding that saved her from shoving him into the wall. How she had come to misjudge him would keep her awake for months to come. Her personal feelings, however, must be cast aside until she was shed of him.

"Let go of the lady's hand," a deep authoritative voice said over her shoulder.

"Why should I?" Sir William asked belligerently, and then, taking a closer look at the man who strode up behind Emma, abruptly obeyed. "Who the blazes are you, may I ask?"

"No, you may not." Adrian stripped off his coat and handed it to Emma. The gesture drew her gaze down the broad contours of his chest. "Do you mind holding this for a moment?" he inquired politely.

"Yes, I mind," she said, folding the garment carefully over her forearm. "In my experience when a man removes his coat—"

Adrian grinned.

"Disregard that last remark," she said hastily, a peculiar sensation stealing over her.

"Who is this person, Emma?" Sir William demanded, staring up into Adrian's hard-sculpted face.

She moistened her lips, whispering, "Lord Wolverton."

"The Wolf?" he asked in an apprehensive undertone.

She nodded mutely.

Sir William seemed to shrink. "Perhaps you ought to fetch Lord Heath to act as an intermediary."

"Please do," Adrian said with a lethal smile. "It's always preferable to have witnesses when one is defending honor."

"Not necessarily," Emma retorted.

"Go, Emma," Sir William said faintly.

"Yes, do." Adrian stepped in front of her to confront the man who appeared to be losing his own powers of speech. "I'm a family friend, in case you were wondering. You, as evidenced by your misconduct, are not."

Emma held Adrian's coat out to him. "Put this back on, Lord Wolverton," she whispered in an urgent voice. "We're still at a wedding."

His gaze lowered to her in a look she could only describe as incendiary. "I think we established that some time ago. Why don't you go back downstairs and supervise the cutting of the cake?"

She shivered at the meaningful smile he gave her before he unfastened his cuffs. A smile such as his signified trouble. At a wedding, of all places. "Do *not* roll up your sleeves," she whispered as he began to do just that.

She felt panic roil inside her. She had watched her brothers tuck up their shirtsleeves too many times with that same careless disregard not to realize that acts of violence, possibly involving missing teeth, would ensue.

"This is not anything you should concern yourself with, Emma," he said in a dismissive voice.

"It isn't something you should do," she whispered in rising alarm. But she knew the signs. It was too late to thwart male pride. Thus had the world evolved, and in the end all a woman could do was tidy up afterward and hope no one was seriously hurt.

Sir William looked as if he were about to faint. "When did you become Lord Wolverton's lover?" he asked Emma incredulously. "You turned to ice whenever I tried to touch you."

"His lover?" she echoed, aghast. For that aspersion she could have challenged him herself.

Adrian walked him backward toward the wall. Sir William edged over to one of the two crested hall chairs that flanked the niche. "Why don't we sit down together and talk this over?" he suggested to Adrian.

Emma turned away, all but resigned to an ominous ending. Her brother Heath had just appeared in the hall below. In flagging hope she thought that if she could attract his attention in time, she might be able to avert a scandalous outcome.

A vaguely familiar woman's cry, a strange man's answering curse from the upper hall diverted her again. She glanced back in reluctance, recognizing the comely maidservant whom Sir William had accosted, and at her heels a strapping young man in footman's livery. The newcomer was obviously her enraged sweetheart, summoned by the girl to satisfy the affront to her honor.

"Where is he?" the footman muttered. "Gentry or not, I'll show 'im a thing or two."

Emma gripped Lord Wolverton's coat in her hands. Distractedly she noted that it smelled pleasantly of vetiver. And the owner—well, his gentlemanly demeanor had apparently been discarded.

He was standing over the chair into which Sir William had either been shoved or collapsed. Adrian's broad shoulders blocked all but William's shoes from view.

"Did you hit him?" she asked in dread.

Adrian straightened, his brow lifting in bemusement. "I think the sapskull has merely pretended to pass out. I never even touched him."

She lowered her hand in alarm. The footman had hefted the other chair into the air and was bearing down upon Adrian like a maddened bull. "Behind you, my lord," she cried in warning.

Sir William chose that inopportune moment to attempt to rise. Adrian, barely glancing at him, bent to push him back down into the chair.

And at the instant he turned, the agitated footman brought the balloon-backed chair crashing down upon the back of Adrian's head. Emma made an inarticulate sound in her throat. The maidservant gasped, swaying back in horror.

"That's the wrong man, you bloody idiot!" she cried at the footman. "Not *him*. The other one."

Adrian raised a hand to his face.

For a moment Emma thought he had withstood the blow. Then he put his other hand out to the wall to brace himself and slowly crumpled to the floor.

"It's the wrong man," the maid cried again. "What have you done, Teddy? What have you done?"

The wrong man, Emma thought in despair, dropping Adrian's coat. Men were wrong in general, or so she believed at that moment. Male pride and imprudence. Was this to be her entire life? Was there no peace?

She glanced down the stairs and saw her brother Heath staring up at her in alarm. A good man, she thought. An example of one who was rarely wrong. He asked her a question, but the words were indistinct.

She could not manage an answer, at any rate. Shaking her head in a wordless plea for help, she rushed over to the man who had fallen in the hall. She dropped to the floor and slid her arm beneath his shoulders, raising him against her.

Wrong man or not, Adrian had only meant to protect her.

Adrian felt her bend over him, felt her hand upon his. She had light bones and a strong, confident manner, a peculiar but appealing combination in a woman. He knew he'd offended her sensibilities, quarreling at a wedding, but from his perspective, there had not been a choice.

He hadn't been away from England for so long
that he had forgotten there were rules to follow. He
supposed the finer points would come back to him
sooner or later. Not that he cared to impress anyone. He had done his wicked best to distance himself from his heritage.

Emma Boscastle had made quite an impression
on him, though. Unexpected, that. He couldn't remember Heath mentioning her, except in the
vaguest terms. But then Heath was a private person, as Adrian tended to be, and he kept personal
matters to himself.

How the clodhopper of a footman had managed
to attack him with a chair was testament to the
lady's charms. If Adrian hadn't been intent on protecting her, he would not be crushed against her
soft, tempting breasts at this moment.

"Your head is bleeding," she said in alarm,
stroking his temple. "Please don't be seriously hurt.
I shall not allow it," she added, and he smiled to
himself, imagining his Renaissance angel taking up
his cause in the good court.

Or the fiery one below. He hadn't exactly lived an
exemplary life.

He ought to tell her he had no intention of sur-
rendering his earthly existence at all. But a pleasant
darkness beckoned.

Something warm touched his cheek. Her lips?
"Did you just kiss me?" he asked with a half-smile.

"Indeed, I did not," she said softly. "I cannot fathom why you would even ask."

The footman who had assaulted him, the maid, and Sir William stared down at him as if at the end of a dark tunnel. Their faces receded. "My God, Emma," Sir William said faintly. "How did this happen?"

Both she and Adrian ignored him.

"Your kiss felt like the brush of an angel's wing upon my face," Adrian murmured.

"What a fanciful notion," she whispered. "It must be your injury."

He sighed. "I think I'm . . . tired. What happened to the half-wit who brained me?"

"Don't go to sleep," she said in panic. "We shall worry about the footman later. Stay awake."

"I'll stay awake if you kiss me again."

"I never—Lord Wolverton?" She lifted his shoulders with her left arm and pressed her head in panic to his chest.

She could feel the reassuring thump of his heart against her cheek. He was a man in his prime, well built, with a soldier's taut physique. It would take more than a blow on the head to snuff out the life of a man his size, wouldn't it? Although the ladder-back framework of the hall chair that had felled him showed deep fissures that she suspected could never be repaired.

"Lord Wolverton," she exclaimed in the voice

that never failed to command the obedience of not only her students but her family. "You will be fine. You are not allowed to expire. Or to fall asleep yet. Stop frightening me. It isn't nice. Wake up."

His heartbeat seemed to have slowed. Was he still breathing? Frantic, she lifted her face to his throat and listened to his respirations.

Without warning he shifted into her. His wide mouth captured hers in a tentative but deliberate kiss that proved beyond doubt he was more than alive.

"Someone should have warned you," he whispered in a barely audible voice.

For the span of several heartbeats she could not think.

And when finally she did, she told herself that while he may still be alive, he could have sustained a lasting injury. Because he had defended her. A chivalrous wolf. She brushed a lock of dark gold hair from his bleeding temple. "Warned me about what?" she asked distractedly.

He heaved a sigh against her bosom. "That an angel has no business kissing a devil."

"I never kissed you—" He sighed and turned his head into her lap.

Her lap.

Yes, appearances mattered. Her reputation mattered, but not as much as the life of a man who had come to her defense in the blink of an eye—in fact, Emma could not help thinking that the entire situation might have turned out better all the way around had Lord Wolverton not been so hasty to play the hero. "You will be fine," she said as much to herself as to him. How many times had her reckless brothers fallen out of trees, windows, speeding carriages, to their apparent demise? More than once the young demons had lain at death's door. And Emma, being one of the only two Boscastle children whom everyone agreed showed a modicum of sense, and who fretted the most of her family, was the only one to despair over them.

"My little mother," her own mama would frequently call her.

But this man, this hard, solid, handsome man whose heavy weight had virtually blocked the flow of blood to her lower extremities, would *not* expire.

A firm hand touched her shoulder. She glanced up into her brother Heath's face. "What the devil happened?" he demanded.

Suddenly she realized that they were alone, Sir William and the two other servants having wisely taken their leave. "What happened, Emma?" he repeated.

Heath knelt beside her, his face grim.

One did not expect to see a duke's heir felled by a chair on the carpet during a wedding reception. Any person of good breeding would understandably be perplexed.

"There has been an . . . incident," she said as calmly as possible.

"An incident?" He lifted his brow. "Have you been hurt?"

She gestured at the splintered chair. "No. He got into a fight."

"That doesn't sound like Adrian."

"He caught Sir William forcing his intentions on—"

"What?"

"—on my hand. William wouldn't let go of my hand and Adrian interceded."

Heath smiled darkly. "Now that sounds like a duke."

She forced herself to remain calm. "Is he going to be all right, Heath?"

"Did he insult you?"

"Not in the least." She shook her head, her worried gaze riveted to Adrian's still face. "He was trying to defend me, and the footman hit him with a chair by mistake."

Heath slid two fingers beneath Adrian's white neckcloth to feel his pulse. "In that case, I can state with complete confidence that he shall be all right."

"Then why isn't he moving?" she asked in a distraught voice.

Heath smiled. "Ask him."

She looked down into a pair of hazel eyes smoldering with unholy mirth. Adrian's lean cheek pressed into the curve of her breast.

A wolf, indeed.

Chapter Three

❧ ❧

Adrian observed the figures that flitted around his bed through half-closed eyelids. He wanted to tell whoever they were to go to the devil and let him sleep for an hour or so. But it had been insult enough to his dignity to suffer Heath and Drake Boscastle examining his head and peering into his eyeballs while he lay uselessly on the floor.

He'd also wanted to inform the pigheaded fools that he could have walked to the carriage on his own if the walls had stopped spinning for a moment and some jokester had refrained from yanking the carpet out from under his feet every time he attempted to take a step.

He would have been content to remain cradled against Emma Boscastle's enticing bosom until he found the energy to chase after the dunghill who had insulted her. And the other idiot who'd brained him into the bargain.

He picked out her graceful figure standing at the window of Heath Boscastle's town house.

From what he could see of her, and his vision was deucedly blurred, she appeared to be unharmed, not a red-gold hair on her slender neck disturbed, which was more than he could say for his pride.

He had meant to come to her rescue, not the other way around. He lifted his head to speak. A piercing pain shot through the base of his skull into his back teeth.

She glanced around at him unexpectedly.

"Hell," he said. "Hurts like *hell*."

"He's stirring, Heath," she whispered to a shadowed form at her right. "Fetch the physician from downstairs."

A minute or so later a brusque white-bearded Scot stood at Adrian's bedside. "He might be perfectly well in the morning," he announced with little conviction.

"Well, thank heavens," Emma said from the opposite side of the bed.

"Then again," the physician added, "he might not."

"How does one know?" she asked in consternation.

"One doesn't," the Scottish doctor replied with cheerful morbidity. "That's the challenge of medicine."

She ventured closer to the bed. Adrian would have recognized her by her subtle fragrance alone, sweet and alluring like roses after a rain. The challenge from his point of view was not medicine. It was hiding his fascination with the woman standing at his side. His head might hurt. The rest of his unfortunate male body seemed to work well enough.

"I believe he's coming around," the doctor said. "Can you give us your name?" he asked, biting off each word with a distinctive burr as if he were addressing a child.

Adrian folded his arms across his chest and sat up, his head pounding. "King Tutankhamen."

"He's fine," Heath said with a droll smile.

"He does not look entirely fine to me." Emma glanced down at Adrian. He stared back at her keenly.

"And indeed he might not be," the physician warned with a grave air. "If he has sustained a skull fracture, he might never be himself again."

"Who will I be?" Adrian asked in a wry undertone.

"A skull fracture is no laughing matter, my lord. There might be bleeding in the brain, and consequences of a lasting nature."

Emma frowned in concern. "What are we to do?"

"Allow him to rest," the physician said. "Give him his medicine if he'll take it. He looks to be a contrary one."

"Just give me your cursed nostrum," Adrian said in annoyance. "And I shall go back to my own hotel—" He made a face as the maidservant behind Emma brought a spoon of foaming brown liquid to his lips.

"You'll not go anywhere after that," Emma said in satisfaction.

"If he does not rest," the physician continued, addressing Heath and Emma now, "he shall have to be restrained. Excessive conversation should be curtailed."

"Then why the hell doesn't everyone stop talking?" Adrian asked, subsiding back against the pillows.

"Darken the room. Keep his head wet. I shall prescribe strychnia."

"Strychnia?" Emma asked, stealing another look at Adrian's face. He stared back at her. "What for?"

"It's a tonic," the physician answered. "It also prevents constipation. I suggest keeping him mildly sedated in case he becomes violent."

Adrian snorted. "In case? Keep cosseting me like an invalid aunt, and it's certain."

Emma's gaze flickered to his. Their eyes held until he glanced down at her mouth. Her lips opened.

The physician leaned over and gingerly probed the back of Adrian's skull. "Does that hurt?"

"Of course it hurts, you damn fool."

"Can you describe your injury to me?"

"Yes. It's a painium in the cranium, and I want you to keep your twiggy little fingers off my blasted head."

"He's becoming agitated," the physician said in a grim voice.

Adrian glanced at Emma. "She can touch my head, but no one else." She could touch him anywhere she pleased, in fact, but he wasn't so dicked in the nob he'd say it aloud.

The physician blew out a sigh of concern. "Shock, it seems; he'll need smelling salts and strong Scottish whiskey."

Adrian grinned inwardly. Shock, his arse. He had a headache, nothing more. He allowed his eyes, crossed though they were, to drift over Emma Boscastle's sylphlike frame. He couldn't remember the last time anyone had worried over him, but he took pleasure in the feeling. "I'll take the whiskey," he said tiredly.

"I also recommend a mustard poultice applied to the soles of his feet and his belly."

"Ballocks," Adrian murmured, stealing another look at Emma before his eyes drifted shut.

"We can put a poultice on them, too," the physician said in a dry voice, "but it won't do your head a damned bit of good."

The seamless life of respectability that Emma had hoped to maintain had suddenly started to unravel. By now the scuttlebutt of what had happened today at Miss Marshall's wedding would be repeated in all the polite as well as impolite circles in London. The bon ton did love to talk.

A physical assault. A duke's heir felled by a footman with a Chippendale hall chair. She understood how it would be interpreted. She accepted her responsibility for having made a poor association in Sir William, and as for what had transpired, she would rise above it.

Still, as the foundress of an academy for the moral edification of young ladies, she had proven herself to be a poor example, indeed. It did not matter that she was entirely innocent of any misdoing. A proper gentlewoman would not have been caught in such a provocative situation to begin with.

Hadn't she known the moment she laid eyes on Lord Wolverton's charismatic personage that he exuded a disrespectable air? It once again proved that instinct should be obeyed.

And yet she could hardly have left the valiant rascal lying on the carpet. Thank goodness no one had witnessed him stealing that kiss or, heaven forbid, nuzzling his strong jaw against her breasts.

To think she had held Sir William in such high esteem and believed him to be a gentleman. Defender of the downtrodden, indeed. He and his trinkets and tailored striped trousers. It had been an entirely humbling day and Emma would be thankful to see it end.

"Whatever am I supposed to tell the girls?" her cousin and trusted assistant Miss Charlotte Boscastle asked outside the private bedchamber designated for Lord Wolverton's recuperation. In recent weeks, the upper-floor room had been used as an evening office or sickroom when one of the academy's students took ill. Ofttimes Charlotte escaped there for the quiet to write.

Emma paused to catch her breath. She'd scarcely been able to think the whole time she had stood at Lord Wolverton's bedside. How a man could sustain such a devastating blow and yet manage to disconcert those around him was past explanation.

Even now she flushed at the thought of his impudent hazel eyes as he studied her from his bed. Clearing her throat, she realized that her cousin was awaiting a reply. The girl was too beautiful for her own good and observant to a fault.

Furthermore, she was a Boscastle, a flaxen-haired, blue-eyed member of the family, and as such, totally trustworthy and worthy of worrying about.

"Tell the girls as little as possible of this incident, Charlotte."

"Easy for you to say," Charlotte retorted. "The young imps have been practically crawling up the curtains for a peek at the duke's heir. I for one feel like murdering the lot of them."

"How vulgar," Emma murmured. "Perhaps I'll ask Heath to have bolts installed on all doors that give access to Lord Wolverton's room."

"That would be better than him awakening with a dozen schoolgirls at the foot of his bed," Charlotte agreed.

Emma sighed. What a trial upon her soul, to gently usher these willful unweds into the arms of some respectable husband. In this, Emma harbored no illusions. While she might wish otherwise, her academy existed for no better purpose than the blatant procurement of a good marriage for her students. Ah, well. Upon such a foundation lay the future of England.

She ushered Charlotte toward the staircase. "Have a stern talk with the girls before evening prayers."

"Good idea." Charlotte paused. "You do not think Lord Wolverton would—well, wander off himself?"

"Wander off?" Emma asked, her voice rising at what her cousin was suggesting. A wolf wandering off.

"And fall down the stairs," Charlotte added hastily. Still, her solicitous look only underscored that she was not concerned about his lordship taking a tumble in the dark. A tumble in some young woman's bed was what she'd meant.

"A nocturnal foray is highly unlikely in his condition," Emma said. "He has been given a sedative and will have to be observed throughout the night for signs that his symptoms do not worsen."

"What exactly are his symptoms?" Charlotte asked.

Immoderate masculinity. Abundant charm. A wicked tongue and temper.

"His lordship has suffered a severe laceration of the scalp and is complaining of blurred vision and hammering headache."

"The poor man could still die," Charlotte said

in sympathy, then added, "although it strains the imagination to think of one so virile being felled by a chair."

"Greater men have been brought down by far less, I assure you. Furthermore, his virility is hardly the issue at stake."

Charlotte appeared to fight a smile.

"I would appreciate it," Emma continued, subduing her own smile as she swept down the stairs, "if you would alert the staff to be on guard against gossipmongers. I shall be more than occupied with the current crisis as it is."

"I'll say." Charlotte trailed after her. "Shouldn't one of us watch him through the night?"

"Heath and Julia have offered to take turns with me. This is an uncommon emergency one does not encounter in the etiquette books."

Charlotte's brow knitted in a frown. "You don't think we shall have to close the school?"

"I haven't thought past tomorrow. We can only hope that whatever scandal ensues will blow over without bringing us down with it."

"We could always move to the country," Charlotte said in hesitation. "I realize we are still short of funds, but—"

"And let Lady Clipstone think that she has driven us away?" Emma's face darkened at the thought of admitting defeat to her rival in London, Lady Alice Clipstone, who had opened an academy in Hanover Square and who was unabashedly trying to steal

Emma's students. She and Alice had been friends once and were now sworn enemies in etiquette. Which meant that, as politely as possible, they never missed an opportunity to best the other. "She won't wait long to take advantage, I tell you."

Charlotte glanced away uncomfortably. "She hasn't waited at all."

"What are you saying?"

"Do you remember Lady Coralie?"

"The earl's young niece?" Emma asked slowly. The earl whom she had been courting forever for patronage. His niece had been expected to enter the academy a week ago. Two of the lady's younger sisters were supposed to follow a few months later. "Her baggage was due to arrive this week. I have a bed in readiness for her arrival."

"Apparently, she is reconsidering," Charlotte said. "She'll inform us as soon as she decides."

"How do you know this?" Emma demanded quietly.

"Our butler's sister has gone to work for Lady Clipstone."

"To work for my rival?" Emma allowed a note of mild indignation to deepen her voice. "Well, I never. She'll be threatening to expose our secrets next."

"You have no secrets, Emma," Charlotte said with a consoling smile.

"I didn't until today, but—oh, dear, I don't suppose that Lord Wolverton's presence can be kept secret."

"He is a little large to hide away."

Emma shook her head. "Still, we shall have to keep the girls removed from him and carry on as if nothing has changed. Thank goodness their wing is on the other side of the house."

"We should be able to manage."

"It's only for two days," Emma murmured. "Good heavens, if I can tame the lionesses I should be more than able to take care of one wounded gentleman."

Adrian pretended to be asleep the three times Heath Boscastle crept into the bedchamber to check on him. He suspected that his light snores did not deceive Heath for a moment, but he had a splitting pain in his skull and was in no temper for conversation.

He *was* almost asleep when Heath's wife Julia tiptoed in with an older maidservant to place a fresh poultice on his scalp. And after that, with the warm herbal unguent dripping down his neck, he could not sleep at all. Disgruntled, he flung off the covers, found flint and tinder to light a candle, and noticed the leather-bound lady's journal on the chest of drawers opposite the bed.

"Well, well," he muttered. "All I need is a lacy nightcap and pair of dentures and I could pass as my own grandmother."

He opened the book, yawning, and settled back into bed to read. He could have told the old sawbones Scot that it would take an entire bottle of lau-

danum to knock out a man of Adrian's size. Not
that he'd needed a sedative, anyway. There was nothing wrong with his head but a deep bruise. He'd
suffered worse.

He started to read. It was a handwritten journal
penned in tidy, feminine script, the subject being—

He blinked. The words jumped about the page
before he could see them properly. Ah.

Winter 1815
 The gypsy fortune-teller at the ball tonight pre-
dicted I would meet my true love within the year.
Of course, she wasn't a genuine Romany. It was
only Miranda Forester dressed in disguise again,
and I doubt she could predict my next dance, let
alone whom I shall love.
 But I predict that it is dear Emma who shall be
wed ere the year's end—I have seen the way she
dotes on Grayson's baby and remember how
once she dreamed of her own children—

The dressing room door that led to the bedchamber opened. By damn, if it was Heath acting mother
hen again, and he caught Adrian reading a young
girl's love secrets, he would never hear the end of
it. He leapt up from the bed, sending the rosette-
embroidered coverlet flying in the air.

With only a moment to spare he vaulted over a
footstool and wedged the journal between the other
books piled upon the chest of drawers. Then, school-

ing his face into an expression of startled innocence, he faced the figure who hesitated on the threshold behind him. For an instant neither said a word. He merely savored the unfamiliar thrill that chased down his spine.

It was her. At last. He gazed into her eyes, waiting in anticipation. His little caretaker, in a high-buttoned blue-gray dressing gown, but with her hair cascading about her shoulders in an apricot gold cloud like a heavenly halo.

Or was it two haloes? he wondered. Suddenly it appeared that his angel of mercy had sprouted another head. Another face. Yet even though his vision was blurred, there was no mistaking the concerned frown on her fine-boned face.

Nor the warm familiarity of her voice, the cultured notes penetrating into the deepest recesses of his pounding skull. "Lord Wolverton, what folly is this?" she asked in exasperation. "What were you doing? You may *not* walk about in your condition."

"I was"—he glanced guiltily at the journal that protruded from the stack of ill-heaped books where he'd stuck it—"searching for the chamberpot."

"We certainly do not keep it upon the bureau." She marched into the room, her finger pointing at the four-poster. "Get back into bed so that I may summon a footman to assist you in your private needs."

Well, *that* was an embarrassment. "I can help

myself," he said, then swayed forward several feet, whereby he was forced to grab the bedpost to steady himself.

"You most assuredly cannot." She hurried to his side, offering her shoulder for support. "You're flapping about like a wounded butterfly."

"A butterfly?" he asked, snorting.

"And with a candle lit," she scolded him. "In your condition. Do you wish to set the house on fire?"

She guided him to the side of the bed, a humiliation he endured only because it gave him another chance to be closer to her. He did, however, refuse to sit at her urging. He was a fully grown man, not a bloody butterfly. He had not personally answered to anyone in years. He had no intention of allowing this bit of silk and satin, even if she was a Boscastle, to give him orders.

"I don't want to get into bed again."

"Get into that bed," she said.

"I shall do so only when and if I please."

Emma steeled her spine. She knew what he was about. Charming when he chose, belligerent when he didn't get his own way. To think he would represent the aristocracy as a peer of the realm, for no matter what the circumstances of his return, he was by law a duke's firstborn and would inherit.

"Physical and emotional strain will not heal your head wound," she said briskly. "Get under those covers right now."

He stood his ground, smiling at her in challenge. The woman thought to master him? "Did you hear what *I* just said?" he asked her.

"It is difficult not to when you are growling in my face," she replied evenly.

He reclined suddenly on the bed. Not because this deceptively demure-looking gentlewoman so ordered him, but because he was overcome by an unexpected wave of dizziness.

"Growling?" He frowned darkly at her. "I'm barely talking above a whisper. If I really wanted to growl, I could bring down the walls."

"I have no doubt of that." She snapped the coverlet over his shoulders, apparently not intimidated by his assertion. "But what would you prove by such an ill-mannered display? You'd only end up making your head ache all the more. It's not me you'll punish but yourself."

He wasn't sure how it happened, but suddenly he found himself tucked back into bed, with Emma standing at his side, looking uncharitably satisfied and all the more irresistible for what she'd accomplished. The most puzzling, if not humiliating, part of the situation was that he half enjoyed how she fussed over him. It wasn't the usual attention he drew from a woman, but it pleased him, nonetheless. Naturally, it also led his mind to consider what other pleasures she might offer to console him.

"Why do you and your brother insist on waking me up every hour?" he asked, studying her closely.

"The physician instructed us to keep watch over you."

"Why?" he asked in a surly voice, curious to see whether he could unnerve her. The few ladies he'd encountered in London who weren't afraid to associate with him seemed intrigued by his past, not to mention his inheritance.

Emma was a more difficult one to decipher. "We're checking you for confusion," she replied. "Changes in temperament and so on."

He grunted. "Really. And how the devil would you know, may I ask?"

She plumped the pillows up behind his shoulders. He'd be spoon-fed next and taken out in a chair to the garden. "How would I know what?"

"Whether my temperament has changed or not." He burrowed his shoulders deeper into the pillows, forcing her to work harder to arrange them. He didn't fool her, either. She gave him a quick, cross look before she leaned against his chest to finish. He drew a breath and felt his damned cock growing hard at her nearness. He'd not had sex with a woman, let alone found one attractive, for so long, he'd begun to wonder if something was wrong with him. Emma Boscastle, bless her, quite pleasantly disabused him of that disturbing concern.

She forced her voice into a patient tone even though she was clenching her teeth. "For one thing, you seemed quite reasonable today before your foolhardy act of bravery. I expect you're regretting the impulse now."

"On the contrary. I only wish I'd hit the other man before he got away."

"You shouldn't work yourself into a state."

"I shall work myself into whatever state I feel like, and you're not going to stop me."

Her pretty mouth firmed. "The physician said you would be restrained if you did not rest."

"It would take more than that bearded bag of oats to keep me down."

"I do have brothers," she said, narrowing her eyes.

That gave him pause.

But not for long. He was not a man to dwell upon his obstacles, only their overcoming.

"Have you ever restrained a man before?" he asked, dubiously eyeing her slight figure.

"Yes. Those brothers I just mentioned."

"Recently?"

"Don't be silly. They are all grown men, even if they don't always act it." Her gaze met his. He glimpsed a spirit quite ruthless indeed beneath her ladylike appearance. "Your family is still in England?" she asked unexpectedly.

He thought of the journal entry he had just read. She had wanted a family of her own, it said. "Yes."

She waited. "Well, is there anyone I should contact about your condition?"

"I have come closer to death's door than a dozen

men," he said dryly. "The incident today does not merit alarm."

"Your family might not agree."

"I have a brother and sister in Berkshire," he offered with a thin smile.

She waited again, aware he had deliberately evaded a complete answer. What little gossip she knew of him was that he had been estranged some years ago from his father, the Duke of Scarfield, who had mistakenly believed Adrian to be the result of his young wife's adulterous love affair. Now, apparently, the duke had admitted he misjudged his late wife and had asked his son to come home.

Adrian's return after an adventurous stint as an officer for the East India Company and other private irregular armies had been assumed by Society to be a sign of reconciliation.

His manner hinted otherwise.

"I think I should leave you to rest, my lord."

"No." His voice was imperious, but his eyes darkened as if to reveal a vulnerability.

She shook her head in bemusement. "You did get the sense knocked out of you today."

He stared at her.

He had never before wanted to undress a woman more than he wanted to undress Emma Boscastle. Strip her naked from her graceful white neck to small feet. Give her a genuine reason to bemoan his lack of manners.

"If you think I'm lying abed for two days, then you have another thing coming," he added.

"Gentlemen seldom suffer their indispositions with good humor."

"Do I have to suffer alone?" he asked in a low, sensual voice.

"Would you like Devon and Drake to sleep beside you?" She stared back at him with a straight face. "I'm sure it could be arranged if you don't wish to be alone."

His mouth curled into a beguiling grin. "I had another arrangement in mind. Kiss me before you go."

"For heaven's sake!"

"You're tempted. I can tell."

She lowered her face to his. "And you're delirious. At least that is the excuse I am using for your behavior."

He regardly her calmly. "I'm a very accepting man, Emma."

She drew her breath at his astounding confidence. "Then accept this—you are staying in bed. Alone."

"A shame."

Their gazes locked a silent battle of wills until Emma realized how absurd it was to allow him to unnerve her. He had been born with a duke's arrogance whether, as rumor went, he accepted the responsibility of his title or not. Well, Emma was the eldest daughter of a no-less-arrogant marquess. If she could hold her own with the Boscastles, she would remain steady on her feet before their friend.

One also had to make allowances for his head injury. Perhaps it would help to think of Lord Wolverton as one of her charges, a person of unrealized potential who needed but a rigorous polishing to shine.

"Now," she said, sternly but not unkindly, "I want you to stay under these covers and have a nice rest. Everything will look better in the morning."

"No, it won't."

She sighed. "Then it won't."

"What if I should require your assistance during the night?"

"It seems quite unlikely. There is, however, a bell on the nightstand for you to summon help."

He reached up and caught her under the elbows. "Now what are you doing?" she asked indignantly.

"Summoning your help."

He drew her down to lie beside him on the bed, testing the very limits of her patience. For a mortifying interval she found herself too overwhelmed by the unexpected intimacy of his hard, lithe-muscled body against hers to do anything but breathe. "What are you doing?" she asked again.

His mouth pressed against her ear.

"I thought you were going to fall," he said in an undertone, shifting his steely frame to settle her onto the side of the bed.

"Yes. Right from the pot into the fire."

His eyes glittered at her in the candlelight. From fever? From pain? Or from something that she'd do best not to identify?

"Lord Wolverton," she said with a sigh. "You are making this difficult."

"That man was wrong today," he said quietly.

Her heart beat in fierce reaction against her ribs. The emotion in his eyes disarmed her. With the exception of her brothers, the men she knew rarely revealed themselves with such candor. "I don't know what you're taking about. I don't think I *want* to know. That blow on the head—"

"You aren't cold at all." His knowing gaze flickered over her. "There are secret fires inside you, Emma."

She blushed at this foolishness. "Don't be—"

"—honest?" He leaned forward to capture her face in his hands. "Kiss me once and I shall prove it. Humor me if nothing else."

Chapter Four

✦

Secret fires, indeed. A kiss to humor him. That horrible insult today. It was more than enough for a day. Yet as his calloused thumbs sculpted her cheekbones, then traced the shape of her jaw, the flames to which he alluded rose steadily inside her. Her body burned. Her nipples contracted, and a pleasing vulnerability pervaded her limbs.

"Warm," he said, lowering his hard, unsmiling face to hers. "And warmer still. If you turned to ice when he tried to touch you, then the fault is in him, not you."

How did he know? How could he dare? She dropped her gaze, held her breath, and waited. Aching in shame, in surprise, in hungry anticipation. At any moment this would end. She would tear herself from this beautiful temptation. It surprised her how Sir William's cutting remark had hurt her. She did not wish to be thought of as cold, and yet she knew it was often how she appeared.

But secret fires—oh, why did women enjoy such

flattery? Why did something in her respond to this man?

"You look even more like an angel with your hair let down," he mused. "I couldn't take my eyes off you at the wedding."

She swallowed, her throat aching. "I look . . . untidy now."

"You made me—" He hesitated.

"I made you what?" she whispered.

"You made me laugh today," he said quietly.

"I did what?" she asked, her voice startled.

"I meant that you put me at ease and I enjoyed your company."

His answer soothed as well as surprised her.

"I was merely being polite."

"You stole three comfits from a wedding cake," he reminded her, smiling.

"Don't you dare tell my family. I'm . . . I'm the good one."

"Are you?"

His strong fingers sifted through the pale hair that framed her face. The gentle seduction of this simple act mesmerized her. She was not a woman easily, if ever, tempted by the sensual. She would allow this novel pleasure to continue for only a moment more. Yet how good his touch felt, how it lowered her guard.

"There's even fire in your hair," he said, his breath warming her lips. "It's like gold silk. And deep inside, I've always been attracted to fire. Are you a dangerous woman, Emma Boscastle?" he asked lazily.

"Lord Wolverton," she said with a sigh. Wolf.

"Stay with me awhile," he said, his gaze holding hers.

"I can't. We both know that."

"Only a few moments more. I detest this inactivity. I detest being alone. That's all I ask."

He reached behind him and snuffed out the candle between his thumb and forefinger. Emma breathed in the pleasingly mingled scent of his cologne and the tang of smoke that wafted toward the bed.

Terrifying. Thrilling. The ordinary act of extinguishing a candle, performed as if he had done so a hundred times in a similar scenario. But so effective. Shadows engulfed them. She sensed him relax, his powerful muscles untensing. Felt his masculine hands close around her waist. Her breath hitched. Pure male. Mystery, strength, and temptation. He was afraid of being alone.

The sudden darkness lowered inhibitions. How many times had Emma warned others to sidestep shadows, and the men who dwelled, beckoned therein? She hovered now, on the verge herself. And if her principles were being put to the test?

"You were married," he said quietly. His hand idly stroked her arm, his fingers possessive, knowing.

His firm lips teased hers, captured her sigh. "Yes."

Slowly he brought his other hand up her side to the silken undercurve of her breast. She quivered, went still, prepared to resist. The hollow between her thighs began to throb. "How long has it been?" he whispered in a gentle voice.

"Are you asking me—"

"Yes."

She arched her neck, afraid her nerves would shatter. No one else in the world had ever asked, would have dared to ask a question that intimate of her. She did not understand why his curiosity was not offensive. It seemed natural. Again she blamed the dark of the night, his indisposition.

"My husband died almost five years ago," she answered against the warm hollow of his neck.

His other arm tightened around her waist in a possessive male gesture that sent a shiver of longing through the depths of her body.

"Five years," he murmured. "And no one's touched you since? How can that be?"

"Please," she whispered, swallowed dryly. The heat in her belly intensified until it hurt. How his voice enticed her.

"It must be your choice," he mused. "Other men have tried, haven't they? That dandyprat today."

She couldn't answer, could barely breathe. And he understood. He told her as much with a touch that moved over her trembling skin, half consola-

tion, half warrior's conquest. No one else had presumed as much until today. Panic and desire mingled
deep inside her.

The worst part of what he'd said was that the absence of love, of passion, in her life had seemed
bearable until now. Oh, she'd suffered the lack, but
a lady would not acknowledge it.

Not even to herself if she were strong.

Certainly not to a practiced stranger who was
subtly awakening all the parts of her that ached so
deeply to be caressed. All the parts that a decent
woman should pretend did not exist.

Dear God. Oh, God. She swallowed a sob.
Adrian barely had to stroke her shoulders, her
breasts, and the curve of her hip, and her body
quivered, answered to his mastery. In disbelief she
became aware of the wonderful tension of her inner
muscles, an overwhelming sense of surrender that
she had known only a few times in her marriage to
Stuart. It was as if a wave of sensation had gathered
deep inside her.

How dare this mercenary . . . this man, how dare
he make her feel, force her to acknowledge her sexual
desires when she had succeeded in ignoring them
for so long.

For years she had struggled to master her emotions. She'd deceived those dearest to her until at
last she had managed to deceive even herself. She
had been born one of the wicked, passionate Boscastles. And while she'd scolded her boisterous sib-

lings, she had at times envied their ability to enjoy their lives, to fall deeply, irrevocably in love. She'd had a chance. She had loved a quiet man and lost him. She'd begun to believe that passion, that true love, would never be part of her life.

She suppressed a whimper. Restrained the instinct to writhe. Instead, she lifted her hand to her mouth as if to stifle another sob.

How dare he commit that valiant act today and then, only hours later, completely undo her?

"Emma," he whispered, "do you wish me to stop?"

She stared up into his luminous hazel eyes and saw not the guile of a practiced rake, but the unadulterated desire of a man who did not bother to hide what he felt. It devastated her.

"I want you to kiss me," he urged. "Just once."

"Just once," she whispered, her voice skeptical, unsteady. "Have two more dangerous words ever been uttered by man or devil?"

He paused, gazing deeply into her eyes. " 'I do?' "

"Oh!" She began to pull away. "Lie down."

"I don't want to."

"Adrian, please. You're a dangerous man."

He frowned. "I'm not dangerous to you."

"You *are*."

"Why? Because I've sold my sword?"

"That's a good start," she replied.

"I would never hurt you."

"Not on purpose."

He drew her tightly into his arms, ignoring her whispered protests. Her body tingled and burned with the forbidden pleasure of being held to the heat of his hard-muscled male body. His gaze hooded, he stroked his long fingers down her shoulders to her sides, stealing sinful little touches here and there until, by the time his hand slipped under the hem of her gown to her knee, she was shaking, utterly prepared for his seduction. And yet unprepared.

His mouth captured hers in such a subtle assault that it did not seem natural to refuse. Her lips parted in expectation. A sweet pain pierced her, quickened the pulses that beat through the depths of her body.

She tilted her head, answering his dominance. Whereas before the candlelight had gentled the hard contours of his handsome face, the darkness stripped away all illusions of refinement. He *was* a dangerous man. One who had turned his back on Society. One who mesmerized her for reasons beyond her understanding.

He had sold his services to other lands. She wondered why. Surely a duke's heir did not need a fortune. Was it danger that he, like so many other young gentlemen, had sought? Perhaps he'd been running away. Had he done something he regretted in his past? She supposed it was more important to ask why he had come back.

Her brothers trusted him. And she—

She acknowledged his allure. It drew her, not merely the danger of him, but his openness. Few men recognized her spirit of fun. She did not often allow it to show. She felt the fire inside her now, too, steadily rising.

His lips brushed her wet, swollen mouth again. His hands sought her most vulnerable places. Her back arched. Her body begged for something she was ashamed to admit. He was a conqueror by choice. A moan rose in her throat.

He heard, his instincts sharp. His eyes glinted down at her in the dark. He knew. Scarcely had she released another breath than his hot mouth skimmed her breasts to suckle her nipple through the thin silk.

She shivered, aroused, her body weightless. Emma Boscastle letting a man she had only just met nuzzle her breasts, suckle at her so indecently. Pleasure lanced like sunlight through her senses, her confusion.

"Lord Wolverton," she said, unable to subdue another shiver, "this cannot be good for your health."

His tongue encircled her nipple, a slow tease of sensation that intensified her breathless pleasure. "Believe me, it is."

"What about your injury?" she asked, her muscles tightening.

He raised his head and kissed her wetly on the mouth. She moaned again. "What injury?" he asked, managing to sound guileless and wicked at once. "You have a beautiful body, Emma Boscastle, and a keen mind. I kept looking at you today during the wedding."

"Because of my mind or my body?" she whispered wryly, wondering why his confession should scandalize her when what he was doing was far worse. Her nipples stiffened impudently against his mouth. She was practically offering herself, her breasts at least, to his advances.

"Both," he answered with a fleeting smile. "You appealed to me. That is all I know."

"You desired me . . . at the wedding?"

"Yes," he said, hesitating only slightly. "Does that offend you?"

"In front of witnesses?" Her voice was almost inaudible. The clamoring in her body drowned out everything else, the measure of her breath, the deep ticking of her pulses.

He was taking soft, sensual bites of her breasts, and she seemed unable to discourage him. Thick warm fluid lubricated the folds of her sex. She could only imagine what it would feel like for his agile swordsman's hand to touch her there, to penetrate her aching recesses.

"It's too much," she said in a raw voice, her spine bowing.

"I have to be honest," he murmured, "it's not enough for me."

She swallowed. "There is such a thing as being

too honest. Certain thoughts shouldn't be expressed."

He appeared to ponder this, but obviously at no great concern, for his attention soon returned to kissing her throat and nibbling tenderly at her breasts again. "I disagree," he said in a low disarming voice. "We are both of us past the age of indecision—and both of us have made love before."

"Certainly not with each other."

"Isn't that what makes this all the more tempting?" he challenged quietly.

Tempting.

"I'm a widow," she whispered. "That part of my life is over."

"You're a woman, Emma. That won't ever change."

She felt a bittersweet little twist of acknowledgment, of longing. "It has."

"I do not remember ever being this attracted to a woman before," he said thickly.

His hand drifted from her hip to the hollow between her thighs. She bit back a sob. His touch, or lack of it, was torture. Her cleft pulsed in silent need. She dared not move.

She glanced down, realizing her legs were bare, and her gown was bunched around her hips. How different they were. How carelessly this man sinned while she diligently pounded sin with her bare fists back into the gutter where it belonged.

In fact, she could imagine her students' exclamations of wicked glee if they could see her now. Emma Boscastle in bed with a dashing aristocrat, having merrily abandoned all the principles that not only the academy represented but those she had made personal sacrifices to uphold.

"I am at your mercy, madam," he said unexpectedly into the lengthening silence.

She gazed up at his beautiful face with cynical resolve. "At my mercy?" she asked faintly.

"I think I've lost my senses," he whispered, his voice penitent.

"Well, you certainly won't find them under my gown."

He laughed and slid his large arms around her waist. "Emma, oh, Emma. I'm dying of desire for you. Why do you have to be a Boscastle?"

"I've asked myself that same question on many occasions."

He slid his hand up her belly to her neck and undid the buttons of her gown. Her soft white breasts swelled, the pink rims peeping above the silk.

"Very nice," he murmured. "And what about down here? All delicious and tender, too?"

She swallowed thickly as his hand wandered down into the warm hollow between her thighs. "Oh, Emma," he said, briefly closing his eyes, "you're so wet, darling. Let me bring you off."

"Bring me—" A blush of shame rose to her skin. Her woman's place softened, opened moistly at his invitation. She made no move to stop him.

"You need it." His scarred knuckles drifted over her mons to the engorged folds beneath. Her inner muscles melted, awaiting his touch. "Don't you?" he murmured.

She closed her eyes against the temptation burning deep in her belly.

He bent his head and licked tenderly across the tops of her breasts. Her face heated, and the heat spread, meeting the fire in her belly.

"I can't—" Her voice broke.

"Hush. I'll take care of everything." His thumb glided across her tender nipples, back and forth, until the pleasure-pain made her tremble. He shifted closer. His erection throbbed through his long cambric drawers and dressing robe against her bare thick belly.

"Why am I allowing this?" she asked with a helpless groan.

One long calloused finger pressed into her pulsing cleft. "Because your body is asking for it. Dear Emma, am I welcome here?"

He kissed her as she struggled to answer. He tangled his thumb in the soft tuft of hair that crowned her cleft. Slowly he inserted two more fingers into her crevice, flexing and unflexing them inside her. She gasped. Sighing in pleasure, he removed his hand and lifted it above her shoulder. Her pearly essence glistened enticingly on his knuckles. She heard him growl his approval deep in his throat.

He kissed her forehead. "Tell me," he said

huskily. "How long has it been since a man has entered your body? Since you touched yourself?"

Her eyes flew open. "You impertinent man."

He grinned, the cleft in his chin deepening. "We'll deal with my impertinence later, shall we? For now we have to take care of you."

She squirmed. He laid his other hand flat on her belly, imprisoning her. His eyes fastened to her face, he gently pinched her hidden bud between his fingers until it tautened and her hips bucked. His gaze darkening, he forced his three fingers back inside her tight, aching passage. She felt exposed, vulnerable, ripe.

She shook her head. In denial? Delight? Perhaps both. He kissed her again, his tongue ravishing her mouth, absorbing her soft moans. His hard thigh pressed against her flank. She put her hand on his powerful forearm. He raised up slightly, his shoulder muscles corded with strength. He was as sexual and beautiful, and as unprincipled, as an ancient god.

In a moment she would put him in his place.

But now, ah, now. She stared up at his gorgeous face. The heat in his eyes sent a current of sexual awareness down her spine. So uninhibited. So male.

Somewhere outside she heard the clatter of carriage wheels and hooves upon the cobbles. She lifted her hand to the back of his sun-burnished neck. She felt his muscles tighten at her hesitant touch. His breathing deepened. His shaft thickened against her thigh as he drew his body against hers.

He rotated her hooded bud again. The pleasure in her body intensified. Hot. Tight. Forbidden. All the while he watched her, understanding her every weakness.

Her brother's home.

Her school.

A practical stranger.

Viscountess Lyons being ravished by a man she'd only known for hours. His large, warm hand wandered in a caress over her breasts. His agile fingers worked her, thrust between her plump wet lips. In and out. Warm blood swirled in a pool to the aching hollow of her sex.

"Too long," he whispered. "And now I'm here. When I met you today, when we talked at the wedding, I felt as if we had known each other before."

"Less than a day," she whispered.

"No. It did not seem so, at least not to me."

She bit the inside of her cheek. He was leaning on one elbow now, intensifying the wicked pleasure he gave her. His gaze was riveted to the shadowed juncture of her thighs. Her excitement grew.

Her hips lifted into his hand. She couldn't control her movements, her need. He exhaled, closed his eyes. "It must have been a long time," he murmured. "You're trembling and so very snug inside."

She could not speak. The warm droplets of moisture that gathered between her thighs betrayed whatever protest she might attempt. How long had it been? Her belly quivered, and a deep pressure built at the base of her spine.

She had *never* known desire like this.

"Give yourself this one pleasure," he whispered darkly. "Come alive for me."

And she did. Her body clenched. She was powerless to stop it. He held her as she peaked, as her ability to breathe stopped, as instinct stormed her senses. She fell under his spell. She sobbed, years of subdued desire unchained. Who was he, this man? What devil's power did he possess to do this to her?

"Emma." His deep voice penetrated her bewilderment.

She shuddered. She refused to look at him, awash in pleasured shame and wonder.

"Emma," he said again, his face pressed to hers. "Are you all right?"

She felt herself slowly return to sanity. Her body pulsed in the aftermath. To her surprise she found herself stroking his hair, the hard planes of his face. Offering him comfort. Who *was* this man? Who was she? After this day, she did not know.

"When I first saw you at the wedding," he said, "I—"

She pressed her finger to his lips. "I am a widow, Lord Wolverton. Despite what just happened, that part of my life is over."

"You didn't die with your husband," he said after a long pause.

She lay unmoving for several moments. His eyes were closed. His face rested against hers. "I thought I'd died once," he said. "God knows I did everything in my power to destroy myself, but I didn't."

She felt tears sting her eyes.

It was evident that his head injury had not affected his more basic functions. Her limbs shivered involuntarily as she finally attempted to disengage her body from his.

Feelings familiar and yet not.

She had married before the middle of her first season, her husband a cultured Scottish viscount and modest landholder. She'd thought that his reserved nature would suit her. They had been good companions, more friends than lovers. In fact, the sum of her sexual experience with her quiet-mannered husband had consisted only of stolen touches and hurried couplings under the covers. Indeed, Emma had emerged from their rushed matings more dissatisfied than not. To this day she blushed remembering how Stuart had announced on their wedding night that it was time to put his little sausage in the oven.

She could not think of a man as well-constructed as Lord Wolverton possessing anything as inconsequential as a sausage. Her limited contact with his heavy male appendage had been proof enough. To think of taking an organ of such proportion inside her own body made her breath quicken. Adrian and her late husband could not have been less alike, in physical form and character.

She slid out of his arms, a poorly planned strategical move if ever she'd made one. Every part of her body came into electrifying contact with his. Her dressing gown dropped back down to her bare ankles. She felt his hot, hard gaze travel over her naked trembling body.

She found her footing and with it the remnants of her control. She wasn't going to cry. "I'm leaving you now." Her voice sounded steady. Her emotions were not. "You must stay in that bed until the physician gives you permission to leave it."

He studied her in smoldering silence. "I have no excuse for my behavior."

She retreated to the door. "Nor I."

He sat up, his hard face hidden in shadows. "I swear to you I will never tell anyone what just happened. On what little honor I have."

She turned away.

"I swear to you, Emma."

"Good night, Lord Wolverton."

She opened the door. His deep voice followed her into the darkened hallway. Her heart pounded in her throat. "You have my word."

The word of a mercenary.

He sank back onto the bed as the door closed with a sharp reverberation that sent a thunderclap of agony through his head. He laughed out loud, defying the pain. Reveling in it, in fact.

He felt incredibly foolish, elated. Yes, his head hurt. But—he was blessedly lucid enough to recognize his infatuation with the tidy Emma Boscastle, a proper lady who'd thought to put him in his place and had almost done it, too.

He knew she didn't trust him. Why should she? But from the instant he sensed her watching him at the wedding today, he had felt his first spark of hope since returning to England. Perhaps there was a purpose to it, after all. Blow to his skull be damned, he had met a woman he wanted to impress.

He'd just made a hell of an impression, too, demanding intimacy on their brief acquaintance. Did she already despise him? Of course she must. What he'd liked most about her was her mettle, her way of noticing every misstep made by others, as if she were silently lamenting the entire world and trying to put it all right.

As if nice manners could mend all the evil on earth. Could she mend a man as broken in soul as he? No woman had ever tried. His dark reputation had attracted the ladies in droves. Emma, on the other hand, had disapproved of him from the moment they met.

She was a Boscastle, one of those spellbinding souls who burned with vitality and purpose. That alone would be enough to explain her irresistible appeal. His best friend, Dominic Breckland, had lost his heart to Chloe Boscastle at the lowest ebb in his life. Fortunately, Dominic had also had the good sense and good fortune to marry her. But the whole bloody lot of them broke hearts as unwittingly as other people breathed. Which answered the question of why he'd felt compelled to defend Emma in the first place.

Still, that hadn't given him the right to seduce her. She had merely been fulfilling some sense of obligation for what he'd done today. Made a cake of himself and gotten crowned by a Chippendale chair into the bargain. Emma Boscastle might conceivably be able to heal his injury, but all her propriety couldn't fix the complicated pain of his personal affairs.

He breathed out a sigh. What if she *could* put him to right? Wouldn't that be a feather in her cap? It was impossible, of course. No one could undo what he'd become. He'd been raised to better, aspired to worse, and there was no denying his manners had slipped over the years.

One had little need for etiquette in his past profession, in the dark, dirty places where he'd fought and loved. But a levelheaded woman like Emma was a different matter altogether, and he'd relied on his wits alone too long in this sorrowful world not to claim a treasure when he saw it.

Chapter Five

❧ ❧

Disgraced.

Emma had disgraced herself. There was simply no one else to blame. True, she had not asked Lord Wolverton to come to her defense today. But neither had he insisted she rush to his rescue, either. Or into his arms.

Those strong protective arms that had anchored her to his magnificently built body. She'd been married for years and had never known a need so keen, so deep reaching that it overcame her judgment. Had she felt sorry for him? Or for herself? With a few simple words he had dismantled her emotions. To think that her brother or his wife might have walked in, and she would have had to explain that—that she had come close to sleeping with a stranger, peer of the realm or not. She lifted her hand to her heart. She wasn't sure whether she ought to pay penance or do something unspeakably wicked like . . . stand at the top of the stairs and bellow a few swear words. She whispered them instead.

"Damn. Damnation."

What had come over her? She wasn't the one who'd been hit on the head.

However, she was the one who had let herself be half seduced by a man of his appalling reputation when no other man had managed to steal as much as a kiss on the cheek from her in years. Not even that Sir William, whose shabby behavior made her feel unwholesome and—Adrian's love play had left her feeling vulnerable but not violated. Upon escaping him, she should have experienced any number of appropriate reactions.

But not this sparkling invigoration, this sense of Sleeping Beauty awakened after a hundred years of dormant desire, of being swept up into the stars, of walking . . .

"The hallstand, Emma," a familiar masculine voice warned behind her. "Watch where you're walking. We don't need another invalid on our hands."

A guilty blush pinkened her face at her brother's gentle reprimand. "Well, who moved it, then?" she demanded, laughing shakily.

The intelligent blue eyes of her second eldest brother, Lord Heath Boscastle, studied her for a moment. Of all her family members he was the most protective and perceptive. And there was certainly something for him to perceive if he looked deeply enough. "No one. The hallstand has always stood there. Are you sleepwalking, Emma?"

"Of course not. It's my habit to check on the girls before bed every night."

"I know," he said in amusement. "However, they sleep in the other wing on the floor above. As they have ever since they arrived here." His gaze drifted past her to Adrian's door. "I thought you might be on your way to check on Wolf," he said in a casual tone she knew better than to trust.

Wolf. She cringed inwardly at the too-apt sobriquet. Spying in the military had refined Heath's instincts. She would absolutely die if he guessed what had just happened. She could not understand it herself. Pray God Adrian was a man who kept his promises, or, well, she cringed to imagine the repercussions.

As calmly as she could, she answered, "I did check on him, naturally. One feels a sense of responsibility when a man has been incapacitated on one's behalf."

His lips thinned into a hint of a smile. "Incapacitated? I think he could have been struck by an entire table and still survive. But I am curious, Emma. Just how responsible for his well-being do you hold yourself?"

This was the test. The trial by Boscastle torture. Heath's blue eyes boring into one's inner thoughts like a tomb-raider exhuming a book that held the secrets to the universe. He knew nothing. How could he know?

Furthermore, she was a grown woman, not a debutante, although until this moment she'd never had cause to lie to her family. "I hold myself responsible in the extreme," she replied, her voice unwavering, her regard challenging him to make more of it at his own peril. Brother and sister, they stood as equals on the Boscastle sibling battlefield.

"In the extreme. Interesting choice of words, Emma."

"Would you expect any less of me?" she inquired in an even tone that gently sent the ball back into his court.

He hesitated. "I cannot recall a similar situation in the past by which to judge you."

"Surely you know me well enough to realize that my duty to obligation will always be met."

He stared down at her with such tender intensity that she was tempted to throw herself into his arms and plead for understanding. For guidance. And if he'd probed any deeper, she might indeed have been brought to that humiliating pass.

But Adrian had given his word that no one would ever know. Their secret. Their shared sin.

Heath's voice penetrated her reverie. "The line between obligation and inclination often becomes blurred, and if one is not looking up—"

"—then one walks into the hallstand." She touched his arm. "Thank you for your concern," she said with deliberate lightness. "Are you on your way to visit him?"

"Is he awake?"

"He was a few moments ago. I cannot vouch for his temper, however. He appears to have a complete intolerance for his infirmity." Although infirm in no manner described the full-blooded devil who had not only discovered a chink in her armor but had aroused womanly instincts she had long believed to be becalmed. In a single day, she had discovered that the one man she believed to be her decent admirer was anything but, and the man of an indecent past who had defended her honor—Well, it remained to be proven exactly what he was and why she now felt constrained to defend her interest in him.

It rained during the first night of his recuperation. Adrian had forgotten how different the English rain was from the storms that swept across the Far East. English rain burrowed deep into the marrow. Despite it or perhaps because of it, he drifted into a fitful sleep. Into this miserable clime he had been born.

He would have found mordant amusement in his plight except that the laudanum had taken effect. He felt its soporific power seep into his system, and beneath it, penetrating even deeper, the warmth of Emma Boscastle. The touch of a gentlewoman's hand. A soft yet reprimanding voice.

The door opened slowly.

Adrian glanced up, a smile playing at the corners of his mouth. Please, let her have come back. She would probably need an excuse. Claim she'd forgotten to shut the drapes or move the stool from the middle of the floor so he wouldn't fall in the night. He didn't give a damn what reason she used. He'd be a good boy for once and not tease. He would beg her forgiveness and promise to behave if she would talk to him.

He knew what Emma must think of him. He was a poor friend who took advantage, a scoundrel, a seducer. The truth, however, was that he'd had only two other lovers in his life. One had been a half-caste courtesan who'd taught him everything he was dying to know about sex. His last long-term affair had been with a French gentlewoman who'd taught him everything he wished he had never learned about love.

"Are you going to come in or not?" he asked quietly. "If you do, I will apologize for what I did."

The bed curtains rolled back on their rings. He reclined in a relaxed pose against the pillows; he had to restrain himself to wait patiently for her to approach him.

A bloody good thing it turned out to be, too. It wasn't Emma's delicate, disembodied features that materialized from out of the shadows.

It was the lean, cynical face of her older brother, Lieutenant Colonel Lord Heath Boscastle, who stared down at Adrian for several meaningful seconds before inquiring with a guarded smile, "Apologize for what, exactly?"

A less seasoned gentleman would have cracked under the strain of that sphinxlike stare. Adrian remembered rumors of French spies who spoke secretly of their respect for the quiet-spoken, enigmatic Englishman who had not ever broken under torture.

Ofttimes Adrian wondered what Heath's bravery had cost him personally. No one would ever know. Heath was the type of man who would shrug off either praise or acknowledgment of what he considered to have been his duty. One presumed he would carry his secrets to the grave. He was a fine officer.

In fact, Adrian had more than once regretted he'd not enlisted in the regular British military and fought alongside the Boscastle brothers and their ilk. He'd never formed the camaraderie amongst his peers that other nobly born military officers had. But then he had been seeking to escape his aristocratic identity. In fact, he'd left England at sixteen, his life made intolerable by his father's taunts. He had met Heath Boscastle not long after at a Prussian military academy. Heath had gone on to a quiet but personal glory. Adrian had given himself to adventure and darker acclaim.

Yet he could still remember his last conversation with the man who now claimed to be his father, Guy Fulham, the Duke of Scarfield. Well, it had been more of an eavesdropping until Scarfield had caught Adrian by the scruff of the neck and humiliated him in the midst of a house party.

"Look at you, listening at keyholes like a dirty little thief. But then I shouldn't be surprised, should I? Your mother was naught but a whore, and your natural sire was a soldier. Not even an officer, if you please. An ordinary, ignorant soldier who didn't even have the wherewithal to survive a year in battle."

His life had started to make sense then. His father had grown aloof since the death of Adrian's mother four years earlier. It hadn't taken him long to figure out a few unsavory facts about his place in the world. The old duke wasn't his blood, as it turned out. Soon enough the abuses and malignant neglect of the man he'd believed to be his father assumed a more dramatic meaning. Adrian's young mother, Constance, had apparently taken a lover, a common soldier who happened to be passing through the village, and that's why the duke had come to despise the sight of Adrian.

The old bugger thought his heir was a by-blow.

The revelation should have broken Adrian's spirit. Another boy would have been shamed by repeatedly being reminded he was the accidental product of an adulterous affair. Instead, it cheered him immeasurably. Gave him a new purpose in life. He decided to become a blood-and-guts soldier like his real father. He would show the duke what he thought of his stuffy old world. He'd become a great military adventurer, a wealthy nabob, and flaunt his successes under the aristocracy's nose.

Only it hadn't worked out that way at all. Revenge, Adrian had discovered, rarely did. Yet by the time he'd set upon his path, he couldn't turn back. He was as much a victim of his vengeance as he was the perpetrator.

He hadn't counted on the rest of the world not exactly agreeing to his half-cocked plans. Or himself. Fighting had knocked most of the anger out of him. In fact, he'd gorged himself on so much violence that he had become numb.

He'd had military adventures, all right. Only his reputation had been built as a mercenary, not a hero. He had trained native soldiers to beef up British forces and subdued insurgents in the battle against French encroachment on foreign holdings. The rulers who appreciated being spared an assassin's knife had rewarded him in gold, rupees, and diamonds. He had been granted trading rights by East India Company and held mercantile interests in Bombay, Madras, China, Persia, and India. He'd made his name by agreeing to fight anywhere for a price.

And then a year or so ago the duke had the gall to ask Adrian home, claiming to be stricken with some mortal affliction. He wrote that he hoped to make amends. Home? For the love of hell, Adrian had only come back to England because he'd be a fool to refuse an inheritance that was his by right. No other reason, although he was ready to settle down.

And if he wanted to claim a woman forbidden to him by friendship?

"Adrian."

He glanced up moodily at the mild reproach in his host's voice.

"Yes?"

"I asked you what it is you are apologizing for."

"Apologizing? Ah." He frowned. The head injury must have jolted his brains, after all. He rarely brooded on the past. "Well, I'm sorry for all the bother. It's bloody embarrassing to have a chair broken on your noggin and then end up being cosseted like a vestal virgin."

Heath sighed. "You were defending my sister. There's no need to apologize for that."

Adrian regarded the other man with a scowl. "Except that I bollixed it up. The true offender sneaked away, and I fainted at your sister's feet like a girl. In fact, now that I think about it, I'm of a mind to finish what I started. Where does Sir William reside?"

Heath shook his head. "Drake and Devon were already planning to have breakfast with him when Emma pleaded for mercy. She's not as scandal-prone as the rest of us. Let this go for her sake."

"I don't need anyone else to stand in for me," he said heatedly. "I could have challenged him myself. Or not."

Heath laughed. "Actually, friend, I'm afraid

you're not quite capable of even *standing* by yourself, let alone fighting a duel."

"Damn it all to hell," Adrian said mildly. "Are you going to insist I stay?"

"I think you need another spoonful of that sedative."

"I think I should take the whole bedeviled bottle."

Chapter Six

❧ ❧

Emma ascended the flight of stairs in what had become a reassuring nightly ritual. Heath had generously reopened the uppermost floor of his town house as a private dormitory for her boarding pupils. For a brief time, her younger brother Devon had also allowed her the use of his home for her school, but Heath could provide more spacious lodgings, and as he and his wife Julia traveled often, this was a more convenient arrangement. Naturally, Emma hoped one day to settle into a proper place for the academy. Now that her siblings had found their own loves, well, it was time. She hoped that by the end of the summer she would decide on a country locale.

For once the thought of her pupils and their fresh, hopeful, sometimes impertinent, faces failed to rally her fighting spirit. She had betrayed them with her lapse tonight. She had become that most hideous of all society entities, a hypocrite, and perhaps she would become something even worse.

She dared not put a name to it. However, what was done was done. The most perplexing thing was how easily she had lost herself in sensual pleasure. She had not realized herself capable of such physical enjoyment.

She paused on the threshold of the tidy attic-chamber to gather her wits. There were thirteen girls now. Enough, she thought distractedly, for a witch's coven. Truly they did brew up enough mischief to befuddle their headmistress.

Four other young ladies who lived outside London had made applications to the academy in the last fortnight alone. One of her current students claimed royal ancestry. Another was betrothed to a cousin of a French marquis. Mademoiselle's parents, naturally, wished to give their daughter's deportment a certain flair before she took residence in Burgundy. To be entrusted with the improvement of young gentlewomen who would influence the world was a duty sacred to Emma's heart.

That an acquaintance from her own school days, Lady Clipstone, had become her archenemy by setting up her own struggling academy only a month ago made Emma all the more determined to succeed.

And now, after today—tonight—

What of her indiscretion? The unspeakable event that she was supposed to pretend had not happened.

I'm dying of desire for you.

Desire. For her. An unbidden smile crossed her face.

She knew what others said of her. The Dainty Dictator. Mrs. Killjoy. No one would believe she was the woman who only a half-hour ago had all but succumbed to a mercenary's seduction. Not at all herself, and yet, well, she *had* been herself. Her veins bubbling with all the wretched passion of her Boscastle ancestry.

To think she hadn't been different at all. She might end up even worse, in fact, than her brothers. At least they sinned openly and made no excuses for it.

Emma had committed her transgression in secret. Or so she hoped. At any rate, she would be less forgiving of herself than anyone in her family should her conduct be brought to light. She had been a hard judge of her brothers' misdeeds. Perhaps they really were all cut from the same cloth.

A soft snore erupted from the bed of one of her sleeping pupils. Sighing, she walked slowly across the room.

She should have guessed the restless girl was her newest student, Harriet Gardner, a charity case from the gutters of St. Giles. Emma had asked herself at least a hundred times since the fateful day she'd taken the flame-haired Harriet under her wing, why she had been possessed of the notion to help a street urchin who swore she would never be reformed.

She was very afraid it had to do with some maternal instincts that, try as she might, would not be denied. And the fact that Harriet, at seventeen, had been preened by her family to enter a life of larceny and prostitution. Emma's heart ached for her. What chance did a girl like that have in London? Her plight both touched and challenged Emma, for she had learned that there were some trouble-bound souls who would not be helped.

As expected, it was Harriet who emitted the offensive snores, her thin white fingers curled around the cudgel she slept with every night. Emma bent over the bed to remove the weapon from the girl's fist, then stopped.

Who knew what horrors Harriet confronted in her dreams? Or had faced in life? If the girl needed a stick to enable her to sleep, Emma supposed, as she straightened, it could be allowed for a few more days at most—

"Effing fancy-man," Harriet shouted, sitting bolt upright in bed with her cudgel raised. "Gimme back my guinea, or I'll bash you into pig guts!"

Emma blanched, then swooped down to wrestle the cudgel from the girl's fists, whispering, "Harriet, Harriet, wake up! It's only a dream, my dear."

Then, even more gently, she added, "You're safe in this house, do you hear? There are no"—her tongue stumbled over the word—"*effing* fancy-men, only friends."

"Lady Lyons?" Harriet blinked several times be-

fore she broke into an abashed grin upon recognizing Emma. "That oughta teach you not to sneak up
on a sleepin' body. I almost thumped you a croaker,
Mrs. Princum Prancum."

Emma regarded her unflinchingly, thinking that
two persons thus "thumped" in one day could not
be allowed. "I have warned you about the language, Harriet." She paused. "And that elocution.
You drop the inital *h* and defy the rules of phonics
more often than not. In fact, your diction could
stop a parade of Horse Guards in their tracks."

Harriet beamed. "Well, thanks, ma'am." She
tucked her bony knees under her well-washed night
rail and settled in for a lengthy chat. "You're prowling about late, ain't ya? Been gettin' friendly with
his grace? Lovely looker, that fellow. Gives a girl the
warm shivers."

Emma felt her scalp tighten. Either Harriet had
almost supernatural instincts, or Emma looked as
guilty as she felt. "Do lower your voice, Harriet, and
refrain from such lowering remarks. His grace—
goodness, he's not inherited yet. He is Lord Wolverton to us."

"Wolf," Harriet corrected her with a knowing
smile. "And don't we all know what that means?"

Emma lifted a brow in astonishment. "If we know,
then we certainly will not admit it, nor share our
embarrassing perception with the other, more innocent girls," she said in a disconcerted voice.

Harriet's mouth quirked at the corners. "Someone has to educate 'em, don't they?"

Emma was feeling a little light-headed, a belated reaction, she was sure, from her own unplanned amorous lesson. "Not in those matters, my girl. When a woman marries, well, her husband is best left to instruct her in such affairs."

Harriet snorted. "There's the blind leadin' the blind, in my ignorant opinion. If you want to give us a proper education, you should take us to Mrs. Watson's house on Bruton Street for a few nights. I heard tell she gives lessons in love."

"My blood chills at the mere suggestion."

"It wouldn't be chill for long in that place."

"Reassure me, Harriet, that you were never employed in such an establishment," Emma whispered, sickened at the thought.

"I was once," Harriet whispered back, "but only as an undermaid until they caught me at a peephole. Cor, the things I saw. Some of them acts just ain't natural, do you know what I mean? The places men put their—"

Emma closed her eyes. "You are never, *ever* to admit to anyone again that you worked in a seraglio. Do you understand? That sort of thing is behind you. We are going to pretend it never happened." At least that was the advice Emma's father had always dispensed when faced with one of his children's offenses. Emma was not sure one could always forget, however.

Harriet studied her with unnerving intensity. "Ain't you ever done one bad thing in yer life, Lady Lyons?"

"Of course. Everyone has."

"Nah. I ain't talkin' about pinching an extra biscuit off the breakfast tray. I mean something truly wicked. Sinful. As a grown woman. Something that keeps you awake at night."

Emma shook her head. "A lady wouldn't ask, and like it or not, by hook or by crook, you *will* become a lady. Now go to sleep. Your voice is disturbing the others."

Harriet sank down only to spring right back up on her elbow. "I won't betray you if you're nice to me."

Emma pivoted at the foot of the bed, the fine hairs on her nape prickling. "Betray me?" She knew she'd be better off ignoring the taunt. "What are you saying?"

"Your rival, ma'am. That flat-chested Lady Clipstone. She's sent letters to all the girls' parents offering 'em free tuition for three months."

Emma narrowed her eyes. "That vindictive woman."

"Yeah. And you wanna hear the worst of it?"

"No. I do not." Although, naturally, Emma did.

"She's trying to steal me away. *Moi.* There. That's French lessons for you. Ain't you proud?"

Emma felt as if she were standing at the edge of

some noxious cesspool. "Why, pray tell, would Lady Clipstone want to steal you away, Harriet?"

Harriet tapped her forefinger to her temple. "To pick these old brains in 'ere."

"To pick them of what?" Emma asked hesitantly. "You have only begun your life as a young lady."

"Yeah. But I do got an attic full of secrets, you know. I see and 'ear everything."

"You see and hear everything," Emma said in a resigned voice. "You have been here less than a fortnight. I would imagine there has not been much of interest to see and hear."

"You'd be flippin' wrong then," Harriet retorted with a sly grin. "I'm like a little mouse, I am, all over the place."

Emma stared at her in chagrin. "Well, whatever it is you imagine you have seen or heard, I trust you will keep it to yourself. You must concentrate on your lessons, Harriet."

"Would I bite the 'and that feeds me?" Harriet scoffed. "Not bloody likely, is it?"

Emma released her breath. "I hope not."

"I'll stick by you thick 'n' thin, Lady Lyons."

"How fortunate for me," Emma murmured, turning to the other beds. How in the name of heaven would she turn this troublesome girl into a lady?

"You keep that chin up tomorrow, Lady Lyons. Don't let 'er knock you down."

"Whatever do you mean?" Emma asked through her teeth.

"That mean Lady Clipstone—once she gets a sniff of scandal, and that Wolf is a scandal if ever I saw one, well—" She swiped her hand across her throat. "The end."

Emma narrowed her eyes. "Do you think I am that easily beaten?"

Harriet slid under the coverlet. "Not with me on your side. You scratch my back and I'll scratch yours. Do we have a deal?"

"I'd as soon make a deal with the devil, Harriet. But—if I must shake your hand to earn your trust, then I shall do so."

Harriet waited another fifteen minutes before she swung her bare toes to the floor and began to awaken the rest of the girls. "All right," she announced whilst the other twelve yawned at her in resentment. "Who's game for tonight's entertainment?"

Miss Lydia Potter crossed her arms across her prominent bosom. "My idea of entertainment is *not* running down a damp alley to peer into another brothel window."

Harriet looked down her nose in scorn. "Who wants to see Lady Lyons's duke and defender in the flesh?"

One by one the other girls ceased their chattering to gaze upon Harriet in uncertain awe. "What do you mean?" one of the prefects demanded.

"I mean exactly what I said," she countered. "Is

anyone game? Or are you too afraid to have a good look at the sort of man you're all aspiring to marry?"

A discordant female voice invaded his pleasant drift of dreams. For an instant he thought it was Emma again. He fought through his drugged befuddlement to respond to her—giggling at the foot of the bed? Surely that was not her making that ungodly noise.

He groaned in an effort to answer her. Finally he opened his eyes to stare up at a gamine-faced girl whose evil grin awakened him to full consciousness like a bucket of salt water splashed upon his face. Her hand was in the process of peeling away the bedcovers.

"Demon's spawn!" he shouted in annoyance. "Where is my sword? I'll cut off your damned little head!"

The girl danced back beyond his grasp. In disgust he noticed the group of young females gathered behind her at the door, watching him in wide-eyed shock.

He lurched into a stand, weaving several feet across the floor with the bedclothes wrapped around his legs. The girls backed away with gasps of fear. Emma, he soon perceived, was not among this group of silly, gasping females, and suddenly, as a black dizziness overcame him, he wondered whether he was still dreaming.

"Be gone, you plaguesome imps!" he growled,

sweeping his hand across the air in a menacing gesture.

"So that's what a duke looks like," one of them boldly whispered. "I never guessed they grew them so big."

So big? Were his improper body parts showing? He had strangely lost sensation from the waist down, but it appeared he was still wearing his drawers beneath his robe. His feet felt like slabs of stone.

As if through a haze, he heard their muffled shrieks of terror, watched them scatter into the dark like timid mice. The gall. Intruding on a sleeping man only to shriek in fright as if *he* had instigated this humiliation, and him as helpless as a . . . what had she called him again? A butterfly.

He made an ungainly effort to chase after them, at the very least to tell them off. But the dose of sedative Heath Boscastle had insisted he swallow would have put a weaker man to sleep for a minimum of three days. In Adrian's cast-iron system it would remain potent only until morning. It slowed him now.

He bellowed once more on principle to demonstrate his wrath, then stomped back to the bed. His head throbbed mightily. His limbs felt clumsy and uncoordinated.

In the morning, perhaps, he would recover sufficient strength to pursue the impertinent mice and inform them he was not a man to trifle with. But not until after he had found Emma Boscastle alone and apologized for the offense he had given her.

Not that he was truly sorry for what had happened, to be perfectly honest. Their pleasant interlude had been the only bright spot in his gloomy return to England. She was quite possibly the only human being, certainly the only woman, who had displayed a genuine concern for his welfare with no thought of what she would receive in return. He'd always had a strange weakness for a woman of sharp wit.

Every other person in this accursed country had fawned at his feet upon learning he was a duke's heir. As if that misfortune of birth elevated him to some lofty status.

Misfortune of birth. For the formative years of his life that was exactly what Adrian had been led to believe his existence was. A misfortune. The result of sin.

And he had not particularly cared one way or another whether he proved this belief to be true or not. Until a few hours ago when Emma Boscastle had stolen a few comfits from a wedding cake to please him.

Emma had gone to bed in the weak hope that when she woke up she would discover the previous day hadn't really happened. But the first thing she thought of when she opened her eyes in the morning was him. Her injured Lord of Scandal. Lord

Wolf lying abed. Still wounded or in wait? She had no precedent upon which to speculate.

She was quite confident, however, that once she faced her day's work, her students, those wild buds of flowering womanhood, she would be able to put Adrian Ruxley from her mind and resume her regular affairs. The demands of instruction never failed to distract her.

It was raining lightly. The coal in the grate had gone out, leaving the scent of old ashes and damp in the room.

She huddled under her quilt and listened to the splash of carriage wheels and hooves through puddles in the street below. Through the rhythmic pattering on the town house roof she heard the faint cry of the pie-sellers offering their freshly baked wares. Her empty stomach grumbled.

She was suddenly ravenous, hungry for something more substantial than her usual light breakfast of tea, toast, and a slim wedge of white cheese. A flaky-crust steak and onion pie, perhaps. A meal in which to sink her teeth.

She pushed her way slowly through the bedclothes. Her body felt unaccountably lush and agile. Even the cold air seemed to caress her skin.

How dare he.

Had he passed a peaceful night?

She washed briskly with her precious orange blossom soap from Spain, usually reserved for special occasions such as court appearances or Christmas mornings. Well, today *was* a special day. The day she rededicated herself to the ordinary life she had chosen. And to the young ladies whose parents had entrusted her with instilling in their daughters the highest values.

She inquired after Lord Wolverton during breakfast and was informed by Heath that Adrian was apparently still alive but asleep. What that meant Emma was afraid to ask.

It seemed best for now to let sleeping wolves lie. If Adrian had passed a restful night, it was more than she could say for herself.

"If you are concerned about him," Heath added from behind his morning newspaper, "I'd be happy to accompany you to his room."

She shook her head dismissively. "Perhaps later. I have a demanding day. I might visit him when he's had a chance to rest."

He raised his brow. At least she imagined he did, his face still hidden behind the morning news. She could only assume there was not yet any mention of the wedding brawl in the papers.

"Should I give him your regards in the meantime?" he asked as she rose from the table.

She took a breath. "Of course."

"And I'll explain," he went on in a casual tone, "how busy you are. Too busy to sit at his bedside."

She stared at the door. She reminded herself how dearly she loved her four brothers. She really did, even when they provoked her. "You might want to phrase that a little less bluntly."

"Don't worry about Wolf's feelings, Emma. He's not the sort to weep over a slight."

"I'm sure he's not."

"I'll take care of him for you," he murmured.

She gripped the doorknob. "That is a comfort to me."

He chuckled. "I knew it would be."

Chapter Seven

❧ ❧

Adrian awakened later that morning with barely an ache to remind him of the embarrassing events that had brought him to his ignominious position. He thought immediately of Emma and wondered when he would see her again or if she intended to ignore him. He yawned fitfully and had just thrust the bed curtains apart when he heard a woman speaking outside his door. It did not sound like Emma's soft, pleasant voice. Perhaps it belonged to one of the mice who had found it amusing to study him last night while he slept.

Rising, he strode to the rose-satin chaise and attempted to arrange his too-big body across the embroidered cushion in an intimidating, male pose. The effort made his temples pound faintly in protest; it was a dull pain he could ignore and it soon receded.

There was a light rap at the door. Then a woman's voice inquired, "Are you awake, Lord Wolverton?"

He lifted his brow. Not a mouse's voice that. "Yes."

"May Charlotte and I visit? It is Heath's wife, Julia, and my cousin-in-law. I won't stay long."

Ah, Julia, the wife of his host, Lord Heath. She was definitely not the sort of lady to accost a strange man in his sleep. Her husband appeared to be another matter. Adrian grinned as he remembered the scandal this red-haired viscount's daughter had caused Heath right before their marriage last year. London had been at turns shocked and delighted when she had sketched his disreputable parts as a cartoon of Apollo and then lost her drawing, only to discover it printed in the broadsheets of the city.

"Please come in, Julia."

"Good. You are awake," she said in relief. "And famished, I expect. Would you like your valet sent up to shave you before or after breakfast? He's been here all morning with your personal belongings. I've kept a plate of bacon and eggs warm for you. I never thought to see you laid low, Adrian."

He leaned his head back against the demeaning piece of furniture. What *he* would have liked was to see Emma standing behind Julia, rather than her comely blond companion who had not lowered her blue eyes quickly enough for him to perceive the laughter in them.

He sighed. Just because he had promised that he would not remind Emma of the Evening-That-Had-

Never-Happened didn't mean he couldn't hope for another chance. He was suddenly irritated at how easily he had alienated her affections with his untimely bid for intimacy.

"Lord Wolverton?" Julia asked, apparently concerned by his lapse of attention. "Shall I send for the doctor? Have you taken a queer turn?"

"Perhaps I should summon Lady Lyons," Charlotte said from the door.

"Wait," Julia said, her eyes full of mischief. "She's teaching table manners this morning. You know how she dislikes to be interrupted in the middle of such crucial instruction."

Table manners. Adrian suppressed a grin. He could just hear her refined voice now as she drilled her debutantes on the importance of not impaling their peas with a knife.

"Lord Wolverton," Julia said again, a little more sharply this time. "Let me look at your eyes."

He blinked. She was a tall, commanding woman and apparently not one to be ignored. Heath Boscastle had allegedly been in love with her for years but had almost lost her when he went to war. Now that he reflected upon it, Adrian seemed to recall that Julia's love affair with Heath had been sparked after she'd shot him in the shoulder. He assumed it had been an accident. He couldn't be entirely sure. The Boscastles tended to marry strong-hearted mates, which would contribute to perpetuating their passionate line.

"Why do you want to look at my eyes?" he demanded suddenly of Julia.

"To judge how responsive you are."

"I'm responding to you well enough now, aren't I?"

Julia raised her brow. "You know, Charlotte, it might not be a bad idea to fetch Emma, after all."

"Why?" Charlotte asked in amusement.

"Because she is accustomed to dealing with the recalcitrant."

"And the socially hopeless," Charlotte added, her mouth curving into a grin.

"I beg your pardon," Adrian said. "Have the pair of you come here to make fun of me?"

"We're only thinking of your welfare," Julia said lightly.

"My welfare." Had he been away from England so long that women had become liberal in expressing their opinions? Or was this a particular influence of the Boscastle men? Not that he'd given the matter deep thought, but if he ever married, he might appreciate a woman who wasn't afraid of her own shadow. Or of him.

Marriage. He supposed it would be expected of him if he chose to accept his legacy. Breeding sons and horses came as part of the package, and it wasn't an unpleasant prospect for the future.

"Recalcitrant," he muttered. "Hopeless."

Julia laughed. "Perhaps the last was an exaggeration. But you have to understand that my sister-in-law is the family's caretaker, and well, we're all a bit intimidated by her."

"A bit?" Charlotte, said, laughing.

Intimidated? Adrian smiled to himself. In a certain light he could see how Emma would intimidate. He'd been a little afraid of her until they were alone and she had softened, let down her guard.

"What she means," Charlotte said, "is that Emma lavishes her attention intensely on those of us in whom she perceives a deficit."

Another person entered the room before Adrian could reflect upon this revelation. He glanced up in the hope that it might be Emma herself, come to lavish attention on him. It was her brother, Heath.

"Is our hero demonstrating his deficits this morning?" he asked wryly, seemingly having overheard at least the latter part of the conversation.

He went straight to his wife's side; his arm slid around her waist. "What we were discussing," Julia said, leaning comfortably into Heath's embrace, "was how Emma thrives on taking care of those in need."

"Ah." Heath grinned. "It's true, I'm afraid. My sister will probably fret over you unmercifully as long as you remain within her care."

"Really?" Adrian managed to sound polite but disinterested even as he absorbed every word. *Within her care*. Why was that phrase so enticing? "I shall have to do my best not to draw attention to myself," he said after a brief hesitation.

Heath met his gaze. "That's a good idea."

A warning there. Adrian had failed to hide all traces of his interest in Emma.

"My sister is never happier," Heath continued, "than when coaxing social improvement in the uncouth."

"I hope she can forgive me for what happened yesterday," Adrian said, smiling faintly. Not to mention last night. Would she forgive him? Could he make her believe what they'd done was as uncommon an occurrence for him as it had been for her?

Heath shrugged. "She seemed herself at breakfast."

Adrian shifted in the chaise; he felt a bit foppish with his legs crossed at the ankles to keep them from dangling in midair.

"Speaking of which," Heath went on, now addressing the two ladies in the room, "yon Wolf has a lean and hungry look. What do you say we feed him breakfast to fortify him before another visit from the doctor?"

Adrian grunted. It was on the tip of his tongue to insist there was nothing wrong with him that required a visit from that mountebank. But something stopped him. He crossed his arms behind his neck.

And he knew what—or, rather, who—it was.

If Emma Boscastle felt the need to lavish her attention on an uncouth being, she had certainly met her match in Adrian. Never had a man begged more for betterment. He wondered idly whether she was up to such a challenge. And how he could present his case to her in a way she could not refuse, or that would not offend her family.

Emma could not concentrate.

His face insisted upon stealing into her thoughts.

That hard, compelling face. It was strange, she mused, but when a certain light captured his strong bones, he appeared as cold and distant as a Norse god. Yet when he smiled or teased, he seemed vulnerable, a man who had simply lost his way.

She stared down at the etiquette manual from which she had been reading aloud. She couldn't find her place. She couldn't even remember what she'd been—ah, table manners. So very essential.

"Woolgathering, are we?" Harriet asked, her impudent voice jolting Emma's attention back to the present.

She cleared her throat. Now even a ragamuffin found cause to scold her. "One starts to learn table manners almost at the moment of birth," she said, warming to the familiar. "A diligent nursemaid never allows her charge to eat his eggs without a fresh linen bib. And even the youngest infant must learn not to spill."

She paused, distracted by the sight of one student slumped forward in her chair. "Good heavens," she exclaimed. "Is Miss Butterfield dozing off? This will never do."

"Blame Harriet," one of the girls grumbled. "She kept everyone up all night."

Emma laid her book down upon the table with a light bang. "Amy. Amy."

Miss Butterfield woke up with a start of embarrassment. The other students smirked. It was never pleasant to be on the receiving end of Lady Lyons's reproach. But it was wonderful fun to witness a fellow student's scolding.

Emma frowned. The image of a pair of warm hazel eyes and sensuous mouth taunted the back of her mind. Her concentration faltered. This would not do. How could a man she'd met only yesterday intrude upon her guiding principles?

It had never happened. He had promised.

She raised her voice. "We will discuss next how one is to hold a spoon and fork."

Harriet slouched in her chair with a huge sigh. "Are we still talking about that messy baby?"

"It's your fault, Harriet Gardner," Miss Butterfield burst out, tears of anger in her eyes. "She got cross at *me* because you kept us up till all hours with your vulgar games."

Emma paled. Another thread unraveled.

"Vulgar games?" She strode to Harriet's chair. "I hope I have misheard. You did not sneak back to the rookeries last night and take along the other girls? You did *not* involve them in your former life?"

Harriet stood, her head bowed in an attitude of

meekness. "No, Lady Lyons, upon my humble soul I did not commit the crime of which I am so unfairly charged."

Miss Butterfield jumped out of her chair. "You dirty little gutter girl! Tell her what you did do, then. Tell her, Harriet Gardner."

Harriet's head jerked up. Fists raised, she shot around her chair like a pugilist only to be hauled back by Emma's hand. "Who the bleedin' 'ell are you calling dirty, I wanna know? Who the effin'—"

Emma clamped her other hand over Harriet's mouth, effectively smothering what she knew from experience would be a blistering earful of shameful invective. Miss Butterfield smirked, only to be nudged back to her chair by Charlotte Boscastle.

Another girl popped up in her place. "Harriet didn't leave the house. She made us all go upstairs and dared us to look at the duke's heir."

"The duke's heir?" Emma said, aghast. "She disturbed Lord Wolverton?" She lowered her hand from Harriet's mouth. "Whatever were you thinking?"

Harriet backed away from her. "I only wanted a peek at 'is nibs while he slept. That ain't no crime, is it?"

One of the younger girls spoke. "She ordered us to look at him while he slept, Lady Lyons. She said that if we wanted to marry a duke, we had to see what one looked like in the dark."

Emma did not dare ask what they had seen.

*   *   *

Less than an hour later Adrian was reconsidering the wisdom of prolonging his recuperation as an underhanded method of attracting Emma's continued attention. He was not even sure he could tolerate being laid up for another day. The rough-hearted men who had fought under him would burst their sides with hysterics if they could see him taking breakfast in bed.

He who had refused brandy when he'd been stitched up by a surgeon from wrist to scapula with only a stick clenched between his teeth to stifle his screams of pain. Hell. The surgeon had been drunk and sweating more than Adrian.

If he remained in this house for another hour, it would only be for one reason. Which had absolutely nothing to do with injury or enfeeblement. It had everything to do with his desire to be near Emma Boscastle.

And since she'd made it painfully clear she wished nothing further to do with him, he would have to be a little more subtle about how he went about it. He would have to prove himself to her. As he'd never bothered about making an impression before, and as he was anything but subtle in manner, he perceived he had a problem.

So he loitered in bed a little longer, studying the church spires and gray sky through the window.

Unfortunately, he had not pondered long before another visitor interrupted his concentration. He groaned inwardly as he recognized Emma's cousin, Sir Gabriel Boscastle, a handsome gambler and hard-seasoned soldier with a dark sense of humor who had walked on the dangerous side of life a few times himself. He'd been at odds with his London cousins in the past. It appeared the two factions of the family had made amends. "Look at our little patient. I heard you ruined a perfectly good chair with your head yesterday."

Adrian snorted. Gabriel was a man's man, a lady's man, and had lived as many years on the fringe of Society as he had. "I might just jump out of bed and throttle the next person who reminds me of that humiliating fact."

Gabriel broke into a grin. "At least they've got your head resting on pretty silk cushions. Would you like me to bring you some flowers?"

Adrian laughed reluctantly. "I thought I might start reading fashion magazines."

"All jesting aside, are you all right?" Gabriel inquired, swinging his long legs over a stool.

"How do I look?"

Gabriel shook his head. "Damned peculiar on that chaise, I have to say. Why are you still here, anyway?"

"I suppose I am easily amused."

Gabriel lowered his voice. He'd been born with the dark Boscastle beauty and passion for life. "You don't know what you're up against."

Adrian angled forward, his interest piqued. "Explain."

"Escape, my friend, while you have the chance. This is not a place for men like us who value their freedom."

"I suppose you're referring to the young ladies of the academy," Adrian retorted. "I believe I can keep them at bay."

"Hell, not them," Gabriel said rudely. "I mean the headmistress, Emma. Get out of this house and run for your life before her gloves of doom grasp you in their dainty but deadly clutches."

Now Adrian's curiosity was not merely piqued, it was aroused uncontrollably. "Run from Emma? She's half my size," he mused. And more than twice his weight in spirit.

Gabriel smiled darkly. "Once she realizes what a miserable past you've led, she will move heaven and earth to make your life one of duty and decency."

Adrian cleared his throat. He liked what little he knew of Gabriel. But, frankly, he was more intrigued by his dire threats of Emma's intentions than discouraged. "I must say, Gabriel, if she tried to redeem you, it doesn't seem to have worked."

"Some of us are beyond redemption," Gabriel replied, unoffended. "I try to avoid her notice as much as possible. Of course you don't have much choice. You do know what the family calls her? The Dainty Dictator."

Adrian hid his amusement behind a bland expression. It occurred to him that Emma had developed her leadership skills of necessity in a family of dominant personalities. A wilting violet would perforce be trampled at an early age in this clan.

"I suppose I would have done the same thing yesterday if I saw her insulted," Gabriel mused. "Mind you, I think you should have ducked before ruining that chair."

"That's good advice." Adrian suddenly reached back for a cushion to hurl at Gabriel's chest. "Duck."

Gabriel caught the cushion with a grin. "Just don't say I didn't warn you. Lying here wounded makes you an ideal target for one of Emma's improving crusades. It's truly painful when she decides to redeem you because, well, because there's something about her that makes a man wish he could be better. She lectures you. You pretend to listen, and then before you know it, you start hearing her voice, like an angel of conscience on your shoulder, just when you're tempted to have a good time."

"Well, she won't have any luck with us in the long run, will she?"

"Not in my opinion." Gabriel tossed the cushion back onto the chaise. "But that doesn't mean she won't take up the challenge and put us through torment in the meantime."

Adrian laughed. No one in his memory had ever taken him as a cause. It sounded almost pleasant.

"She improves young girls, Gabriel. Not battle-scarred soldiers like you and me."

Gabriel backed toward the door. "Now there's a thought. She can buff you up with beeswax for one of her debutantes. I might even suggest it to her before I leave."

"Why, in God's name?"

Gabriel grinned. "Because as long as she's got her hands occupied with one sinner, she's not likely to try reforming me. Don't let her delicate appearance fool you, Adrian. Emma is the equal of her brothers when it comes to having her way."

Emma's temples began to pound with tension. Why had she been possessed to think she could change a girl from the gutters of Seven Dials into a gentlewoman?

A peek at Lord Wolverton while he slept.

Had he even been asleep? "What time did you perpetrate this unforgivable intrusion, Harriet?" she asked in a choked voice.

Harriet shrugged her thin shoulders. "Not long after you walked your nightly patrol."

"It is not a patrol," Emma said in vexation. "Did Lord Wolverton awaken during your misdeed?" she demanded.

"Didn't you 'ear him?" Harriet asked with a grin. "He roared to bring down the walls."

"You should send her back to the slums, Lady Lyons," Lydia Potter suggested. "My parents would be ever so upset if they knew I was rubbing shoulders with the likes of her."

Harriet smirked. "I'm sticking a big brown spider up yer nose while you're asleep tonight—"

Emma took hold of Harriet's arm. "You shall do nothing of the kind. Please, Harriet, do behave."

"Why do you even bother?" Harriet asked, as if it were a question she'd heard a thousand times in her life. "I'm a hopeless cause. Everyone knows that. I'm only gonna come to a bad end and bring the rest of you down with me. Why bleedin' bother?"

She spoke the words without pity or even defiance, as though she'd long ago resigned herself to the fact. Emma found herself torn. She had an obligation to her paying students, the vow she had made to their parents, that their daughters would emerge from their cocoons of awkwardness into enchanting social butterflies.

But nobody wanted to help the street girls of London, the orphans, the abandoned, the abused. Were they truly hopeless? Surely not all. Surely a woman of conscience could not sleep at night without trying.

She released Harriet's arm. "I shall attempt one more time." She picked up her manual from her desk. " 'The invention of eating utensils such as the spoon precedes the wheel.' "

"Well, hell," Harriet said. "Who'd have guessed? Or cared, for that matter?"

Emma continued as if she had not noticed the interruption. "Does anyone know what is said to distinguish a gentleman—and I cringe even using the term—from a clodpate?"

"His ancestors?" Miss Butterfield asked brightly.

"No." Emma allowed a fleeting look of disdain to settle upon her aristocratic face. "It is the use of a fork—"

"A fork," Harriet said. "Well, blow me down with a friggin' feather."

"—over a spoon," Emma continued calmly. "The *use* of a fork over a spoon separates the gentleman from his lessers. And I daresay we still raise countrymen on our proud island who may as well eat with a shovel, so abysmal are their table manners."

Harriet regarded her wistfully. "Lady Lyons, if you honestly think that using a spoon to eat is the worst crime a man can commit, I would be willing to enlighten you otherwise."

"Please, don't," Emma said quickly. She pressed her knuckle to the tickling vein beneath her right eyebrow. Her head felt as if it might indelicately explode. "Actually, I think this is a good time for you girls to gather your shawls and take a walk in the garden with your sketchbooks. I shall expect each of you to draw in detail whatever object of beauty catches your eye."

"I know what Harriet is going to draw," Miss Butterfield said in a disgruntled voice.

Harriet snorted. "Well, I wouldn't be the first one in this 'ouse to draw it, I can tell you that."

"Go upstairs, Harriet," Emma said tersely. "Read a book or . . . take a nap."

"A nap?"

"Under no conditions are you to disturb Lord Wolverton again, do you hear?"

"Anything to please you."

"Good gracious," Charlotte said, hurriedly throwing on her cloak as the girls filed out of the room. "I shall have to accompany them. Harriet is liable to start a revolt if left unsupervised."

Emma sighed. "I know."

"What are you going to do about her, Emma? She's quite incorrigible."

"I'm not sure."

"I should be tempted to turn her out on her ear."

"I am tempted, believe me. And, yes, I know everyone thinks I'm a trifle mad for trying to reform a street girl in the first place. Perhaps I am."

"Perhaps everyone else is wrong," Charlotte gave her a sympathetic smile. "You've worked wonders on some of your students."

"I've had modest success."

She had, in fact, done her duty by the three other altruistic cases she'd undertaken. One had become a competent housekeeper; her sister had married a judge. The third was a dedicated schoolmistress in Gloucester who was engaged to an apothecary.

No one knew how those minor triumphs had lifted Emma's spirits. How her personal mission to transform all of England into a haven for the refined had lifted her above the pall of grief that had befallen her when she had lost a brother, her father, and her husband in a short span of time.

Perhaps it was sheer Boscastle arrogance, believing herself imbued with the power to improve others.

At least in her case, as opposed to the behavior of her siblings, she had channeled that Boscastle spirit into a force for the good of humankind.

Until last night.

Last night . . . when she had proven, if only to herself, that Emma Boscastle really wasn't any different, or any better, than the rest of her scandal-prone family. She might well be the most wicked of the lot, and if this were true, well, there would be no one in the family to take her to task.

Adrian rubbed the thick towel against his smooth jaw. His valet, Bones, could shave a man in under a minute. He could behead one, too, if it came to it, which had been a useful talent for a mercenary's subaltern and makeshift undertaker, but one that would hardly stand him in good stead with English Society. He and Bones had met while defending East Indiamen from French pirates on the Persian Gulf, their duty having been to discourage the growth of French industry. A year later Bones had lost an eye while defending Lahore and had consequently offered to sail as Adrian's valet to Java under the orders of Stamford Ruffles. Bones had done his part to enable the British to conquer Batavia.

"How do I look?" Adrian inquired, stooping to examine his face in the gilt-edged cheval glass.

"The very picture of health, my lord."

"That's what I was afraid of."

"I beg your pardon."

Adrian regarded his sun-burnished complexion in disgruntlement. "I don't look as if there's a thing wrong with me."

"Indeed, you do not," his valet agreed. "I thought you said you'd never felt better in your life, that something had happened to snap you out of the doldrums."

"Damnation."

"My lord?" Bones asked, busily repackaging his soaps and blades.

"You dressed a few men for their funerals after battle in the Punjab, didn't you?" Adrian asked.

"Alas, more than a few. It was the least I could do, with no professional to prepare their bodies for burial. I viewed it as an artistic compassion. Remember that at one time, I had hoped to work in the theater—"

"Do you think you could make me look a little less wholesome?" Adrian interrupted. "Not deathly ill, you understand. But a trifle poorly. A man you'd feel needed a little tenderness."

"I could make you look as if you had been trampled by a herd of elephants," Bones said with a contemplative air. "Or by a stagecoach, considering we are back in what one arguably calls the civilized world."

"I doubt we need go to those extremes," Adrian said pensively. "An impression of underlying malaise will suffice for my purposes."

Thankfully Bones did not inquire what those purposes might be. He was already poking about the pots of rouge and rice paper that sat in neat rows upon the dressing table. "Ah, if I could only find a little ceruse—are you quite sure about this, my lord? The physician is waiting outside the door. He will insist you remain in bed if you appear unwell. I know how idleness displeases you."

Adrian dropped down onto the chaise, tilting his head back in anticipation. "I shall simply have to take his advice if he does, won't I? Who am I to argue with a superior mind?"

It seemed to Emma that scarcely fifteen minutes of relative peace had elapsed before another crisis presented itself. Charlotte intercepted her at the door, her cheeks high with color.

"I was just on the way into the garden." Emma was tying the ribbons of her low-crowned silk bonnet beneath her chin. "Have the girls settled down?"

"The girls are fine." Charlotte paused to catch her breath.

"That reminds me, Charlotte. Did the earl's niece send any more news of when she would arrive? I should hate for her to witness a scene such as that with Harriet on her first day. When she—"

Charlotte broke in quietly. "It's *him*."

"What?" And yet deep inside she knew. How could she not when nothing else had occupied her thoughts?

"It's Lord Wolverton." Charlotte's voice was soft but distraught. "I heard the footmen asking about the house for Heath. It seems the physician has just finished examining Lord Wolverton and fears he's taken a turn for the worse. He did warn us this could happen."

"Oh, no." A chill raised gooseflesh on her arms. "He looked so . . . vital when I saw him last night." Rather too vital. "I should have visited him personally this morning. This is all my fault."

"Of course, it's not," Charlotte assured her, ever loyal to her social sponsor and cousin. "His condition must have declined during the night. How could anyone fault you?"

"During the night?" Emma lapsed into worried silence. If she hadn't exactly encouraged Adrian's amorous advances late last night, she had not rebuffed them, either. To think that the exertion of their unplanned episode could have been the catalyst for his decline. No. She refused to entertain such a mortifying possibility. The passion of Emma Boscastle doing physical harm to a man? She felt faintly ill herself all of a sudden.

"Have you seen him yourself, Charlotte?" she asked, her eyes ink dark with distress.

"Yes. But only for the few moments I left Julia with the girls and accompanied the physician."

"How did he look?"

"A little pale. His skin had a waxen look. Not, I don't know, well, but then I didn't want to appear as if I were examining him."

"Dear me." Emma could not easily envision his deterioration, having left a man whose energy had been striking.

"He was ever so cavalier about it, Emma. I could tell he was struggling to hide how he felt. A true gentleman at heart that man, if ever I saw one, and I don't care what he may have done in the past. He even insisted I not disturb you with news of his relapse."

"Which, of course, quite properly, you did."

Charlotte gave a heartfelt sigh as Emma edged around her to ascend the stairs. "Yes, well, I knew you would kill me if I didn't."

Chapter Eight

✥ ✥

As she entered the bedchamber, Emma took grave note of the Boscastle physician bent at Adrian's side. The air was redolent with the pungent scent of an herbal poultice and burnt feathers. "How is he?" she asked with a worried glance at the large man lying upon the bed.

"His pulses seemed fine until you entered the room, Lady Lyons," the doctor answered, sounding a little perplexed. "Perhaps the excitement of hearing your voice after what happened yesterday has overstimulated him."

"After what—"

"Forgive me for bringing it up again," the physician said at her distraught look. "I know it is an incident a lady would wish to forget."

He had no idea. Emma took another step forward. The excitement of seeing her after what happened . . . He could not possibly be referring to those events of the past evening, unless Adrian had become delirious and talked in his sleep.

She tiptoed closer to his bedside. From the doorway he had appeared more subdued than the last time she had seen him, which, considering exactly what he'd been doing to her, was a relief.

But as his head turned on the pillow, as his unfocused eyes lifted briefly to hers in question, she was struck by his obvious decline during the night. His beautiful sun-bronzed skin had taken on a chalky pallor. Dark circles carved shadows above his strong cheekbones. The devilish twinkle in his half-lidded hazel eyes could only be a sign of fever. "He doesn't look himself at all," she exclaimed.

The physician shook his head. "I agree. I'd have applied leeches to his veins had he not kicked up such a fuss."

She took a deep breath. "Perhaps you will have to restrain him. I don't mind helping if it is what he requires."

"We can wait a bit. I've just gotten a decent dose of opium into him—Lady Lyons, you look a little peaked yourself. Should you not have a sit?"

"Thank you, no." Her horrified gaze latched on the jar of leeches at Adrian's bedside. The poor rogue. Was it possible that he had not even known he was seducing her last night? Had *she*, in letting herself be taken advantage of, taken advantage of a senseless man? Perhaps he had not been himself at all. Perhaps he had not even known what he was about.

"Dear heavens," she whispered, backing so abruptly

into the bedpost that she not only alarmed the physician but also startled Adrian into opening his eyes to stare at her.

A shiver of electrifying sensation chased down her back. For the most peculiar instant he appeared so lucid that she was tempted to believe he had made a sudden recovery. And then he slumped back against the pillows with a disheartening moan. She was not certain what his behavior meant.

She turned her head to the physician. "Did he just awaken only to fall unconscious again?"

The Scotsman leaned over Adrian's unmoving form, searching for the pulse in his throat. "He appears to be asleep. I've drugged him heavily. I do believe you aroused his passions and thus stimulated his response."

"I *what*?" she asked in an embarrassed whisper.

"The passionate humours that govern a patient's— my gracious, it is only an old medical term, Lady Lyons. I did not mean it in a literal sense nor to offend you." He rose. "The smell of these herbs is aggravating my lungs. Excuse me while I step out into the air a moment to clear my head. Do you want me to summon a servant? I don't think he is liable to awaken again for some time."

Emma shook her head. "I'll wait until you come back."

Adrian was surprised how guilty he felt at Emma's concern over his apparent, and fraudulent, decline.

In fact, he was suddenly ashamed of himself for attempting to deceive her. The truth was that he enjoyed her attention, and he wasn't entirely ready to give it up. The concern of an attractive woman, he was learning, was a powerful beguilement indeed.

She touched his shoulder, murmuring that he would be all right. Her voice held him spellbound. Adrian could not remember when, if ever, he'd known such a pure and beautiful attraction. Without doubt she was the most desirable, the finest woman he'd ever met. She came from a family he had long respected.

And how had he repaid that respect?

His thoughts drifted.

The drug blunted his awareness. He slipped into elusive darkness, a dream.

"Don't be afraid," Emma whispered.

"Of what?" His voice was hoarse. It must be nightfall. Had he been asleep?

"Of the dark. I'm here to take care of you. I know what you need."

What he needed.

He managed to sit up in bed and stared into the dark, his throat closing. He wasn't sure how long she'd been at his side. But she appeared to be removing her dressing gown, slowly dropping it to the carpet. Her beautiful breasts shone like large pearls in the darkness. Her slender limbs danced enticingly beyond his reach. Delicate yet voluptuous. A woman's ripe body. His groin burned.

"Beautiful," he whispered. "Don't let anyone else . . . see you."

His gaze traveled over her perfect body. Her brown-pink nipples, her rounded belly, the fluff of gold-tinged curls above her sweet quim. He wished to God he could shake off his fatigue. His mouth watered at the sight of her. "Turn around," he ordered her huskily, his penis lifting against the bedclothes.

She did, her red-gold hair teasing the tempting white cheeks of her arse. He grabbed her by the waist, one hand settling between her silky thighs. She was warm and fragrantly wet, riding his wrist like a naughty little nymph. He bit her nape. She bucked, thrusting her breasts out, and uttering a soft cry. He squeezed one ripe nipple until it turned cherry-red and taut.

His cock rose hard and throbbing. He pushed off the bedcovers and drew her down onto his lap.

"I don't want you to overexert yourself," she whispered, sitting delicately between his heavy thighs. "You're not well."

"Are you going to make me well?" he asked, not feeling weak but powerful, so desperate to house his aching prick in her pouting little cleft that he couldn't seem to focus. He thrust upward.

She smiled and cupped her firm breasts in her hands. The taut pink tips protruded between her fingers. "You have to stay in bed while I take care of you. I know what you need."

"What I need," he whispered.

He groaned and locked his hands around her hips. She slid forward with a gasp of pleasure until his penis probed between her damp gold curls. Penetration eluded him. He writhed in frustration. "I think this would help," he whispered, raising himself into her.

She lifted herself daintly from his lap to accommodate his turgid organ. "Like so?"

He groaned in agonized delight. "Yes. Sit on me, Emma. My shaft is about to burst."

She slid her hands down to the base of his enormous erection. He was going to explode soon, in or outside her tempting body, between her fingers or against her belly. "Will it fit?" she asked in a taunting whisper.

He flexed his back, the tip of his cock stabbing the drenched lips of her womanhood. "We'll make it fit, sweetheart," he said. "We'll stretch you slowly until you take it all the way. I can't quite . . . I can't . . ."

In a faraway voice she whispered, "Adrian . . . are you all right?"

Was he all right? He would be as soon as he found relief.

He surged upward, impaling her in answer. It felt so good. She gave a soft cry of surrender. He felt her hands on his face, his neck. His body moved spasmodically.

She eluded him. His stones ached. His body drew taut, every muscle aching for the release that evaded him. Suddenly he felt her slipping away. He groaned in despair.

"Please," he whispered.

Her soft voice filtered through a fog. "You mustn't thrash so."

"I'll be good." His body trembled. He could smell the sweetness of her hair, her skin. Her breasts brushed his face. "Please, Emma," he whispered. "Don't leave me. I need you."

He opened his eyes and knew it had been a dream. In the back of his mind he heard his father's damning prediction. "You'll ruin lives, Adrian. You've already ruined mine."

"Liar," he said. "You're a liar."

"Are you awake, my lord?" Emma whispered, her voice worried. "How unsettled you are. I do admit I was afraid for you."

"Someone drugged me." He was suddenly lucid. Emma was sitting at his bedside, her eyes heavy with fatigue. For a hopeful moment he thought they were alone until he noticed Julia dozing a few feet away on the chaise. He sank back down onto the bed in disappointment. He'd been dreaming, half-delirious. Why did he have to awaken?

"The doctor thought you needed sedation," Emma told him gently. "You were so restless that we didn't want to leave you."

"Did I say anything in my sleep?"

She stared down at him. "Yes, but I couldn't understand you. How do you feel?"

"Thirsty as hell." Aroused. His body ached unbearably, hot and heavy with unfulfilled passion. And if she hadn't noticed, he wasn't about to draw his discomfiture to her notice.

"Is he awake?" Julia asked groggily from the chaise. She rose, hugging a cashmere shawl around her shoulders. "I didn't mean to doze off. How is he, Emma?"

"He's thirsty," Adrian replied. Among other things, and now there were two of them to deceive.

"I'll fetch some fresh water," Julia said.

Emma glanced up. "No. I'll call a footman—"

"I need to move about," Julia said, already at the door. "I've a horrible pain in my neck."

Her voice trailed off. The candles fluttered as the door shut.

"Are we alone now?" Adrian asked, easing up on one well-muscled shoulder, his eyes intent on Emma.

She glanced back at the closed door. "Yes, but she won't be—"

She gasped in surprise as he pulled her onto the bed and wrapped his arms around her waist, his face buried in her neck. "I had a dream about you," he said. "I've never dreamed like that before."

"A dream—Adrian, she's going to come back at any moment."

"I don't care."

He sank his fingers into the tight knot of hair at

her nape and sought her mouth. If they had only a moment, he was not about to waste it. He could hear her breath catch sweetly. For an instant he felt her resistance start to slip; her mouth parted for his kiss, her back arched against the hand he'd planted above her bottom. Desire leapt to life in his belly. He might have been dreaming of her before, but this was real. Her breath mingled with his. Her soft flesh yielded.

He wanted her. Not only her surrender but her company, damn the danger of being caught. They were past the age of reproach. She had been married and he'd been to war. His blood came to a slow boil, and she knew it, too. He enjoyed the challenge. In proving himself to her, he might convince himself of his own worth.

"Emma." He brushed the back of his hand down her shoulder to her breast, shivering at the silky texture of her skin, remembering how real his dream had been. His lips teased her mouth.

"Adrian, please," she whispered. "Not now."

He released a sigh. His hands moved down her graceful back, learning her shape, kneading her vulnerable curves. His body was so aroused that it hurt.

They both heard the approach of someone on the stairs at the same time. She raised her hand, inadvertently touching his painful erection. He groaned in resignation and subsided back onto the bed.

She disengaged herself at the same instant the door

opened, whispering in reproach, "This really isn't going to make you feel better, Lord Wolverton."

He stared at her wet, swollen mouth and thought that she was entirely wrong. Talking with her, making love to her, would bring him immense relief. His great body shuddered in need as she threw the covers back over him. "Yes, it is," he said stubbornly. "Just being with you is pleasant. Do you not enjoy my presence?"

She wavered. "I've scarcely known you long enough to think of it."

"Well, you don't steal comfits from a wedding cake to please every stranger you meet, do you?"

She laughed softly to hide her confusion. "No. I don't."

"Then why did you flirt so charmingly with me yesterday?" he challenged her.

She studied his hard-boned face. "Perhaps I was hoping to keep you out of trouble."

"And now," he said quietly, "I'm in the deepest trouble of my life."

She had little time to reflect upon what he meant, or even to respond.

A familiar masculine figure bearing a water pitcher materialized behind Emma. Heath. Not Julia. "What is he saying?" Heath asked, lowering himself onto the stool by the bed. "Julia said he was half-delirious."

"It's nonsense," Emma said evasively. "He was

dreaming. What are you doing here? I should think you were in bed yourself."

Adrian could hear the quaver in her voice. Heath would surely notice it, too. He was of a mind to explain himself to her brother, to confess that he'd developed an inexplicable attraction to Heath's sister. But he'd promised. He couldn't say anything until she gave him permission.

"I thought I'd keep you company," Heath said after a measured silence. "Do you mind?"

Emma looked up at him. Her faint smile seemed to say that if he weren't her trusted older brother, she might have resented his presence. "Why would I mind? He's your friend, isn't he?"

"As far as I know," Heath said, his voice thoughtful. "Our brother-in-law trusts him implicitly."

Emma lowered her eyes. "Dominic is a good man," she said quietly. Dominic had survived a brutal murder attempt and brought his would-be killer to justice with the help of their sister Chloe. "He allows precious few people into his life."

Heath stared at her. "As do you and I, Emma."

She nodded. "I feel responsible for him."

"Is that all?"

"How could it be anything else?" she asked quickly.

"I don't know." His concerned gaze searched her face. "He's led a hard life."

"Yes," she murmured, swallowing. "What of it?"

"You're my sister, that's all."

Chapter Nine

❧ ❧

The physician had come and gone when Emma began her routine the following day. According to Julia's report, Lord Wolverton had been awake when he arrived and had chased the man from his room. After that no one except his valet had dared disturb him again. It was to be hoped by the entire household that this was a sign he was recovering and would soon be himself again. Exactly *who* he was, what sort of man, was a topic upon which Emma reflected as she sat down with a cup of tea in the informal drawing room with its long scrolled-back sofa and matching rosewood table.

She'd gathered three of the girls together for a lesson on the finer points of paying a social call when Julia and her high-spirited aunt appeared and asked to be included.

Emma could hardly refuse. This was, after all, Julia's home. Practical experience in the arts of etiquette was essential.

Furthermore, if any well-received person in London were capable of distracting one from troubling thoughts, it was Lady Dalrymple, or Aunt Hermia, as the entire Boscastle family had fondly come to call her. The robust beldame still had gentleman admirers. One could not help liking the lively Hermia and the ladies of her painting club, although Emma had privately warned her students not to emulate this unconventional circle of older women who thought themselves past the age of propriety.

"Don't tell me we're 'aving tea again," Harriet said as she burst into the room unannounced and flopped into an armchair, dislodging the other three girls who were standing patiently awaiting Emma's permission to sit.

Emma frowned. "What are you doing here, Harriet? I did not summon you."

"Miss Charlotte sent me out to you. I was disrupting history."

"I don't doubt it, my dear. Hold your tongue, please."

"How do I drink me tea if—"

"Silence, please."

Harriet sighed.

Lady Dalrymple examined Harriet's scrunched-up face with an encouraging smile. "Another diamond from the coal scuttle, it appears."

Emma's eyes gleamed. "We make exceptions at the academy for the young and the infirm."

"Infirm as in Lord Wolf?" Harriet asked slyly.

Lady Dalrymple shifted around in attention, a

woman with a keen instinct for mischief. "Lord who?"

"Not now," Emma said hastily. "It isn't a topic for young ears."

"My ears are quite aged," Lady Dalrymple said. "Are you keeping secrets from me, Julia?" she demanded of her niece. "What is this mention of a wolf in London? I do believe that the poor beasts died out almost two centuries ago."

Emma exhaled slowly. "Miss Gardner was ill-advisedly referring to Lord Wolverton, and not a *genuine* wolf."

Lady Dalrymple might be in her dotage; she might be as wrinkled and plump as the next fairy godmother. Her mind, however, was anything but ancient. Her fingers fluttered coyly in her pale butter-yellow gloves. "Did you say Lord Wolverton?"

Emma set aside her cup with care. The elixir of scandal wafted in the air, and clearly Hermia had caught an intoxicating whiff of it. "Yes, unfortunately, I did."

"Adrian?" Lady Dalrymple pressed her gloved knuckle to her chin. "Adrian Ruxley?"

"I believe that is his given name," Emma said evenly.

"That's 'is nibs, all right," Harriet chimed in, taking advantage of Emma's inattention to stuff a whole gooseberry tart into her mouth.

"I saw that," Emma said in an undertone, "and I am quite revolted."

"Well, excuse me," Harriet said, crumbs on her chin. "No one told me we was just supposed to look at 'em. Or are they for dippin' in this piddle here?"

"You may leave now, Harriet," Emma said, not raising her voice at all. "Your lesson is over."

"Do I 'ave to take another nap?"

"Why don't you help in the kitchen?" Julia suggested gently. "Learning what is needed to run a home is a useful skill for any gentlewoman."

Harriet stood. "I'd rather rob a—"

Emma's eyes widened in warning. "You are excused, Harriet."

After a moment of apparent indecision, Harriet took heed of the militant fire in Emma's voice and made a quick escape. Aunt Hermia, however, had not been sufficiently diverted to forget the scandalous topic of conversation.

"What is Adrian doing in this house?" she asked in a conspiratorial whisper.

Emma rose. "He is recovering from an unfortunate mishap. I'm surprised you haven't heard."

"Well, I just got back from Tunbridge—what sort of mishap?" she asked sharply.

"I'm sure Julia will be happy to answer your questions, Aunt Hermia," Emma murmured. "I've really left the other girls alone far too long."

A silence enshrouded the room upon her departure. Julia sipped her tea, and studiously nibbled at her tart. Lady Dalrymple sat and stared at her until Julia began to squirm.

"I will not leave this house until I am told the truth, Julia."

"Oh, *really*. How do you know Adrian, anyway?"

"It has been brought to my attention by one of my friends that he would make a fine addition to our deity collection. I knew his father and his aunt some years ago."

"You are not going to paint an injured man au naturel," Julia said heatedly. "I will not allow it."

"This is a matter of art, my dear," Hermia said with an offhanded shrug. "Is the man possessed of a grand physique?"

"Art?" Julia asked with a disbelieving laugh. "You aren't deceiving anyone. You and your friends like to draw naughty pictures of handsome young gentlemen. There is no excuse for any of you. I'm quite ashamed, at your age."

"Need I remind you, Julia, of a certain woman who unleashed upon the populace a sketch of her lover's primary appendage as a cannon? The Wicked Lady Whitby. Wasn't that your signature?"

Julia was beyond blushing over that particular faux pas. Most likely the notorious cartoon of her husband's royal scepter would be immortalized on her gravestone. "I don't know whether Adrian has a grand physique or not," she said irately. "He has been abed with a head wound, and it did not occur to me to examine him."

Lady Dalrymple drained her cup. "I must pay the heroic man my regards."

Julia's gray eyes widened in shock. "You are *not* going to disturb him. It's indecent of you, Aunt Hermia. It's—"

"—none of your affair, darling. I'm old enough to be his grandmama. I shall simply offer the gentle consolation that only a lady of some years can give."

Julia sprang to her feet. "Don't you dare ask him to pose for your painting circle. He's a duke's son. Moreover, he has suffered a blow to the head and hardly knows what he's about."

"Goodness, my dear, you make me sound as if I mean the brave man harm. I've met his family, as I just told you. His father, old Scarfield, had a passion for me many years back. It's only common courtesy that I pay his son a call."

"Alone, Aunt Hermia?"

Lady Dalrymple stood. "Unless you would like to accompany me?"

Julia flushed. "I should like to restrain you. Short of that, however, I'll only ask you to promise that you will not harangue my guest about posing for your embarrassing club."

Chapter Ten

❧　❧

Adrian swept his sword into the air, his knees bent in a classic fencer's pose. He had come to the regrettable conclusion that his ruse would not work. He'd been bedridden for—how long? not two whole days—and he was ready to jump from the window and climb the rooftops from lack of activity.

Even as a child he had not been able to sit still for more than three minutes at a time. His nursemaids had chased him for hours on end across his father's vast country estate. As a soldier he'd held the conviction that a man's prowess began to deteriorate from the day he did not demand sacrifices of his body. Even if he did come into the dukedom, he had no intention whatsoever of sitting plump-arsed on a bejeweled saddle and trotting about his acres while others broke their backs in labor.

He wanted to fight, to move, to—to make wild love to Emma Boscastle. But as that appealing option seemed to be temporarily denied to him, he wasn't about to laze about in bed like a cosseted empress waiting for a daily bowl of stewed prunes to move his bowels.

Riposte.

Retreat.

He kicked over the stool, leapt onto the chaise, and attacked a nonexistent assailant at the door.

Unfortunately, at that instant, the door opened to admit an unsuspecting chambermaid bringing fresh towels and a pitcher of wash water. She took one look at Adrian, standing on the chaise with his sword directed at her, then emitted a shrill cry and barely managed to unburden her delivery on the floor before whirling to escape.

Adrian lowered his sword. "I'm sorry. Did I frighten you?"

The gamine-faced maid shook her head, suddenly looking more curious than alarmed. Adrian climbed down from the chaise and frowned at her. "Have I seen you before? Aren't you supposed to knock before coming into a gentleman's room?"

"I dunno," she said with an impertinent shrug.

He narrowed his eyes. "Who are you, anyway?"

"I'm whoever she tells me to be."

"Lady Lyons?"

"Yeah." She went down on her knee to collect her towels. "I thought you was laid up."

"I was—I am. There was a cobweb on the ceiling. I was trying to reach it with my sword. I can't abide spiders."

She glanced up shrewdly. "I don't see any cobweb."

"No, you wouldn't. I sliced it to kingdom come."

Her knowing gaze sized him up. "You don't look like there's anything wrong with you, either."

He sat down on the end of the bed. "And you don't look like a chambermaid."

She straightened, a look of delight brightening her elfin features. "I know what you are."

"Do you?" he asked disinterestedly, his sword balanced between his knees.

"You're a scaldrum-dodge."

"A what?"

"You're a fakement."

He gripped the sword hilt. "I beg your pardon."

"There ain't nothin' wrong with your 'ead."

"There must be," he retorted. "Or I wouldn't be talking to you."

She dropped her voice. "You ain't a duke's son, then?"

"That's—this is none of your business."

"Why are you fakin' it? You gonna rob the house?"

He looked up in irritation. "You cheeky monkey."

"Then why—" She started to laugh. "If it's not money, then it has to be— There's only two things a man goes after."

"How old are you?" he demanded.

"Seventeen. I think."

"Well, you sound as if you were brought up in a brothel."

"How'd you know?" she asked, genuinely surprised.

"Go away," he said wearily.

"How much?"

"How much what?" he asked in mild vexation.

She leaned her bony shoulder up against the door. "How much will you pay me not to peach?"

"What?" he said, his voice soft with disbelief.

"How much will you pay me not to tell Mrs. Killjoy you're puttin' her on?"

He stood suddenly, the sword gripped loosely in his left hand. He'd never hurt a female in his life. Then again, he'd never been blackmailed by one, either. "Do you know how I spent the last ten years of my life?"

"Growin' marigolds?"

He walked up to her until she stood pressed flat against the door. "Death. Dismemberment. I've been accused, rightly or wrongly, of a beheading or two."

"I see." She swallowed, nodding in understanding. "So that's why she likes you."

Adrian knew he shouldn't ask. A guttersnipe in any land was hardly the most reliable source of information. But, on the other hand, the girl didn't seem stupid. "How do you know she likes me?"

" 'Cause you're in a bad way. She prides herself on fixin' up people, making them all proper and pretty. Ye're pretty, no doubt. But you ain't proper. There's the devil in your eyes."

He smiled coldly. "In that case, you'd better not cross me."

"I wouldn't dream of it." She thrust her hand at him. "The name's Harriet and I'm gonna be a lady. Shake?"

"No. Just fetch me some clean towels. You've stepped all over the ones you brought, and I'm a bit particular about my personal habits."

She bobbed a shaky curtsy. "I'll have 'em bloody well embroidered in gold thread and ironed, if you like."

He grinned. It never hurt to have an ally. "Then we understand each other?"

She had the nerve to grin back at him. "We cheats and swindlers got to stick together, I always say."

An hour later Adrian had reached the end of his tolerance for inactivity and escaped his room to wander downstairs and into the garden.

He hoped he would catch Emma alone. Her well-meaning scolds cheered him up. He liked the thought of walking with her in the garden, teasing her into a bit of temper. She'd probably admonish him for being out of bed. Perhaps she would take his hand and offer to sit with him for a few minutes.

He walked past a shed and suddenly found himself surrounded by a gaggle of sketching debutantes. He froze. By the expressions on their young faces he knew he'd done something very wrong by interrupting their class. Either that or they'd been warned he was a man to avoid.

Emma would strangle him if he embarrassed her in front of her students. Still, it was too late to make an escape unseen. One of the girls had spotted him over her sketchbook and gave a cheery shout of recognition.

"Crikey! Look who's risen from the dead. It's the duke 'isself."

That voice. He cringed. That impudent young face. The guttersnipe again. He nodded pleasantly as Emma looked up from the bench to stare at him in . . . well, her face gave nothing away. She wasn't exactly strewing rose petals of welcome at his feet. She merely sat in a pose of guarded attention as if she were a figure in a painting. Perhaps she was afraid he would give her away.

"Excuse me," he said, bowing politely and coming to a halt. "I didn't mean to cause a disruption."

A disruption.

Emma breathed out a rueful sigh. A disruption would be defined as a cat chasing a squirrel up a tree, or one of the maids arguing with a butler. Adrian's presence before a dozen or so sheltered debutantes was more akin to the heavens opening up to deposit a demigod in their youthful midst.

Gasps. Squeals. She lifted one hand in annoyance to quelch this little rebellion. "Control yourselves, please. A young lady does not twitter at the sight of a gentleman."

But what a gentleman.

She was discombobulated herself at his appearance. He'd strolled across the grass with long-boned grace, his artless beauty enhanced by his white Irish linen shirt, tight buff pantaloons, and well-worn boots. That his short dark-wheat hair appeared a little disheveled only enhanced his devilish appeal. Beautiful pagan. Her secret lover. Oh, how he made her ache for the forbidden.

Try as she might, Emma could not discourage the girls from staring at him. Unfortunately, she had a hard time ignoring him herself. It did not help matters that he was staring quite frankly at her. Grinning with genuine delight, in fact. She shook her head, apprehension muddling her wits. What on earth did he think he was doing?

If she didn't know better, she would think he was smitten with her. But didn't scoundrels always play their games with such conviction? Half their pleasure came not from the conquest but from the pursuit.

After all, he had admitted he was not inclined to heal the rift with his father in any great hurry. Could a man who had lived as he ever be content with the quiet life of gentility that Emma envisioned for herself? He decided he could.

But could she be content with him.

"I didn't mean to interrupt," he said. "I was dying for some exercise." He waved his arms about in a physical way. "Fresh air, you know. Nothing like it."

She managed to nod. "Yes. However, we were in the middle of a lesson on—" Adrian's arrival appeared to have sent every thought out of her head. "On the correct form of etiquette should one ever be invited to a foreign court."

"A subject close to my heart," he said gravely.

Emma regarded him blankly for several moments. Was he trying to impress her? Could he possibly be as sweet as he seemed? "Indeed. Anyway, as I was about to explain to my students, the wife of a foreign ambassador shares her husband's rank. Therefore, she should be announced after his entry at an entertainment—"

"What if he's late?" Miss Butterfield asked in a worried voice. "My father never arrives anywhere on time."

"She will wait for him," Emma replied. "Now, let us continue to the order of seating."

"Lord Wolverton was a foreign diplomat, wasn't he?" one of the girls cried in excitement. "Perhaps he could enlighten us on diplomatic society, Lady Lyons."

Emma's eyebrows arched at that suggestion. She met Adrian's wry regard for a moment. She doubted that diplomatic society counted a disreputable English mercenary in its elite ranks. "I believe Lord Wolverton was more acquainted with—"

He shrugged modestly. "I don't mind sharing my knowledge. I had to break the news once to the occupants of a harem that their master had been slain in an uprising. Granted, this is not a situation any of you young ladies are likely to encounter."

"One trembles at the thought," Emma murmured.

"He was a rajah," Adrian added, his eyes twinkling.

"Did he own tigers?" Harriet asked.

"Yes. And they escaped after his death."

"I do not see how this is an example of foreign diplomacy," Emma said, terrified at what he would reveal next.

"Well, I was getting to that," Adrian replied. "We had to get the rajah's closest relative on the throne before we had a bloody revolt on our hands. And if you think that doing so was easy in a palace overrun with hungry tigers and weeping women, you don't know what diplomacy really is."

Emma glanced around in dismay; Adrian held thrall over an enrapt audience if ever she had seen one. The girls were hanging on his every shocking word. As she had been. She would indeed have enjoyed hearing more colorful stories from his past, but in private. An adventurer. What did he see in proper Emma Boscastle? Would she become one of his wicked little stories?

She surged to her feet. "Thank you so very much for that elucidating perspective, Lord Wolverton. As it is a social challenge my students will hopefully never face, as you yourself pointed out, I suggest we return to our more mundane instruction. Can anyone tell me the correct form of address for a French ambassador's wife?"

Harriet stood up. "May I ask a question of his dukeship?"

"No," Emma said quickly, "you may not."

"What I want to know," Harriet continued, "is what a girl has to do to marry a duke."

The other pupils gasped in ill-concealed delight at this forward inquiry.

Emma sat down on the bench, resisting the urge to raise her voice.

"I think," Adrian said carefully, "that such a question might be better answered by your headmistress."

Everyone looked expectantly at Emma, who found, to her chagrin, that *she* was awaiting Adrian's response to the highly improper question as eagerly as her class. His answer would certainly not be the usual advice. He was anything but the typical aristocrat.

He coughed quietly, a smile hovering on his lips. "Lady Lyons?"

"Class dismissed until after late afternoon," she announced in a wry voice.

* * *

Emma and Charlotte had decided several months ago that they would write an etiquette manual for those young gentlewomen who strove for refinement but could not afford private instruction. Both women wrote for recreation. But a guidebook was a vast undertaking that would possibly require years of effort and deep practical reflection. Once or twice a week, at the end of the day, Emma would scribble a few notes on a crucial issue to be included.

Sometimes she and Charlotte would indulge moments of sheer silliness and insert a satirical chapter just for fun. The Delicate Art of Disengaging Oneself from a Belching Baronet. How to Pour a Bad Glass of Wine into a Potted Fern at a Party.

Where in this guidebook would there be a chapter entitled: "A Gentlewoman's Disgrace—How to Feign Dignity After the Fall"? She laid down her quill with a sigh, dismayed to notice the nib dripping ink onto her papers. And on her brother's desk, too.

She had never spilled ink in her entire life.

This was the careless state into which her one sin had led her. Where was the sand? She watched the stain spread until a dark velvet voice spoke over her shoulder.

"May I offer you some help?"

She slid from her chair as Adrian reached over

her and blotted the ink with the clean handkerchief he had produced from his vest pocket. "You've ruined that, too, you know," she said in embarrassment. "What a pair we make."

He folded his handkerchief across the ink blot. "What's another stain to a life as corrupt as mine?" he asked in the neutral voice that made it impossible to know whether he was serious or not.

She stood, her heart racing as her eyes met his brooding regard. "You should not be walking about without an attendant," she said lightly. "I meant to mention that in the garden."

His gaze held hers before he glanced away. "And I meant to tell you that I really feel much better. I'm leaving, actually. I've taken advantage of you and your brother long enough."

She crossed her arms under her breasts. What an infuriating person. On the one hand, he made her feel guilty and ashamed for what she'd done with him. On the other, she suffered the same emotions for driving him off before he'd had a chance to heal. "Why is it that men can never admit to any weakness? I'm going to have you taken back to bed. By a footman."

He leaned his hip against the edge of the desk. "Don't bother."

"It's no bother at all," she said, turning toward the bellpull—and finding herself suddenly trapped between a tall virile male and the desk. "What are you doing?" Her voice dropped to a whisper. "What did you want of me?"

"I was looking for Heath," he said quietly, his body a breath from hers.

He edged a little closer. She shivered in response. She raised her face to his. "Really?"

"No." He lowered his gaze. "No. I was hoping to see you before I left."

His confession, the memory of the brief but blissful pleasure they had shared, hung between them, both a taunt to Adrian and a temptation. He wanted her so badly, he refused to believe she did not want him back.

Before she could stop him, or he could stop himself, he bent his head and kissed her. Her lips parted, perhaps in surprise. He drove his tongue deeply inside her mouth. Her body shook. Even then he forced himself to hold his hands at his sides because if he touched her, he would want more and more until he'd taken his fill. He wanted her, and if she were any other woman he would have found a hundred ways to have her. But for now, because she was Emma Boscastle, he had to pretend to observe certain rules of conduct that he'd never bothered to properly learn in the first place.

"No," she murmured, but her lips yielded, warm and lush, and underneath her denial he tasted desire and remembered driving his fingers into her silken flesh. Groaning, he deepened the kiss. "Please," she said faintly.

"Please, what?" he whispered.

"I don't know. Someone might . . . see."

"I locked the door behind me."

Her shoulders gave a delicate shiver that hinted she craved this as much as he did.

"The problem," he continued softly, "is that you're in my every thought. I am tormented by the memory of how it felt the moment I breached your defenses."

Her breathing quickened. "Don't say it."

"You came apart for me," he went on, low and relentless. He trailed his fingers down her throat. "There could have been more. Perhaps you need time. It was my fault, I am a fool to have rushed what should have taken months to grow."

"It doesn't matter now," she said brokenly. "We'll forget it."

"I'll wait," he whispered. "I believe I may need you, although I've never needed anyone before, not like this. Have you? It's not a particularly comforting feeling. I'm not used to being so bloody emotional."

She took a breath. "I'm not going to answer that question."

"I think you just did," he said, smiling at her. "Will you be honest with me?"

She exhaled slowly. "I shall try."

"What would a man like me have to do to win your affections?"

He was teasing her, Emma thought, and a blush

heated her face. His disingenuous banter was so effective that it must have been practiced, perfected, on a dozen other women before her. "I have reached the age, my lord, when discretion overrules desire. When virtue must subjugate Venus."

He looked deeply into her eyes and then, to her indignation, burst into laughter. "That's rubbish. You've never even tasted life. Don't deceive me or yourself."

"How do you know what I've tasted?" she asked in irritation.

He smiled ruefully. "I'm sorry. I didn't mean to insult your vast experiences. However, I doubt that you have seen as much of life as I have."

"Is . . . is everything they say about you true?" she asked in hesitation.

He shrugged. "Such as?"

"Oh, I don't know. Fighting Chinese pirates—"

"They were French pirates, as a matter of fact. Freebooters. The East India Company hired me to put an end to their aggression on what we claim as British territory."

She regarded him with relief. "It all sounds rather noble like that."

He paused. It did. But it hadn't been noble at all. It had been fierce, bloody, and hellish.

"What exactly did you do in the company?" she asked.

He almost answered, anything they bloody paid him for, but he reminded himself that a man had to watch his words around a lady like Emma. It hadn't mattered much how he spoke around soldiers on the other side of the world.

"I am anything but noble, Emma," he said with rueful honesty. "But neither am I a liar."

"Then what are you?" she whispered.

He shook his head, his voice rough. "A man who finds your company irresistible. I don't know the words to explain what I have never felt before. Please, reassure me, I am not alone in this madness."

She lowered her gaze.

His knuckles grazed her collarbone. Her breasts tightened, swelled as if awaiting his touch. How she could pretend to be unmoved when his nearness tormented her, she could not say. Her every sense urged her to submit. It was shaming to realize how this one man had made her so aware of her womanly yearnings. A flush worked slowly down her face into her breasts, then below. He breathed sexual desire into her very bones.

"Adrian," she whispered, closing her eyes.

"You shiver when I touch you."

She shivered when he entered the room, too. "I forgot my shawl in the garden."

"I can't forget what we did, Emma."

"You haven't even tried," she said with a moan of distress. "Adrian, honestly, you aren't being fair."

"Will being fair win you?"

He bent his head, smiling, and kissed her again. His tongue slowly circled hers, sweetly tormenting, until she arched her throat in surrender. Sensual enticement burned in the air they breathed. "I like to think about you," he whispered. "About those little groans you gave as I played with your quim. How wet you were."

"Adrian." Her lower body buckled. The inner walls of her body softened. A stinging surge of blood tingled throughout her veins. "You promised me."

"What I promised," he said thickly, "is that I would not tell. I never said I would not desire you nor try to coax you back into my bed."

She shook her head. Yet he surely knew her body desired him. She could not hide the signs. A soft gasp escaped her lips as his erection jutted into her soft belly. Her pulse beat a wild betrayal at the base of her pale throat.

"Emma." He breathed a groan into her delicate mouth. "Why not? I am a well-born man who lost his way."

Why not? His hips shifted in restless sensuality at the plea. She trembled delicately, further arousing his hard, aching body. He needed to touch her, to feel her flesh. He clenched his hands, swearing he would master his lust for her, and prove his worth.

But in his mind he was undressing and possessing her in every sexual act under the sun. Blood thundered between his temples, in his groin. He ground his teeth, cursing the male instincts that reminded him of the sweet treasures under her skirt, her subtle perfume. Like vanilla and female heat. Comfort and sex with the same woman.

How could he convince her he was not past redemption when his past, his behavior toward her, proved otherwise?

He stared down at her. Her mouth looked damp, swollen, so delicious he would die to taste her again. Somehow he grasped the remnants of his sanity, remembered where they were.

"For the sake of fairness," she whispered, her blue eyes steadily holding his, "I choose to believe that it is your head injury making you behave with impropriety."

He snorted in amusement. Now he felt like twice a devil. Did she not understand what a desperate rogue he was and that for the first time since he could remember, he cared what someone thought?

"Emma, listen to me," he said in a stark undertone. "There is nothing wrong with my head. I'm perfectly fine."

"What are you saying?" she asked him impatiently.

"I only wanted your attention," he said with a sheepish grin. "I admit I took advantage."

"And you expect me to believe that you got hit on the head to attract it?"

"Not exactly. The chair wasn't part of my plan."

He sighed ruefully. "I did hope, however, to stay in bed as long as you were willing to take care of me. I could have walked out of this house anytime I chose. But I chose to play on your goodness and now I'm confessing and asking for your understanding. I deceived you, but only because I took pleasure in your care."

"I see," she murmured. And he thought that she did. "Well, the physician said you were to be kept under observation for several days."

"I don't need bed rest," he protested, his eyes glinting down at her. "I need . . . you. Your personal attention."

"Ah." Her tempting mouth flattened. "I believe that there are any number of women in London who would be more than glad to answer your needs."

"I'm not referring to my carnal needs," he said swiftly. "I haven't been in good society for over a decade, and I've forgotten how to behave. What I need is"—he grasped for inspiration, for the key to her sympathy—"instruction in deportment. I need someone to smooth my rough edges."

"You'll not get an argument from me there."

"I can't have a reunion with the old bugger of a duke unless I'm proper," he elaborated. "He's particular about appearances."

"You should be more particular about your language," Emma exclaimed.

He grinned unexpectedly. "That's exactly what

I'm talking about. I didn't even realize what I'd called him. The word just slipped out. How can I present myself to him in such an unpolished state?"

She drummed her fingers on the desk, her gaze frankly skeptical. "I'd be shocked by all this if I hadn't grown up with five brothers of my own. And—" She shook her head in sudden realization. "Do you mean to tell me you've been in England for almost a year and you have not even *visited* your father?"

"Give or take a few months."

She studied him in dismay. "Your *dying* father? An elderly person who is willing to overlook your past grievances and offer an olive branch of—Why are you looking up at the ceiling, my lord?" she asked annoyedly. "It is most unsettling."

"I was just wondering when the heavenly chorus would break into a hymn." He shrugged at the scolding frown that she gave him. "And, by the way, I'm the one who should be offering forgiveness, not him. He made my life miserable, Emma. He drove me away with his unfounded suspicions. I've lived almost half my life believing I was not his son." He glanced down at her in cynical amusement. "He's also not as old as you think, and he isn't dying."

"He's recovered?" she asked in surprise. "Are you sure?"

"If there was ever anything wrong with him to begin with. I think it was a ploy to bring me home."

"Do you expect me to believe that your father feigned a deathly illness to bring you back home?"

"Yes." And he assumed she would take his side. He had done nothing wrong to his way of thinking.

"You are his son, Adrian," she said, meeting his gaze. "It is your duty and your birthright to honor him."

"Honor him?" he said in disbelief. "That old—"

"It is what you were born to," she said gently. "He cannot disinherit you. It's time to put your personal feelings aside."

"Is that right?" He stepped into her small frame, a tactic, he knew quite well, that was usually distracting. "Scarfield told me for years I was born of a whore and that I wasn't his. Do you expect me to put aside years of abuse?"

"Let him make amends, that's all, and then you can decide. At least you can hear him out."

"Why should I?" he challenged her.

"Have you ever considered what would happen to England if all our blooded aristocrats simply decided to abdicate?"

"I despise him," he admitted, still waiting for her to agree his enmity was justified.

She vented a sigh. "No matter how bitter your feelings, you have to face him. For your sake even more than his."

"Don't tell me what I feel or what I must face," he said, raising his brow. "Just help me."

"I'm not sure how."

"Neither am I. But there you have it, Emma," he said, pressing his forehead to hers. "This all proves I need—"

She laughed. "What?"

"A wife. Perhaps what I need is—a wife."

God help him. Where that notion had sprung from he could not say, but all of a sudden it made sense.

"A wife," she said, shaking her head. "I couldn't agree more. Yes, you do. A duke definitely needs a wife."

They both heard the quiet knock upon the door at the same instant. Adrian swiftly moved aside while Emma returned to her chair, calling out, "Yes. Who is it?"

"It's Charlotte. May I see you a moment?"

Emma bit her lip, glancing up guiltily at Adrian. He gestured to the side door behind the desk that gave into a private corridor. She nodded in obvious relief as he made a discreet escape.

She did her best to behave in her usual manner as she unlocked the door to admit her cousin. At first Charlotte seemed too agitated to notice anything amiss.

She prayed her cousin would not hear Adrian's footsteps fading away in the anteroom corridor.

"What is it, Charlotte?" she asked in concern.

"Why did you lock—oh, never mind." Charlotte glanced around the library. "It's *her*. Lady Clipstone is here and demanding to see you. At this hour, without invitation or forewarning. Hamm did his best to send her away, but I thought it imperative you should know."

Her. Her enemy. Battle flames burst to life in Emma's heart.

Ever a Boscastle at the ready to defend her field, she straightened her back. No wonder Charlotte looked flustered. There was only one woman in London with the effrontery, with the instinct, to arrive in the wake of Emma's personal dilemma and use it to devious advantage.

"Where is she?" she asked tersely.

"The formal drawing room. I served her tea."

"From the best china?"

"Naturally."

Emma gave her an approving pat and charged forth to face her rival. She held high hopes for the future of young Charlotte, whose perception and reticence had thus far protected her from their scandalous ancestry. It remained for Emma to demonstrate by example how a proper gentlewoman should defend herself without sinking to low behavior.

Hypocrite, a small voice taunted her as she strode briskly down the hall. *What sort of example did you set the other night? For that matter, what unspeakable transgression were you tempted to commit only a few minutes before Charlotte interrupted?*

The possibilities, however intriguing, did not bear contemplation.

Not that she was in a frame of mind to ponder the ramifications of a secret romance. Her temper flared the moment she set her eyes upon the trim, fashionably cloaked brunette awaiting her in the drawing room. She paused for a moment to admire the adorable straw hat with a jaunty ostrich feather that gave Lady Clipstone a certain piquant air.

Alice Clipstone. Oh, how her very existence taunted Emma.

It went without saying that neither woman allowed her hostility to show. Indeed, they might have been two long-lost relatives reunited at a family affair. They exclaimed over how well the other looked. They inquired after the health of their loved ones—as if they had not been figuratively at each other's throats for months.

"May I offer you more tea?" Emma inquired when the initial period of pretense drew to its inevitable end.

"Heavens, no," Lady Clipstone replied. "I shouldn't take you from instruction, having so rudely arrived without announcement. Or have you canceled lessons for the day? I shouldn't blame you what with all the recent . . . excitement."

Emma's nostrils narrowed. Ah. There it was. The first cut. A rapier tip dipped in arsenic.

The scented, high-buttoned gloves had come off. It appeared that for Alice, at least, all pretense of gentility would be abandoned for this private moment. Emma felt the calmer for sensing her adversary's lapse into antagonism. Alice had never been able to graciously accept that Emma's academy drew more applicants than she could accommodate and that she, the usurper, had to make do with those her rival rejected.

"There are always classes," she said with a negligent shrug. "One studies the social graces from dawn until dinner. Charlotte, as you know, is well qualified to instruct, and I have employed the redoubtable Miss Peppertree. Right now she and the girls are in the library enjoying a sketching lesson with Lady Dalrymple."

Alice's eyes lit up. "Hermia? You'd trust those tender minds to a—"

"A what?" Emma said in an ice-edged voice.

"Well, to a woman who paints unclad aristocrats for public consumption," Alice said with a sly pause. "I wouldn't be surprised if she wasn't avidly sketching a certain duke's heir as we speak."

A guilty flush stole into Emma's face. *There* was the rub her rival had been waiting for. Adrian and the incident at the wedding party. It might conceivably have sunk to the bottom of the scandal broth in a month or two, had Emma immediately placed as much distance possible between herself and her outrageous defender.

Still, Alice knew nothing of *that* indiscretion— Emma would be forced into exile alongside an even more infamous dictator before she would allow the truth to be known. "If Lord Wolverton wishes his portrait painted, then I . . . I am—"

She broke off.

A sense of foreboding stole over her at Alice's sudden, enrapt silence. In trepidation she turned to see what had so captured the woman's attention.

Some furtive movement at the window. Her brother Heath—and Adrian, his handsome, broad-shouldered figure a silhouette against the dying sunlight. For a surprising moment Emma's throat constricted in regret. He was fully dressed in a heavy charcoal-gray coat and black silk hat. As if, well, from what one could deduce from his dashing shadow as he walked past her sight, he were leaving.

Wasn't that what he'd been telling her? Both of them knew it was for the best. A man of his talents could take care of himself, but—

She forced her gaze back to Alice, only to find the woman studying her in brittle curiosity. "What were you about to say, Lady Lyons?" she inquired in an innocent tone.

Emma would not allow herself to be unsettled by her opponent. "Actually, my dear, I was about to ask what brought *you* here this late in the day."

Uninvited. Unaccompanied, too, unless that surly old footman Emma had spotted lingering in the entry hall meant to pass as a companion.

"Surely we did not have an appointment planned

that I had forgotten?" she went on artlessly. "If not, I really must excuse myself. You see, we're expecting a new arrival, a special student—the Earl of Heydon's niece. I expect you've heard of her." Emma paused. "I believe her bags have already arrived."

"Hasn't everyone heard of Lord Heydon?" Alice asked. "He once considered offering the academy his sponsorship, didn't he?"

Emma wavered, reminding herself a lady would end a conversation before it drifted into more dangerous ground. Nor would she keep stealing peeps out the window at a certain beautiful rogue. "He has been gracious enough to consider us, yes. As for—"

"Goodness," Alice said, clapping one hand to her cheek. "What a featherbrain I am. That's the reason I've come."

Emma swallowed over the knot of apprehension that tightened inside her. "The *earl* sent you?"

"In a manner of speaking." Alice gathered her gloves and reticule from the table. "His secretary advised me to collect Lady Coralie's baggage. It seems there's been a misunderstanding and it was delivered here by error."

Emma watched Adrian vanish around the corner into the garden. "What sort of misunderstanding?" she asked in a stiff voice, forcing her attention back to Alice.

"Lady Coralie won't be attending your academy

after all, my dear. It appears her uncle has changed his mind about her education. I thought I should see you in person to explain on her behalf, and to pick up her belongings."

Emma struggled against an ungentle impulse to pluck Alice's adorable hat from her head by its feather. "She's changed her mind?" she asked lightly.

Alice sighed with unconvincing regret. "I am sorry if this inconveniences you—I do hope you weren't counting on her funds?"

Emma managed a shrug of insouciance, rising to her feet. "Of course not. Shall I instruct Hamm to help you out with Lady Coralie's luggage? I assume you still have not been able to afford a footman yet . . ."

Alice virtually breathed fire from her nostrils. "I employ two of them, and intend to take on another two soon."

"Shall I hire a dogcart for the two of you or will you be walking back across town?"

"I have a new vehicle, in fact," Alice said, standing to stare directly at Emma. "I bought it with—"

A trill of delighted giggles from the garden interrupted Alice's coup de grace. Emma could not decide whether she appreciated the timely outburst or not. One more word from her nemesis, and she would indeed have been provoked to do something nasty enough to make the morning papers.

As luck would have it, however, the disturbance

in the garden, a scandal in the making of its own, absorbed her full attention. Adrian stood poised on the steps of the small summerhouse, his coat slung over one well-built shoulder, his hat at his feet. His grin, although not directed in Emma's direction, for she doubted he could see her at all, nonetheless, took her off balance. He was a deity with a dozen female admirers at his feet.

Was he *posing* for Lady Dalrymple's infamous sketches? Oh, how . . . how—

"Is that Lord Wolverton?" Alice asked breathlessly from behind her.

Emma drew the drapes tightly together and spun on her heel. "Do you think you should leave your school unattended, Lady Clipstone?" she said crisply. "I for one must return to my duties."

Alice's gaze drifted back toward the darkened window. "Indeed," she murmured. "You have your hands quite full, by the look of him."

Adrian was not sure himself how he had ended up posing for one of Lady Dalrymple's sketches. He had merely been waiting outside with Heath, discussing his plans. He did know, however, that he felt quite absurd, especially with Heath watching in amusement from the garden bench. How many times had his friend Dominic made jokes about the outrageous sketch of Heath Boscastle's manhood that had ended up on the streets and in the salons of London?

Well, Adrian wasn't removing his pantaloons for any of the females sketching him in the garden. He'd had a deuced hard time refusing Lady Dalrymple at all. No matter what abhorrent violence had defined his professional years, he harbored a strange weakness for sweet old ladies and uncouth little children. His grandmother had spoiled him and his siblings until two weeks before her death. He wondered now whether Lady Dalrymple had reminded him of his beloved nana. Had his grandmama's eyes twinkled at him with such irresistible wickedness? He suspected they had.

"Do you mind turning at the trunk a little and arching your back?" Lady Dalrymple asked in her quavery, angelic voice, then struck a classical pose to demonstrate.

He frowned down into her pleasant face. "Excuse me?"

"As if you were engaged in some labor that required every ounce of your strength," she explained with an evasive flutter of her wrist. "Oh, dear. Pretend you're lifting a heavy load."

"Of what?"

"I don't know. Coal. Bricks. Whatever makes those marvelous muscles work."

He glanced past her to his host, Heath, who, by this point, had covered his offensive grin with his hand. For Adrian, that insult coupled with the startled look on Emma's face as she stood at the window before hurriedly closing the drapes, warned him he had walked into a very wicked trap indeed.

And here he'd thought Lady Dalrymple to be a sweet, harmless scatterbrain. "Exactly what manner of sketch is it that you have in mind?" he asked, his hand planted on his left hip.

She smiled up at him over her easel. "Hercules," she murmured. "We have yet to add him to our Deity Collection. You don't object, do you?"

"Object?" he echoed as Heath slithered farther down the bench in a paroxysm of suppressed laughter. "Well, I'm not entirely sure—what exactly is the Deity Collection, if you don't mind my asking?"

"All the proceeds go to charity," Hermia assured him.

"Hercules? He wasn't a deity, was he?"

"Don't move," she muttered. "The light won't last long as it is, and my knees feel a storm moving in. Hercules became a deity after he died. Could you do me a favor?"

She had that naughty twinkle in her eye again. "That all depends, Lady Dalrymple. What is it?"

"Do you mind pretending you're wrestling a lion?"

His forehead creased. "Wrestling a *lion*?"

Miss Butterfield raised her pencil above her head. "I say, Lady Dalrymple, I think he's supposed to be naked in this labor. At least that's how he looked in the museum."

Adrian glanced up in alarm. Heath was practically rolling on the ground. "I hope you're talking about the lion, and not me."

"Not *you*," Lady Dalrymple said with a reprimanding smile. "Hercules—Lydia, do fetch my cloak for his lordship to use as a prop."

Lydia ran back into the house and breathlessly returned a minute later with Hermia's heavy gold velvet cloak. She held it up to Adrian, who took it in his hands with a snort of resignation.

"What am I supposed to do with this?" he asked Lady Dalrymple.

"Wrestle with it," she said.

He twisted it around his wrist, tossed it into the air, and caught it. "Like that?"

Her mouth thinned. "One doesn't wrestle a Nemean Lion as if it were an orange at a country fair, does one?"

Adrian stared her in the eye. "I don't know, but I am developing a Herculean headache. May I please get down?"

"In one moment," she replied, unruffled. "Do be patient, Hercules."

It was at this point, with all the girls of the academy avidly sketching, and Emma hiding behind the drapes, that Adrian decided enough was enough. Of course extricating himself from the situation was another matter. Every time he attempted to move, Hermia gave him a look that reminded him of his grandmother. And he stayed.

Obviously, Heath had no intention of intervening, and as there was no telling how long Hermia would hold him, Adrian was debating making an unheroic if desperate escape when Charlotte Boscastle appeared in the garden.

"It's time for deportment, everyone!"

The girls abandoned their sketches with sighs of regret and awkward curtsies in Adrian's direction. For a moment he could not figure out who the deuce the lot of them were curtsying at. He chuckled when he realized it was him. Relieved, he stepped down onto the grass, glancing past Charlotte to the house. Emma waited at the door to gather her flock.

Adrian gazed at her delicate profile.

She seemed so sure of herself, too self-assured to appeal to most men, but her strong presence rather appealed to Adrian. She wasn't one to mince words. He could trust whatever she said, even if he might not like it. And yet she still managed to carry herself like a lady should with a natural grace and regard for others.

He glanced around, suddenly realizing that both Charlotte and Heath were watching him with unabashed interest. "Well, that was an unplanned diversion," he said, turning his head so that he would not be tempted to stare again. "I hope I do not discover my likeness printed all over town tomorrow."

Charlotte's blue eyes danced with laughter. "Take heart. All monies collected are distributed to London charities."

"Do you mean someone would actually pay to have a sketch of me?" Adrian asked, grinning.

"Unbelievable, isn't it?" Heath strolled past him toward the house. "Your driver is here, by the way. If you'd care to stay for supper, I'll have him wait."

Well, that was pointed, but polite, and Adrian knew he'd more than worn out his welcome. "I'm going. Thank you, anyway. In fact, thank you for all that you've done."

"You're more than welcome, but— You are coming back again, aren't you? I'll wager Hermia will pester you to finish wrestling that lion."

He hesitated. He could hear Emma informing one of the girls she'd dropped her pencils. "Of course, I'll come back," he said vaguely. "Soon."

Heath studied him with a thoughtful smile. "A good friend is always welcome in my house."

A good friend. Adrian nodded, wondering whether it was his own guilt or Heath's intuition that gave the invitation a deeper implication.

Chapter Eleven

A chilling rain challenged the integrity of the ancestral pink granite manor house that bordered the Berkshire valley. The voices within were muffled by infrequent claps of thunder. Two sleek deerhounds dozed before a roaring applewood fire. A bottle of hearty port and three crystal glasses sat on the Jacobean table that had occupied the same corner two centuries ago.

The Duke of Scarfield stood, his back straight despite the rheumatism that had settled deep into his bones alongside a decade of bitter regrets. His heavy brows were knitted in a perpetual frown. His craggy face betrayed no weakness or self-pity. He was a man who believed fiercely in the duty of his birthright.

Begging the forgiveness of his firstborn son did not come easily to his pride. In fact, it had taken him years to admit that he had wronged his late wife. Almost a lifetime had elapsed before he'd found the courage to accept the fact that his jealousy had destroyed his family, and to invite Adrian home. He knew his son had arrived in England a year ago. And still he had waited for his return. Either this was Adrian's revenge, or perhaps he merely did not care.

"A week," he said, studying the dreary wooded landscape. "It's been raining for a week."

Miniature pools of rainwater glistened in the crushed oyster shells that comprised the circular drive. He had kept a vigil for several months for sign of Adrian's return, always to be disappointed.

"The weather makes travel difficult," his golden-haired daughter said from the chair where she plied a needle into one of her endless tapestries.

"Perhaps he is ill, my lord," murmured Bridgewater, the estate manager, from the candlelit desk where he awaited the duke's attention to his neglected accounts. Indeed, the entire estate had slipped into neglect as if everyone counted on Adrian's return to awaken whatever hope Scarfield had once known for the future.

Scarfield turned with a rueful laugh. "We play this performance every afternoon, do we not?"

His daughter Florence glanced up with a smile. "Every morning, every afternoon, every night."

"At least Cedric could have sent word," the duke said in a fretful voice.

"The weather, your grace," Bridgewater said vaguely. "Travel is difficult at this time of year."

Florence rose, dropping her needlework in a basket at her feet. "Well, I for one like the rain. I think I shall walk over to see Serena before the day darkens."

"To tell her that her betrothed has not returned?" her father asked with a sigh.

She laughed again, the two deerhounds following her to the door. "You have not paid attention if you think it matters to her after all this time."

"Of course it matters," the duke snapped as he sank into his leather chair. "A promise is a promise."

His daughter caught Bridgewater's sympathetic glance before he looked away. "I shall be home before supper."

"You must have the groom drive you, Lady Florence," Bridgewater said. "There's been another report of brigands on the road."

Her father did not appear to hear, resuming the vigil for his prodigal son. Once she too had wished for Adrian's return. But now the entire estate waited in suspense for the reunion of the duke with the firstborn he had banished on the basis of nothing but a false accusation.

She walked across the thick Turkey carpet, Bridgewater rising hastily to open the door for her. He was a white-haired elf of a man whose family had served hers for over a century. For a moment the flash of naked worry in his keen amber eyes saddened her. He saw everything that went on in the house.

He knew all of their secrets. He had witnessed her

father unfairly accuse her mother of adultery, her mother's brief illness and sudden death. Bridgewater had served here during her father's subsequent decline into spells of melancholy. He knew which footman had impregnated the chambermaid, and what the butler was up to in the pantry late at night.

Did he fear, as she did, that Adrian's return might be too late for Scarfield?

After the emotional upheaval of her older brother's departure the house had settled into a predictable rhythm, if not a pleasant one. Adrian's absence had ended the constant quarrels that erupted almost daily between him and his father.

In Florence's estimation, the question of Adrian's parentage should never have entered anyone's mind. Still, by the time Adrian escaped, there was no one on the estate, from the scullions to the family's maiden aunt, who had not been convinced that he had been conceived of an illicit seed.

Then, two years ago, all had changed.

On her deathbed, the children's retired governess had told witnesses that the duchess had been indeed faithful to her husband, if not devoted. Miss Mallory then confessed that it was she who had maliciously sent the duke anonymous letters describing his young wife's love affair with a soldier who had stayed in the village. Adrian, the author of these unsigned missives had claimed, was not Scarfield's natural son. His early arrival as an eight-month baby had proved this shameful fact.

Scarfield's mistrust of his duchess grew. She was fifteen years younger than he. She was so vivacious that it hurt him to gaze upon her. He accompanied her everywhere, and his dark suspicions ruined their marriage. When she died of a sudden lung infection, he refused to mourn her. His sorrow, his resentment were turned upon his son Adrian, who at a young age resembled his mother.

When Adrian had left home and set upon his notorious career, it seemed to Scarfield that he had been proven right. The boy was wild, uncontrollable, and showed none of the sense of duty that was the duke's lodestar. The base instincts of his birth father drove him. He shunned his obligations because recognition of privilege was not in his blood.

And then Scarfield had learned that he had been deceived by the vindictive lies of a former governess, a simple act of revenge. The duchess had caught Miss Mallory physically restraining Adrian in the nursery one day. The young mother had dismissed her on the spot, accusing the woman of being unfit to care for the heir.

Miss Mallory had pleaded for another chance, which the duchess had refused to give. Years later the governess had paid her back.

So many years wasted. Scarfield had allowed a lie, his jealousy, to destroy everything that mattered in life. Self-remorse had not erased all traces of his arrogance, however, and never would.

He wanted his heir home. Never mind that those

who cared for and served him, his elderly aunt, his daughter and second son, even his assiduous estate manager, who had pulled the estate from poverty more than once due to the duke's ill-chosen investments, had cautioned him that a reconciliation of such a breach might take time.

Scarfield did not listen. The law proclaimed Adrian his rightful heir, past deceptions and suspicions notwithstanding. It remained for him now to bring the boy home and make amends. The duke was not a well man. He would not live much longer.

He did not give a damn what anyone said, or that Adrian's profession had brought shame to the ancient family name. Scarfield would have his way.

Adrian would wed a neighboring young lady, the girl he had been unofficially pledged to in childhood, and the rightful order of things would be restored as it had been written in the stars centuries ago. The village would prosper again. The brigands who haunted the outlying woods and roads would be chased off by a man strong enough to challenge them, for in a particular way, Scarfield took pleasure in his son's self-assertion.

It never occurred to the Duke of Scarfield that his son would turn his back on his inheritance and refuse his offer of forgiveness.

But it had occurred to Florence and she could not sleep for dreading what was to come.

Chapter Twelve

Emma arose for the following three mornings at her customary time, if not in her typical good temper. As a rule she frowned upon indulging in any extreme of mood. To be at the mercy of one's emotions was a weakness of character. Such distemperaments should be subdued in private.

That her father, the fourth Marquess of Sedgecroft, and her older brother, Drake, had suffered from this dark affliction of disposition did not persuade her that her struggle against one's personal demons were in vain.

One must battle the subtle devils of self-doubt and discouragement almost daily. This had been the advice her practical-minded mother had bestowed upon her unruly brood. Of the Boscastle siblings, however, only Grayson, Emma, and Devon seemed to have inherited their mother's ability to rise above their father's private struggles with personal darkness.

Emma, of course, understood the reason for her

own present disquietude. Whereas she should have felt relieved, it was a pea in her shoe that Lord Wolverton had not attempted to contact her again since their last encounter in the library.

She knew it was for the best.

She knew she had made him promise to keep their indiscretion to himself. And so far he had. In fact, the papers had made only a fleeting mention of the embarrassing incident at the wedding. Apparently even Lady Clipstone had not stirred up the scandal pot. All was well that ended without commotion.

It even began to seem possible to Emma that she would be able to put the week behind her and return her full attention to the academy where it belonged.

And where it was so desperately needed.

Indeed, as she entered the ballroom after breakfast she found her entire class gathered suspiciously around one bright-haired girl. And in that girl's hand was a sketch.

Emma swallowed and prayed for personal fortitude as she strode forth to wage an entirely different kind of battle. "Give it to me."

"It's our lesson from Lady Dalrymple," one of the girls exclaimed.

"Harriet Gardner, hand me that drawing now, or I shall—heaven forgive me, I shall—"

Harriet looked up with more astonishment than

fright. "I thought a lady couldn't raise neither her voice nor her fists."

"I might be persuaded to make an exception," Emma said. "Give it to me now."

Harriet did, watching Emma's face for her reaction as she glanced down at the rough but skilled sketch Hermia had made of Adrian in the garden the day of his departure.

Her initial thought as she studied the charcoal figure was of a profound, knee-trembling relief that he had not been rendered au naturel, except for one bare arm and shoulder, which Hermia's artistic imagination had captured in all its muscular glory.

To her embarrassment, Emma felt her eyes misting with tears as she beheld Adrian's imperfect angular profile. Lady Dalrymple had caught the beauty of his face, his stark bone structure. Truly he did resemble a young hero, although Emma thought wistfully that Hermia's depiction had not succeeded in capturing Adrian's more endearing traits.

She sighed. She would like to keep this sketch even if she would have nothing more to do with him. Well, she'd be polite if they met at a party because one could hardly ignore a duke's son in good society. Especially when—

"Emma," Charlotte said, touching her arm. "What are we going to do?"

She gathered her wits. "For one thing, we mustn't leave the girls unsupervised while Lady Dalrymple gives instruction."

Charlotte glanced down at the drawing. "Oh, but it's lovely—very artistic, I think. Just look at that ferocious lion. It's—quite believable."

"Lion? What—oh, yes. Beastly."

"Furthermore, I was supervising," Charlotte added, "and there wasn't anything untoward about the lesson. The girls are developing an appreciation for Greek culture."

Emma quirked her brow. She doubted her little band of debutantes cared one way or another for ancient history.

"Greek culture notwithstanding, the girls are chatting away while we stand here. Today's lesson is supposed to be a continuation of the art of deportment in a foreign land. Where is Yvette, by the way? I shall use her as our queen at court."

Charlotte hesitated. "She's upstairs packing with her maid. She was supposed to come and inform you herself."

"Inform me of what?" Emma asked.

"That her papa is removing her to Lady Clipstone's school." Charlotte looked away. "It seemed that he felt our academy was perhaps not the most favorable milieu for Yvette, considering the recent violence."

"*Violence?* At the academy?"

"Well, at the wedding. The scuffle. It reminded the marquess of the Terror."

"Being hit upon the head and beheaded are hardly

events one can compare. But . . ." Emma's voice trailed off. She could not defend brawling at a wedding in any terms. "We must not wallow in our own dirt," she said briskly. "Nor shall we lower ourselves by bemoaning our fate. Come, girls! Gather around—Harriet. Yes, let us pay court to Miss Gardner. Today she is a French *princesse*."

"A princess—Harriet?"

"She is 'Votre Altesse' to you, Miss Butterfield," Emma said. "And if one of us were fortunate enough to be presented to a French prince, what would we do in his presence?"

"I'd faint at his bleedin' feet," Harriet said, flouncing to the chair that was her throne. "Better yet, I'd 'ave him kiss my feet, seeing as how I'm a princess and—" Without warning she burst from her dais and flew to the window in a manner more befitting a parlormaid than a royal princess. "He's 'ere!"

"Your prince?" Emma inquired under her breath.

"No," Harriet said absently. She twisted off the apron one of the girls had tied about her shoulders as a robe. "The duke's heir. Poor feller can't stay away. Cripes, look at his pumpkin."

"Look at his *what*?" Emma asked.

"His pumpkin—cart and wheels."

"Are you speaking of Lord Wolverton's carriage?"

At Harriet's distracted nod, Emma edged forth a few steps to peer over the heads of her excited students. The "pumpkin" in which the prince had made his untimely arrival was a white ducal carriage emblazed with rampant gilt lions and unicorns. The stiff-backed driver wore a black frock coat and knee breeches trimmed with gold lace.

Indeed, it was an impressive sight, but not nearly so awe-inspiring as the handsome figure in a double-breasted black coat who descended onto the sidewalk. Emma stole a look at his rugged profile and resolutely turned away, ignoring the bittersweet ache inside her.

Her attention was immediately diverted.

Anarchy in Harriet's imaginary court had ensued. Emma clapped her hands in dismay to draw the girls away from the window. Charlotte took a more direct course of action and pulled the drapes closed on their disappointed faces.

"Spoilsport, miss!"

"It isn't fair. What if he's come to see Lady Lyons? What if he's going to ask her to marry him?"

Emma frowned at this frivolous speculation, fighting not to run back to the window herself. "He is no doubt here to visit Lord Heath, *not* that it is our affair."

"What if he's in love with Lady Emma?" Miss Butterfield cried to a chorus of scandalized gasps.

Harriet jumped up onto her chair. "What if he's going to abduct her? What if he hurls her over his shoulder and spirits her away?"

"What," Emma said in a well-modulated voice

that cut across the ballroom like a bullwhip, "if you all go to bed without dessert for a week?"

Silence followed this unpopular threat. Then Harriet cleared her throat. "We'll 'ave order in this court right *now*. So shut yer gobs and—"

Adrian swept into the room, so breathtaking in his tailored black coat and snug trousers tucked into black leather boots that every pair of eyes widened to watch him.

Resisting his blatant charm, if only to make an example of herself, Emma remained in the center of the room. She was chagrined as the girls rushed to encircle him, even if she felt a similar tug of temptation. Her job was to set a proper standard of protocol, not to fling herself against that manly chest.

He disengaged himself from the girls with an embarrassed smile and made his way to Emma's side. He appeared to be a man, like her brothers, who did not mind what sort of example he set.

"Lord Wolverton," she said, managing to appear chagrined beneath her undeniable pleasure. "We are in the middle of lessons. May I help you? Perhaps you're looking for my brother?"

"Yes." Suddenly he looked intimidated by all the attention he had drawn. "I was going to invite him to attend a horse auction later today." He cleared his throat. "I don't suppose you've reconsidered taking me as a student?"

This inquiry set the class off into a fresh round of

giggling. Charlotte quickly shushed them, looking a little curious herself.

"I'm afraid," Emma said in a polite, professional tone, "that there has been a misunderstanding. May I ask how your head is?"

"It's still on my shoulders."

"I can see that. I wonder, though," she said with an arch smile, "whether you have regained your clarity of thought."

"I've never felt more clearheaded in my life." He stared levelly at her. "And you?"

She shook her head.

Adrian, holding his high black silk hat in one hand, smiled in a manner that suggested he understood her uncertainty. Had she just thought all this attention intimidated the man? Not in the least.

He drew her out of earshot. "May I ask you another question? Since you didn't answer my first."

His hard body brushed against hers. Forbidden heat flooded her. He should not have come here, but she was glad of it. Too glad for her own good. It did not bode well for the safekeeping of her heart.

"The girls are watching us," she whispered.

He looked around innocently. "Well, we're not doing anything wrong."

She frowned. "It's the way you looked at me."

His brow lifted knowingly. His gaze wandered over her with lazy sensuality. "Yes? What of it?"

She blushed. "You know."

"Tell me anyway."

"Teasing is most impolite."

"That's why I need your advice."

"I'll give you some advice, Lord Wolverton," she said, her voice climbing. "You should return to Berkshire and—"

He drew her in the direction of the window. "Did you happen to notice my carriage?" he asked.

"I could hardly miss it." Nor had she missed how he had changed the subject at the mention of returning to his home. She had glimpsed a genuine pain in his eyes. Perhaps he was not even aware of it himself. Perhaps there were unpleasant memories of his past that haunted him still.

His voice dropped to a whisper. "The old duke sent it to collect me in style. It's a little pretentious, don't you think? I'm embarrassed to be seen in it."

"Your personal code of conduct is what should embarrass you," she whispered back.

"Then it's a good thing I've come to you, isn't it?" he asked, his warmth returning.

In fact, the heat in his hazel eyes could have melted stone. Emma was chagrined at how much she enjoyed being again in his provocative company. "I'm not at all convinced of that. I am in the middle of class."

"I prefer private lessons myself," he murmured. "Are you available to give guidance to the socially lost and lovelorn?"

She looked up slowly with a little smile. "Not unless you wish my brothers to be included in our instruction. I'm sure it could be arranged."

"Your brothers?" he asked, bending his head into hers.

"Yes." She leaned away, indicating the door behind him. "Heath and Drake have arrived as we speak, and oh, yes, here comes the youngest Boscastle demon, Devon. Sometimes it's difficult to tell them apart. You did say Heath was expecting you?"

Adrian straightened abruptly as the three dark-haired Boscastle brothers strode forward to greet him.

"Good day, Lord Wolverton," Emma murmured. He sighed.

"Hello, Wolf," Devon said, throwing his arm around Adrian's broad shoulder. "Come to show off your ancestry today? There's a crowd gathered in the street to see who owns that fancy piece. Let's rescue you from the dangerous little debutantes and take a drive around the park. Innocence can be rather overwhelming at times, don't you think?"

What Adrian thought, as he was skillfully escorted into the presence of Emma's three masterful brothers, was that he had just been given another friendly warning that their sister was under their protection.

At least until such time as another man assumed the responsibility. And as Adrian had come to the decision that he was the most appropriate, the only current candidate for her affections, he would need permission from her brothers to court her. This posed a dilemma, considering the promise he had made to her. For now he was forced to pretend she was a mere friend.

He wouldn't impress Emma by embarrassing her. Would she think better of him if he visited his father? He frowned. He supposed he appeared to be a coward in her eyes by avoiding the inevitable. And to his surprise, being in the company of the close-knit Boscastles had made him wish to see his own brother and sister. He remembered that they had cried when he left home. Had they found happiness?

"Has Grayson seen that gilded monstrosity of yours?" Heath asked as they walked back to the door that looked upon the street. "I vow he'll be quite jealous."

"It arrived from my father only this morning." Adrian paused. He knew better than to assume Heath would believe he'd wandered into the ballroom by mistake. Or that after only three days he had missed Heath's company.

Heath confirmed his hunch in the next instant. "I suggest you take a drive over to visit Grayson in the next week or so. I'm sure he would be interested in talking with you."

And not about carriages, either, if Adrian understood what Heath meant. Grayson Boscastle, the fifth Marquess of Sedgecroft, was the family's patriarch and former scoundrel himself. He was the man to grant dispensation as well as to issue social death sentences.

Heath's message could not have been clearer. If Adrian intended to pursue Emma, he would have to ask permission of Grayson first and declare himself.

And he would. He honestly would. Just as soon as he persuaded Emma he was sincere and proved to her that even a ruthless misadventurer could be redeemed.

Perhaps in the course of this endeavor, he might even persuade himself that his redemption was possible.

Sir Gabriel Boscastle glanced back from the entrance of the town house at the ducal carriage that swept down the street. An audience of admiring pedestrians, street vendors, and urchins had congregated to witness its departure. "That wasn't Adrian, was it?" he asked his cousin Heath a few minutes later, after a housemaid had directed him to the library. "One would think he were a—"

"—duke?" Lord Drake Boscastle said with a cynical smile. He and Gabriel had been at odds in the past, but since Drake's recent marriage to his governess, their old enmity had begun to fade away. "He and Devon have gone driving. You can probably catch up with them if the crowd lets you through."

Heath was seated at his massive military desk, his arms folded behind his head. As usual his expression revealed nothing of his thoughts. "Are you coming with us to the opera tonight, Gabriel?"

"Of course," he said, nodding gratefully at the glass of sherry Drake had poured him. "I never sleep so soundly as during an aria." He paused. "There is a definite pall over this gathering. Have I done something to offend anyone? I know that in the past, we were not as close as—"

"We have a slight family problem." Drake glanced at his brother. "Do you think we should tell him?"

Heath laughed shortly. "You damn well have to now, after dangling that tidbit under his nose."

Gabriel shook his head, his face amused. "Does this mean I'm actually to be included in some Boscastle intrigue—and do I *want* to be?"

"It's Emma," Drake said.

"And Wolf." Heath ran his hand through his thick black hair. "Emma and Adrian. An improbable pairing if ever there was one."

Gabriel took a long swallow of sherry. "Stranger affairs have occurred throughout English history. Take Nell Gwyn, an orange girl, made a duchess by the king."

"A duchess. Now there's a point. Adrian isn't married. His father will be arranging a suit." Heath glanced meaningfully at Drake. "I think this calls for a family cabal before Emma is involved beyond our help."

"Grayson is in Kent until Friday, teaching Rowan how to hunt," Drake replied.

"The boy can't even walk yet," Gabriel exclaimed, choking on his drink. "Isn't it a bit early for him to be shooting a gun?"

"Not if you're being groomed as the next marquess," Heath said with a mordant laugh. "Drake, I say we meet on Friday evening. Will you do the honors of making sure that Devon attends? I would invite Dominic but he and Adrian are too close. It isn't fair to put him on the spot."

"So *I* am included?" Gabriel asked, looking pleased.

Drake grinned at him. "It wouldn't be a complete cabal without your jaded perspective, cousin."

"A caution." Heath held up one hand. "The women are *not* to be informed. As dearly as we love them, their interference must be avoided at all costs. We do not want emotion to cloud whatever we decide."

Gabriel finished his sherry. "My lips are stitched shut."

"Mine are shackled," Drake said.

Heath nodded in satisfaction. "None of us can break, not even under the duress of—well, you know their wiles. The women of this family, and I include our sisters and wives, have an uncanny sense for these affairs. If they suspect that we are making a decision without consulting them, our lives will not be worth living."

Gabriel looked at him in disbelief. "Are you trying to tell me that the pair of you, former spies who did *not* break under torture, are really afraid that your wives will somehow find out about our meeting?"

Heath stared at the map of Egypt mounted on the wall. "You have no idea, Gabriel, what power the women in this family wield."

Grayson Boscastle's wife, the former Lady Jane Welsham, sister-in-law to Emma, and present Marchioness of Sedgecroft, lowered her field glasses as the head Boscastle footman, Weed, trudged breathlessly up the grassy knoll of the Kent estate toward her. Her son Rowan lay gurgling upon his blanket while his father and the family gamekeeper attempted to share their hunting knowledge with a child who could not even talk. Jane vowed that if Grayson showed Rowan that crossbow one more time, she would confiscate it.

She felt a flutter of anxiety in her chest. Weed waved a folded missive at her, puffing with exertion from what was apparently a frantic dash from the house.

"Who is it from, Weed?" she asked quietly, imagining that some tragedy had befallen any number of elderly aunts and uncles, her beloved parents, her wastrel brother, her sisters—

"I do not know, madam," he wheezed, holding his side. "I was told only it was a matter of the gravest importance and that it must reach you posthaste."

One of the three female attendants sitting at her feet arose with a worried look at Jane. "Please inform my husband that young Orion is in need of his afternoon rest," she said, her gaze dark.

As the attendant scurried down toward the wooded preserve, Jane carefully broke the letter's seal and scanned the missive. It was from Julia, Heath's wife, in London.

And it was an urgent request indeed, tersely worded.

> *Emma. Adrian Ruxley. I trust you are able to read what discretion forbids me to write. Heath is cognizant of the situation and intends to call a cabal to decide her fate. May I ask you to intervene on behalf of the female contingency?*
> *In the name of true love,*
> *Your sister-in-law and no stranger to scandal,*
> *Julia*

Jane whipped around so abruptly that Weed, smiling at the sight of the marquess and young master below, nearly lost his balance. In fact, he might have slipped down the knoll had Jane's hand not shot out to grasp his sleeve.

"I am a clumsy girl," she said, hauling him back up beside her.

His gaze flickered to the letter she had unceremoniously stuffed into her bodice. "Not bad news, I pray, madam?"

"It will be if I don't intervene," she muttered, then bit her lip.

Weed worshipped the Boscastle family. Jane did not doubt he would lay down his life to save her if she were in danger. But when it came to choosing sides between her and her husband, she suspected that Grayson would win. Weed, after all, was a man and a Boscastle loyalist.

"Shall I order the carriage for immediate departure?" he inquired, gently disengaging himself from her grasp as he regained his dignity.

Jane cast a fond glance in the direction of her husband and child. "There's no need to spoil my husband's plans. I shall be leaving for London with Mrs. O'Brien and my son." Mrs. O'Brien was Rowan's Irish nursemaid, a woman not afraid to challenge Grayson's authority when it came to the best interests of her charge.

The senior footman had witnessed too many Boscastle scandals for his suspicions not to be aroused. "Madam?" he asked cautiously in a voice that said everything and yet nothing.

She lowered her voice to a throaty whisper, her green eyes sparkling with mischief. "There's an adorable shoemaker just arrived from Milan and I mean to engage his exclusive services before any other ladies steal him for their own."

"Ah." He nodded knowingly. A passion for fashionable attire he understood.

"You won't tell, will you?" she asked with a beseeching smile.

"Need you even ask?"

"Good. I will be leaving for London as soon as I have explained the situation to the marquess."

Grayson suspected something was afoot when his wife informed him of her intention to return to their Park Lane residence. They both knew the shoemaker could be brought to their Kent estate to do her bidding, as had the corsetiere, milliner, and numerous jewelers on several past occasions. An hour later, when the marquess received the missive from his brother Heath apprising him of the startling news about Emma, his suspicions were confirmed.

He did not know what devious plot his wife was hatching, but he deemed it wise to take action before she could gain any advantage on him. He and Jane took delight in outfoxing each other.

She was not at all pleased when she discovered his decision to travel to London with her. "There is no need to spoil your plans on my account," she said as they met in the entrance hall where a mountain of their mutual luggage had been assembled.

"But my plans are of no account if they do not include you, darling."

One delicate brow lifted. He gazed steadily into her dark green eyes and felt his heart stir. Marriage had not dimmed his passion for her in the least. Nor had it diminished her clever spirit. At a time when some men might have lapsed into wedded complacency, he was still kept on his toes by the desirable Lady Jane.

"Really, Grayson." She held still as her maid draped a velvet-lined pelisse over her shoulders. "I don't need your help to meet a shoemaker."

He took over the task of fastening the braided frogs of his wife's wrap. "I'd miss you more than I can bear. You don't mind, do you?"

Her full mouth firmed. "It's only a shoemaker."

He smiled. The shoemaker.

Something was definitely afoot.

Adrian studied Emma Boscastle's perfect cameo profile from the pair of pearl-inlaid opera glasses that belonged to one of the two gentlemen who sat beside him in his Haymarket opera box. Adrian had been mildly astonished that his appearance at the house tonight had drawn an embarrassing amount of attention. In fact, as the crowded lobby fell silent upon his entrance, he had glanced around curiously in search of the important personage who had sent the young ladies present into such a dither.

Female regard was not exactly a novel experience. He understood his appeal to the opposite sex even if he had not always bothered to take advantage of it. Certainly, he did not celebrate his manhood by how many notches he could carve into his bedpost.

Therefore, he found it absurd that because he was a duke's son there existed numerous women who judged him so desirable that even before the opera began he received seven invitations to supper, three to breakfast, and two to darker entertainments.

"I wish I had your luck with the ladies," the baronet who sat at his right commented.

Adrian would have liked to tell his newfound admirers that to pursue an affair with him was a complete waste of time. Instead, he amused himself by fashioning the notes into pointed missiles that he directed at the Boscastle opera box on the opposite side of the house.

He would have really liked to lure Emma into his box, close the curtains, and pay attention to *her* for the rest of the evening. But with her band of brothers looming about, the pleasant fantasy seemed unlikely to be realized tonight, or in the immediate future.

It wasn't going to end that easily between him and his elusive lioness, however. If Emma imagined for one instant that he was the sort of man who seduced a woman in secret, then sauntered off to other conquests, she had a few surprises coming. Actually, no one could have been more surprised than Adrian himself by his desire to pursue her for a more lasting association.

Yet something in him understood, had recognized from the instant he heard her voice, that she was the woman he'd been waiting for all his life. And he hadn't even realized he had been waiting, or that true love would be in his future.

He knew many men, soldiers of fortune especially, who did not believe in love. Abandoned by parents, abused at home, they'd taught themselves not to seek anything but instant gratification. Not to feel. But Adrian remembered his mother's love. And his brother and sister tagging about like hapless puppies, willing to follow him into any mischief.

They had loved him. And he loved them. So he never admitted to his crude-minded cohorts that he did believe in the reality of love.

It had existed once.

Why could it not be his again?

He sat up, his heavy black cloak cascading down his back. Was she leaving? Alone? Just when the head-splitting singing had begun? Ah, what a blessing. "Excuse me," he muttered to his two acquaintances, one of whom was already asleep. "Don't wait for me if I don't come back soon."

He nearly bowled over every footman and late arrival he encountered in his hurry to intercept her in the entrance vestibule. He would be satisfied if he could convince her to meet him once again to discuss the future she asserted they didn't even have.

"Goodness gracious!" an ominously familiar voice trilled in his ear. "Is that my Hercules?"

Not her. He stumbled back from the robust older

woman blocking his progress. She followed until he stood flush against the wall. Over the top of her peacock-feathered turban he caught sight of Emma fanning herself. Hamm, the footman in Lord Heath's town house, stood idly by. "Dear Lady Dalrymple," he said politely, then practically lifted her out of his path. "I should love nothing more than to continue this conversation, but I've just seen a friend I cannot ignore."

"A friend?" She swung around in interest, gasping as she realized whom he meant. "Not Emma? Yes. Emma. She's—Emma is your *friend*?"

Too late he understood that she understood exactly what he meant. "Of course she's my friend," he said awkwardly. "And so are you, and your niece Julia—"

Her voice dropped to a frightening whisper. "You can trust me, Lord Wolverton."

"Can I?" he asked. Emma was turning back toward the steps that led to her box. He could see his opportunity slipping through his fingers.

He bolted across the vestibule, reaching Emma before she could elude him. "Lady Lyons." He bowed, then caught her gloved hand to draw her back into the corner. "What a pleasure it is to meet you here."

For a satisfying moment her face lit up and she did not fuss when he edged nearer to her than he should. Then she laughed. "As if it were a coincidence. Did you know we'd be here tonight?"

"Your brother might have mentioned it earlier. I only hoped you would accompany them."

She glanced down. "You enjoy the opera?"

"I detest it."

She tapped her fan against her shoulder. "I won't ask then why you came."

"You know why, Emma."

She lifted her gaze to his. "Is that Hermia over there staring at us?"

He drank in the sight of her, did not even bother to look around. She was buttoned up at every point of entry. Her neck, her sleeves, her bodice. Small pearl buttons that would take forever to undo but only a moment to tear from their moorings. Her prim appearance made him only want her more. "Who's Hermia?" he asked absently.

"Lady Dalrymple. The artist."

"Hide me from her, would you?" he said with a groan.

She laughed again, tilted her face to his with an unconscious beguilement that warmed his entire being. He lowered his head, starved for a taste of her mouth. If he'd thought for a moment that she would let him kiss her in public, he would have showered her with kisses, devoured her—

A hard fist punched him playfully on the shoulder. "By God, Wolf, it *was* you in the box opposite us. And here I thought you'd given up on good society."

He turned his head. Drake Boscastle's indigo blue

eyes stared directly into his. "Haven't you heard?" he asked in an even voice. "I'm on a course of self-improvement."

"Really?" Drake's smile was skeptical. "You should have come with us. My brothers and I are always glad to keep a fellow rogue company."

And to keep him away from their sister.

It was a theme to be repeated throughout the following week.

Emma had excused herself from the box for a breath of air. The truth was that if she witnessed one more woman giggle or preen to capture Adrian's attention, she would abandon all sense of refinement and . . . mutter an unsavory remark. To prevent this demeaning possibility, she escaped her brothers' company and sought a moment by herself.

She had, of course, glimpsed Adrian from behind her fan the instant he entered the vestibule. Her first suspicion was that he was meeting a lover. His appearance here tonight had certainly stirred amorous hopes in the audience. But then she had seen the unguarded look of pleasure on his face when he had espied her in the corner.

She'd watched in disbelief as he had practically lifted Lady Dalrymple from his path to reach *her*, Emma. There were no other young ladies in sight.

Still, she ought not to even acknowledge him in the vestibule. But then he was standing in front of her, warm, vital, so devilishly handsome she couldn't quite think of escape. All she could do, unfortunately, was bask for a few forbidden moments in his presence.

And when he lowered his head to hers, she'd felt her heart accelerate wildly, felt herself suspended between apprehension and hope. He wouldn't dare kiss her in public. He couldn't—

Her brother Drake ended her agony.

Although Emma could barely see Drake's face, concealed by Adrian's large frame, she realized in embarrassment that his interruption had been staged. Hamm, the footman, was standing only a few feet away. Therefore, her person was protected, which could only mean that Drake was deliberately keeping her and Adrian apart.

She fanned her face, listening to the brief exchange between the two men. "Seriously, Adrian," Drake said, "I'd have invited you to come with us tonight if I'd known you were attending. How was the auction today?"

Lady Dalrymple chose that inopportune moment to bustle up between Drake and Adrian, inviting Adrian to join her and her escort, the Earl of Odham, for a late dinner after the performance. Emma glanced away, aware by the speculative gleam in his eye that Drake knew perfectly well how flustered she felt. But what else did he and her other brothers know? Were they merely guessing or overly perceptive?

When she dared to look around again, Lady Dalrymple was dragging Adrian by the elbow across the vestibule, and a small group of young ladies, evidently tracking his whereabouts, had contrived a dozen excuses to appear in his path. He did not spare a single one of them a glance.

"How uncouth," she muttered.

"Who, darling?" Drake asked languidly, leaning back against the wall beside her. "Me or Adrian?"

"Those forward women over there."

"Ah. So that's it."

She snapped the sticks of her fan shut. "So that is what?"

"Nothing." His innocent shrug bespoke more than she truly wished to know. "Shall we return to our box?"

"Of course."

"And you are all right?" he asked, offering her his arm.

"Why would you think otherwise?"

"Well, you did express a desire for a little air."

"I'm fine now."

He patted her hand. "That's all I wanted to hear. And remember that I am always here if you wish to talk."

"Talk about what?" she asked tightly, her gaze fixed straight ahead.

"Well, I don't know."

"The weather?"

He glanced at her. "If you like. Rain, sun . . . love affairs."

She grinned inwardly. "I shall bear that in mind."

She should be grateful for Drake's timely intervention. Thankful that the protective arms of the Boscastle family would not only shield her from harm but from temptation. Thankful that her brothers cared enough about her to guard her like a citadel.

Yes, indeed. The Boscastles took care of their own.

Chapter Thirteen

❧ ❧

Adrian was still plotting how to meet Emma alone the next day when he accepted an invitation to fence at Angelo's with Dominic Breckland. Dominic was not only his closest friend, he was also married to Emma's younger sister Chloe, which meant he might be able to serve as a neutral party as well as a potential go-between for Adrian and Emma.

Adrian thought that during some friendly swordplay he could casually drop a few hints about his position. Presumably Dominic, an intelligent man in love with a Boscastle woman himself, would offer to act as Cupid.

Unfortunately, Dominic thwarted this scheme by inviting Heath Boscastle to join them at the last minute. At any other time Adrian would not have objected to practicing with another capable partner. But Heath took a few jabs at him that might have been considered less than sporting. Adrian, who could have easily countered with equal skill, decided to allow Heath the advantage.

Even Dominic commented on Heath's uncharacteristic aggressiveness when the three of them dropped Heath off at his town house. "I think Adrian and I should be glad to count you as our friend," he said jokingly as the coach drew to a halt. "I was afraid for a moment that you forgot who your opponent was."

A spell of silence fell.

Adrian merely shrugged as if the matter were of little consequence. Only a fool would quarrel with one who had treated him as well as Heath had.

Still, it had become apparent to Adrian that he would be reduced to subterfuge if he wanted a few private moments with Emma to state his intentions. He did not relish hatching any intrigue against the family who had befriended him. If he had not promised her secrecy, he'd have gone straight to her brothers and bared his soul.

Should he write her a letter? No. It could easily fall into the wrong hands and disgrace her.

Should he send a message to her to express his deepest feelings through an intermediary? His valet, perhaps? Even Adrian realized that sending a servant would offend her sensibilities. And he could not imagine Bones being able to keep a straight face in the situation.

But Heath Boscastle was an honorable man no matter what his personal suspicions about Adrian. He regarded Adrian steadily as he stepped from the coach to the sidewalk.

Somehow Heath knew that Adrian was pursuing Emma. Of course Adrian hadn't gone about it in the most discreet manner possible. But he hadn't revealed their secret, either.

"Perhaps you would care to come in for some refreshment, Adrian," he said in a guarded voice. "Just to reassure Dominic that I have not lost my manners."

Adrian was torn. He and Heath both knew what had instigated Heath's physical display at Angelo's. The proper thing to do would be to accept Heath's apology, to laugh it off, and go on his merry way. But to do so would be to miss an opportunity to see Emma. And, God help him, he was desperate for a glimpse of her.

"A brandy would be pleasant," he said, meeting Heath's scrutiny.

Heath's face betrayed no emotion. He nodded pleasantly enough. "Dominic?"

Adrian heard his friend murmur something about a previous appointment. In truth, he was not paying attention—his thoughts had shifted forward in anticipation of seeing Emma. He knew it was unlikely that he would be allowed any unsupervised conversation with her. At this time of day she was most likely giving lessons.

"Come inside, Adrian," Heath stood at the door his butler had just opened to admit them. "We do not want any of the ladies to see us looking so disheveled. My dear sister does love a lecture."

Adrian realized what Heath meant by that remark as he followed him into the drawing room and caught a glimpse of his reflection in the overmantle mirror.

He grimaced. Tousled hair, cloak askew, his muslin shirt damp. "Dear God," he muttered. "No wonder that lavender seller almost dropped her basket when she saw me outside Angelo's."

Heath laughed. "You might want to unroll your cuffs. I look no better than you, I fear. In fact, I shall leave you for a moment to change my own shirt. There's brandy in the cabinet. I'd prefer a coffee, myself. I'll ring Hamm."

Adrian stood in the middle of the room for several moments. He couldn't believe that Heath had actually left him alone. Of course the clever fellow had to know that Adrian could hardly approach Emma looking as if he'd just survived a street brawl.

He stared at the closed door, slowly unrolling his cuffs, slowly losing the battle against common sense. He wondered whether he could see her without her seeing him. Just a glimpse of her. After all, she'd nursed him when he had looked worse, hadn't she?

The door opened. Hamm, the gigantic footman who had served in the war under Heath, appeared. "May I bring you something, my lord?"

Adrian hesitated. "Coffee, please, for Lord Heath."

"Nothing else?"

"No. Unless—unless the ladies are joining us."

Hamm's scraggly eyebrows lifted. "The ladies, my lord?"

"Yes." Adrian shrugged nonchalantly. "Lord Heath's wife. And his sister. They may wish for tea."

"Ah." Hamm nodded in understanding. "I believe that the ladies have gone shopping."

"I see." And, apparently, so did the footman. Adrian felt suddenly like the biggest bufflehead in all England. Why had he ever promised Emma he would not openly pursue her?

Hamm bowed. "I shall bring the coffee, my lord."

Adrian pulled off his cloak as the door closed and had just realized he was still wearing his sword when he heard a muted scream from the rear of the house. It did not occur to him to ignore it, even though neither Emma nor Julia were at home.

But the scream, which held a note of genuine alarm, had definitely been issued by a female.

He left the drawing room, fully expecting that he would discover nothing more threatening than one of Emma's students standing on a chair because a mouse had run across her slipper.

And that he would probably catch hell from Emma for making another indecorous appearance at her academy.

*   *   *

Emma nearly dropped her etiquette manual at the short-lived scream that arose from the library behind her. Harriet again, she thought in vexation. What mischief had the troublemaker brought upon herself this time?

She could not trust that Gardner girl for one hour. It was fortunate Emma had decided at the last moment she would not accompany Julia shopping today, although Emma could not honestly say that she had done so from any virtuous motive.

She enjoyed buying a new bonnet as much as any other lady; Charlotte and Miss Peppertree could manage the academy for a few hours. The fact, however, was that she had stayed home in the secret hope Adrian would pay her brother a visit.

She missed her disreputable duke's heir more than she'd anticipated when she had virtually banished him from her life. She missed Adrian more in these past few days than she had missed her late husband in the year following his death.

She raised her shoulders as she approached the library door to investigate the cause of Harriet's latest mishap. Rarely did she wish she had not begun the academy. It filled her lonely hours and gave her a great deal of satisfaction.

How gratifying it would be to guide Harriet into the graceful ways of womanhood. At least the perplexing girl had not emitted another of those blood-curdling screams.

She hefted her beloved manual onto her hip and

opened the library door. For an incalculable interlude she was too shocked at the scene she beheld to
wage a response. Indeed, there was no precedent
in her life to prepare her to handle the shocking
tableau in progress and, as a Boscastle, Emma had
suffered more than her share of shocks.

Two of the scruffiest young ruffians she had ever
had the displeasure of encountering were in the
process of hauling Harriet through the garden window. A neckcloth, dirty, of course, had been tied
across the girl's mouth to silence her.

This indignity apparently did not discourage Harriet's strenuous struggle for freedom. Although each
of her abductors claimed an arm and leg apiece,
Harriet fought them with the astonishing bodily
contortions of a monkey and a spate of muffled
curses that gave Emma a moment of guilty thank-
fulness for the neckcloth that gagged the unfortunate girl.

"How *dare* you!" she said in a soft growl that not
only startled the abductors but herself.

Indeed, now that her initial shock had passed,
she felt herself possessed of a searing anger. Not
only her brother's home, but her own academy,
sanctuary for the socially inclined, was being violated by what she could only describe as the dregs
of London's underworld.

A multitude of considerations flew through her
mind. Heath had gone to Angelo's earlier to meet
Dominic. Presumably they would dine afterward or

stop off at the club. Her sisters-in-law, Julia and Eloise, were at this moment probably studying fashion plates at the modiste's.

Charlotte and the other girls should be studying Latin in the east wing at this hour. Hamm, Heath's behemoth footman, was somewhere in the house.

She gauged the distance to the bellpull. Taking apparent advantage of Emma's unexpected arrival, young Harriet had just delivered a kick in the hollows to one of her captors. The ruffian emitted a low bellow of pain and crossed his hands over his bruised parts. His partner laughed in crude amusement until Harriet lifted her shoulder to deal him the same offense.

Freed from her inept abductors, Harriet wrenched off the soiled neckcloth and flung it to the floor. "You're done for now, you stinkin' sons of a sow's turd! Help me, Lady Lyons! I'm bein' kidnapped by a pair of louse-ridden murderers!"

The taller of the two young men threw one leg over the windowsill whilst he sized up Harriet's defender. "This is our sister, and I reckon we got a right to bring her back. Our dad's sick, and he wants his daughter at his side."

"Is this true, Harriet?" Emma asked. "Are these two persons related to you?"

Harriet snorted. "They're me halves, Luke and Rob."

She fell briefly in the pile of broken glass on the

floor, only to spring right back to her feet. "The old sod's no more sick than I am."

Emma glanced down at her in horror. "Your elbow is bleeding, Harriet."

"Her hide is gonna be raw as a beefsteak if she don't come with us," the other man announced, grabbing Harriet by her injured arm. "Ain't no point in pretendin' she belongs here. We all know she'll never be no bleedin' silk purse."

Emma marched over to the window. Her throat had closed, and yet somehow her voice resounded in the air, in her very ears. "The authorities do not agree. Miss Gardner stays under *my* supervision."

His grimy hand slid to the leather scabbard protruding beneath his worn leather jerkin. "She's got work to do at home." His head lowered with the belligerence of a country bull.

"What sort of work?" Emma asked, willing Harriet to use her wits and remain calm.

"A job right here in Mayfair," the other man answered from his wobbly perch upon the windowsill. "Decent work as a maid for a countess, no less. Can't beat that with a stick, can you?"

Emma noted that his brother's hand had completely disappeared inside his jerkin. "I believe I can. Perhaps I might speak with her employer and explain the situation."

Harriet gave a bitter laugh at that. "Go on. You, Lady Lyons, walkin' right up to 'er door to explain that her new maid is being set up by her pigs of brothers to rob her blind during a party."

It was at this point that the criminal called Rob drew out from his jerkin an ominous-shaped knife known as a balisong, or butterfly. Emma would never have recognized such an appalling apparatus had her brother Grayson not had one mounted upon the wall in the weapons room of his country home. "Get out of my way," Rob shouted at Emma, "or I'll cut off yer interferin' little nose."

Harriet broke free and flung her scrawny frame in front of Emma while raising her fists in the direction of his face. "You so much as nick 'er and I'll sew yer nutmegs together when you're drunk. I swear it on our whore of a dead mum's grave."

"Put the knife away," Luke muttered from the window. "We haven't got all day. Harriet always mucks up a lay, anyways. We'll find someone else."

Rob nodded in seeming agreement. Then he shot his arm out without warning and ensnared Harriet by the waist. "All right now. I'm the one to give the orders." He pressed the butterfly knife against the back of her ear as he glowered at Emma. "And *you* keep your pretty little piehole shut until we're gone or I'll slice this sow's ear here."

"Someone's coming," Luke muttered and swung both legs over the sill. "Hand her over and hurry."

Emma started after them. It went without saying that she deplored violence of any manner, but she had grown up in a family of five physical brothers and one earthy, exuberant younger sister. More than once Emma had broken up a bout of fisticuffs, as well as rescued a sibling tied to a stool during a family torture fest, in the butler's pantry.

Therefore, without hesitation, she hefted her personal bible of good behavior in one hand and, taking only a split second to aim, sent it hurtling at the head of Harriet's abductor.

It hit him square in the temple, her precious manual of polite graces, all that valuable advice wasted on a primitive's forehead. The blow rendered him momentarily senseless. He shoved Harriet down onto her hands and knees. When he straightened, he was pointing the balisong in Emma's direction and advancing on her.

Emma spun into motion.

She threw a cushion into his face, followed by the complete leather-bound works of Shakespeare. He swore, his arms shielding his face so that he did not see Harriet tackle him from behind and shove him against the window.

As he staggered, losing his balance, Emma darted to the bellpull and tugged in panic. She had quite lost track of time, but surely two seconds did not pass before the door flew open.

"Adrian!"

With a relief that shivered down the seams of her stockings, she recognized the tall long-boned figure who stepped into the room. His hard unsettling gaze questioned her, the book on the floor, the broken window. In two strides he crossed the room and stood as if to shield her.

A rather terrifying transformation seemed to have settled over his handsome features. Before her very eyes he changed from a dashing gentleman to a dark avenger. His very smile filled her with foreboding.

This was not Adrian Ruxley, heir to a dukedom. The man who strode into the room might have just leapt off a pirate junque into a battle on some foreign shore. The image only sharpened in her mind as he wrenched off his cloak and drew his sword from its scabbard.

His white linen shirt clung damply to his chest. A gasp composed of as much admiration as protest rose in her throat. At any other time she might have been offended by the sight of a man's sweaty chest, as attractive a view as she admitted to herself it was, had she not been so grateful to see him.

"Tell me you are all right, Emma," he said without looking at her.

She nodded, heard her brother calling down from the top of the stairs. Then the loud clatter of Hamm's footsteps in the hall. But all of her attention suddenly centered on Adrian, beautiful, heroic, and blessedly here.

"I'm fine, but Harriet—"

Suddenly Adrian's focus shifted. One of Harriet's brothers was already racing through the garden, silverware and snuffboxes spilling out of his pockets.

Rob had edged to the window with his knife held out in an effort to keep Adrian away.

"Don't sleep too sound, none of you," he said roughly. "We'll come back."

Adrian unsheathed his sword. "What did you say?"

Emma blinked. She was too riveted by Adrian to even acknowledge the three other people crowded in the doorway. Her stomach fluttered at the hard smile that curved his mouth. His dark menace mesmerized everyone who watched him as he moved forward.

Harriet retreated behind a satinwood library table.

Rob cast a wild look around the room. "Ain't no one going to stop him? Harriet?"

Adrian circled him with unnerving concentration, raising his saber to the throbbing pulse of Rob's throat so swiftly that even Emma had not seen it coming. "I want to kill you," he said, shaking his head as if the confession amused him. "I'm not entirely sure I can stop myself."

Emma clutched the bellpull. From the corner of her eye she saw Heath and his footman standing in the door, their presence blocking the view of Julia and her aunt. She was profoundly grateful that Charlotte and Miss Peppertree appeared to have kept the girls occupied in the other wing.

They must never learn what had happened today,

at all costs. It would give them nightmares for months.

Rob's forehead glistened with sweat. His brother had disappeared. The tall blond man with the sword had a murderous glint in his eye that even a fool would respect. "Look. There's been no 'arm done."

Adrian walked him against the window. "Says who?"

"Ask me sister," Rob said, his voice thick. "Ask that lady at the bellpull."

Adrian's lips thinned. "What say you, Harriet?"

She pushed her hair from her eyes. "Slit him open like a salmon. Scourge of the earth, he is."

Adrian glanced at Emma. "The decision is yours."

Emma could not seem to think clearly. She wished only that this ordeal would end. "Let him go," she whispered.

Adrian stared up at the ceiling. His hard expression said it wouldn't bother him to send Rob to the next world. "Are you sure?" he asked lightly.

"Please—"

He pressed the tip of his sword into Rob's throat. Rob's face drained white. "The lady wishes for me to be merciful. I release you with reluctance."

Rob stood in hesitation, glancing covertly from Adrian to Emma.

"Go, you big witless nit," Harriet said in contempt. "Get out before he changes his mind."

A moment later Rob spun on the shattered glass and dove out the window into the rose bushes below. He broke into a run before he even straightened, thorns and leaves stuck to his clothes. Adrian shook his head in disgust and sheathed his rapier.

Harriet clapped her hands in delight. "Criminy! I've waited my whole life to see 'im get what he deserved. You're a hero, Lord Wolf, that's what you are. Wait'll I tell the girls—"

"Harriet Gardner." Emma raised her voice. "You will not speak of this affair again. To anyone. Do you understand?"

"Why not, ma'am? Wolf ain't done no wrong. It's me lousy family."

"Please go with Hamm to the kitchen and have Cook put salve on your elbow."

"I'll take her," Julia offered from the door. "Heath wants to make sure none of his treasures were taken from his study. Hamm is going to fetch a glazier to repair the window. I suppose it would be a good idea to assign one of the under-footmen to go outside and retrieve whatever valuables Luke lost during his cowardly escape."

Adrian glanced around. "May I do something to help?"

Emma sighed. "I think you've been more than helpful."

He bent to pick up her manual. "I suppose that's one way to drum manners into a fellow's head."

She laughed a little unsteadily. "I do not recommend it."

Suddenly they were standing alone in the library.

Adrian stared at her, knowing he looked unkempt and sinister. "I could have killed those two when I saw you standing there, and all that broken glass—"

"But you showed admirable restraint. Still"—she could not quite hide a dark sense of humor—"I've a feeling Harriet's brothers will not return soon, if ever, after your appearance."

"I only showed restraint because you were not harmed." He lowered his voice. He could hear Heath talking to one of the servants in the hall. "I shall go mad if we cannot meet in private. I'm behaving like a man—"

"I shall be at the park tomorrow," she said with a guarded smile.

"By yourself?" he asked, studying her face.

"Of course she won't be by herself," Heath said as he reentered the room. "Look at what happened to her today. A brother cannot be too careful when it comes to his sister's welfare." He looked directly at Adrian. "I'm certain you'll agree."

"How could one argue otherwise?" Adrian replied gracefully.

Heath shrugged. He'd changed into a clean shirt and buff trousers. "Are you staying for dinner? It is the least our hero of the day deserves."

"No." He shook his head. He could not trust himself to sit across the table from Emma and not reveal his feelings. It was, in fact, killing him to leave her now with nothing resolved. "I have intruded upon you enough. As well as bringing scandal to your house." He grimaced. "Not to mention looking like a pirate at the moment."

Heath laughed, his good nature apparently restored. "Scandal is nothing new to the Boscastles. Indeed, I do not believe we would know what to do with ourselves if a week passed without some disgrace."

Emma had laid her manual on the library table to examine it for damage. She could sense her brother, in turn, examining *her* in his subtle yet unnerving way. She wondered exactly what he saw.

"I do like Wolf," he said as he turned to the window. "He is a natural defender. However . . ."

She continued to turn the pages of her beloved book. One had to be on guard against Heath's "howevers" and his inscrutable stares. He did not pry. And yet he always seemed to know what a person was most desperate to hide. He understood human nature. He must have been an excellent spy.

She glanced up. "You were saying?"

"I said that I liked Wolf," he answered after a deep silence. "He is a brave man. However . . ."

Emma continued to examine the pages of her manual for creases. "However?"

"Well, he has lived a hard life, fought battles that some would deem brutal."

"He has, hasn't he?" she murmured.

He arched his brow. "What I meant to say is that

ofttimes, when a man is forced to defend his life, the lives of others, he sacrifices a part of his soul."

She closed the book and looked at him. "Did you, Heath?"

He looked so taken aback she almost giggled.

"I thought so once."

"And now?" she asked gently, feeling guilty for provoking him when she knew he had intervened only out of his deep concern for her.

"I have enough in my wife and family that I do not feel the lack," he replied.

"Dear Heath," she said with a rueful smile, "what would we have done without you?"

He sighed. "Is there something you wish to confide in me? I would never violate your trust."

"There is only one thing," she answered, her gaze downcast.

"Yes?"

"I want you to know I perceive that whatever sacrifices you made, whatever you feel you lost during the war you have more than gained back in wisdom and kindness."

"That is all?" he asked in patent disappointment.

She looked up again, her blue eyes playful. "The Boscastle Inquisition is over. We are no longer children, and I am old enough to choose my own course."

"That is not the answer I hoped to hear." He grinned helplessly. "In fact, it is not an answer at all, you clever woman."

* * *

Be happy, Emma.

Those had been her late husband's last words to her, his benediction.

But he had not told her how.

Be happy.

And then he had expired, leaving her bereft but not alone, for no sooner had his coffin been lowered into the ground than her brothers had swooped down to convince her that she must abandon her young ladies' academy in Scotland and move to London where they could watch over her and protect her from all the evils the world inflicted upon young vulnerable widows such as herself.

As it had turned out, and not exactly to Emma's regret, she had been the one to watch over the Boscastles and warn them of the constant perils they sought and miraculously escaped unscathed, with the tragic exception of their youngest brother Brandon.

But Emma was not about to complain. Guarding her siblings had filled the void in her life, and now with all of them married, she could turn her nurturing instincts to the young ladies of London who so desperately needed the guidance of an experienced gentlewoman.

But suddenly the tables had turned.

The rogues were paying her back in kind.

They'd always accused her of meddling in their affairs. Now they were the meddlers.

It was over the next two days, however, that she realized how the strong arms of her family had begun to tighten about her like shackles. Scarcely could she take a cup of tea without one of her brothers hovering at her elbow. One or another of the demons seemed bent on accompanying her everywhere.

Since when had Devon taken such a keen interest in haunting the library the exact hour that she did? And when on earth had Heath ever enjoyed shopping for lace and haggling over the price of a hanky?

Still, it was not until her next unplanned encounter with Lord Wolverton at the museum that she knew a bona fide conspiracy had been hatched to prevent her from being alone with Adrian. She and Charlotte were guiding the girls for a history lesson, when Drake appeared from behind an Egyptian sarcophagus and meandered past her to a collection of ancient pottery. Drake and ancient art?

Clearly her wicked brothers had decided they had reason to intercede.

"How did *you* know I would be here?" she whispered to Adrian as he followed her into the Roman gallery ahead of the girls.

"I have a spy in your house who informs me of your whereabouts."

"You don't," she said softly. "It's Harriet, isn't it? How could you, Adrian? You haven't told my brothers?" she asked in an undertone. She swallowed hard. "They know. There's no other explanation."

Adrian trailed her at a respectable distance. "Well, they didn't hear it from me. I would rather die than betray you."

She noticed Harriet sneak away from the group. All of a sudden she seemed to have lost control over her entire life. "Harriet, do not place your hand into that urn. You don't know what might be in there."

The air was chill inside the museum. Rain had fallen steadily throughout the day. Yet with Adrian's warm, wool-cloaked figure at her back, Emma felt almost overheated. In a barely audible voice, she asked, "Why exactly are you following me, Adrian?"

"Because I want—because I—oh, hell, Emma, may we walk alone in the hall for a moment?"

She glanced around. "*One* moment only."

He looked back, noting Drake's figure only a few feet away. "It isn't over between you and me," he said under his breath. "It can't be. I have spent every hour since—"

He broke off as they turned a corner together and discovered her younger brother Devon sitting in a chair perusing a collection of state papers. "Well, isn't this a surprise," Adrian muttered. "The entire family is here. There's your brother."

Emma glanced back through the doorway in consternation. "It can't be my brother. I can see him standing right over there with Charlotte."

"The *other* brother. Devon."

"Devon? In a museum? Now I have seen everything."

Devon lowered his sheath of documents, pretending to look astonished to see them, and gave a friendly little wave.

"This has gone too far." Emma came to a halt. The girls crowded into the arched doorway behind Adrian. "I shall put a stop to it as soon as I return home."

Adrian looked at Devon, whose friendly expression had gone faintly discouraging all of a sudden. "All I want to do is talk to you, Emma. Without a full complement of guards."

She glanced back meaningfully at her brother. "It seems as if you shall have to do so by committee."

He crossed his arms. "Unless we can arrange a private meeting."

"We can't," she whispered. "At least not until they stop pestering me like this."

His gaze darkened. "Well, I'm not giving up. And just so that you'll know what you're dealing with, I have never failed in any mission before." He stared at her in male arrogance underlaid with a very appealing vulnerability. "And I don't intend to start now."

"We'll see," she murmured.

To Adrian's surprise, his declaration of amorous

warfare would demand a good deal more strategy than the straightforward military conquests he had waged in the past. He had earned his reputation as a hard fighter.

He had not, however, masterminded a campaign against the Boscastle brothers before. He had to admire their ingenuity and determination when it came to protecting one of their own.

His admiration would not deter him from his purpose. In fact, it only made him more determined to win.

He just wasn't quite sure how to go about it.

They were four Boscastle brothers and one of him. Obviously he needed a powerful ally. And a bolder plan of action.

Chapter Fourteen

❧ ❦

Heath's sleek black carriage rumbled over the glistening cobbles of the city street. The three brothers borne within stared back at the receding museum in silence until Devon tossed his black leather gloves onto the seat in disgust, if not defeat.

"This is getting a bit ridiculous. We can't follow Emma everywhere. She's planning on attending a Flemish needlework display this evening in Cavendish Square. A man does have his pride."

"Dear God," Drake muttered. "I thought ancient pottery was bad enough."

"At least none of you had to buy pink lace in public," Heath remarked dryly. "And tomorrow morning she's been invited to inspect a parish school for the children of unwed prostitutes."

"Well, count me out on that one," Devon said. "I think Chloe is accompanying her."

Heath snorted. "And Chloe, as we all recall, knows absolutely nothing about illicit affairs and staying away from dangerous men. If anything, Chloe will push Emma right into Adrian's arms."

"Well, we cannot accompany her forever on all these forays," Devon muttered. "I'm beginning to feel like my dowager auntie. Moreover, I think Jocelyn is beginning to suspect I'm up to no good."

Heath blew out a sigh. "We must hang in only until Grayson returns and we have a forum to decide on action."

"Our presence doesn't seem to have convinced Wolf to stay away from her," Drake said.

Heath laughed. "Perhaps he can't help himself."

Drake grinned at him. "Emma and Wolf. He's the complete opposite of our sister, the antithesis of all she holds dear."

"Actually, he's not," Heath said reflectively. "He'll be a duke one day. And with a little bit of polish, well, who knows? No one would have laid odds on any of us reforming not long ago."

"As far as I can tell, she's doing her best not to talk to him at all," Devon said, folding his arms behind his head. "When is Grayson due to return, anyway?"

Heath drew aside the curtain. "By tonight if the storm doesn't worsen."

Jane, the Marchioness of Sedgecroft, and young matriarch to the Boscastle clan by marriage, had arrived at her London residence two hours ahead of her husband Grayson. It was dark by the time she had settled her son Rowan into the nursery with his nursemaid, Mrs. O'Brien.

She barely had time to fortify herself with a cup of brandy-laced coffee before she set back out in her own small carriage for her brother-in-law's town house. She hoped Heath would not be home, but even if he was, it was safer to hold a ladies' meeting there than at home where Grayson was liable to come bursting in and interrupt.

Besides, Heath's wife Julia had called this emergency gathering. Perhaps Emma herself would attend, although Jane rather doubted it.

Julia's message insisted upon secrecy and hinted at panic. Jane concluded there was not a moment to waste.

Indeed, Julia's initial greeting at the door underscored her suspicions. "Thank heavens, you are here, Jane. Quickly. Quickly! Into the family drawing room."

Jane divested herself of her cloak and gloves, following the taller woman to a private stairs at the side of the house. "Such intrigue. Would your bedchamber not offer more privacy?"

"Not from my husband," Julia said offhandedly.

"Ah."

"I meant—"

"No explanations are necessary, Julia. I am myself married to a Boscastle male." And a hot-blooded breed they were, including the female members of the family, one of whom was already waiting in the candlelit drawing room.

Chloe Boscastle, Emma's younger raven-haired sister, rose from her chair to embrace Jane. Chloe was not unknown to notoriety herself. In fact, she had married Adrian's oldest friend, the dark-tempered Dominic Breckland, Viscount Stratfield, after a romance that had been sparked when Chloe had found him hiding half-dead in her dressing closet.

Seated comfortably on a tufted sofa behind Chloe were Emma's cousin Charlotte; Devon's young bride, the former Jocelyn Lydbury; and Drake's wife, a past governess, Eloise.

Julia's aunt, Hermia, occupied the French fauteuil that sat by the fire. While associated to the Boscastles only through her niece's marriage to Heath, Hermia had been unofficially adopted by the entire clan. Her zest for life and penchant for trouble had earned her a place of favor. The one true love of her life, the Earl of Odham, had been unfaithful to her years ago and was still earnestly trying to win her forgiveness.

"How is that darling son of yours, Jane?" Hermia asked fondly.

"As plump and lively as ever."

"Always getting into mischief, is he?" Hermia asked approvingly.

Jane sighed. "Especially when Grayson plays with him."

Hermia chuckled. "I should love to paint him as young Cupid to add to our collection."

"I assume you mean Rowan and not my husband." Jane took the glass of port that Julia handed her. All of the women had been tippling since late afternoon, a sure indication of their concern. "It seems I have come from Kent not a minute too soon."

"That all depends," Julia said. "It might even be too late to thwart our male counterparts."

Hermia set her glass upon the table. "Too late for what? It's only ten o'clock or so. In my day, an evening's entertainment would just be getting under way. You younger women must have been fed on milksops."

"I am referring to the situation that has developed between Emma and Adrian Ruxley," Julia said in annoyance. "Don't you ever pay any attention to me, Aunt Hermia?"

Chloe, who had been playing idly with her pearl bracelet, glanced up with an incredulous expression. "Emma? And Wolf? A *situation*? This is too delicious."

Eloise Boscastle, the former governess who had once hoped to work at Emma's esteemed academy before marrying into the family, looked aghast. "Lady Lyons and that . . . mercenary? You must be mistaken."

"Of course she's mistaken," Jocelyn said, almost choking on her sherry. "Emma and Lord Wolverton are the most unlikely match in all of London."

"In England," Chloe amended merrily.

"The whole of Europe for that matter," Eloise said, clearly defensive of the paragon whom she still held in her heart as an untarnished example of all a lady should aspire to be. Indeed, it was no secret to the family that Eloise had esteemed Lady Emma for years.

"Julia, you must speak plainly to us," Jane said. "If this is a matter upon which we are compelled to act, there is no time to mince words. All I know is that Adrian came to Emma's rescue at a wedding. Perhaps not in the most graceful of ways, but—"

"It is already too late," Charlotte Boscastle broke in very quietly.

Jane drew a breath. "I see. Then exactly how does the situation stand between our two—dare I call them—lovers?"

"I would say the situation is at a complete standstill," Charlotte replied. "I don't believe that Emma can take a step these days without one of my cousins peering over her shoulder."

Chloe snorted lightly. "I do remember their smothering guard myself. It's a miracle Dominic and I ended up marrying with the four devils boxing me in. And now they've added Gabriel to their ranks. Poor Emma. To think she's found love this late, at last, only to—"

Jane wandered over to the window. "You're probably right. They'll ruin this for her—oh, Lord above. He's *here*."

"Lord Wolverton?" Hermia asked eagerly, half-way out of her chair.

"No. Grayson, the cabal leader, come to decide Emma's—"

A dull *thunk* shuddered through the wall. "Did you hear that?" Jane asked, whirling around in alarm.

Chloe examined a loose bead on the instep of her slippers. "Yes. Grayson has never gone through a door he didn't slam. You should know that by now, Jane."

"It wasn't the door," Jane exclaimed. "It—"

"—came from the other side of the house." Charlotte leaned forward, pointing over her shoulder. "From the side where Emma's suite is located."

Adrian climbed up the rickety wooden ladder and swung one arm, then his right leg over the sill, grateful to that imp Harriet for remembering to open Emma's window. Of course he'd paid the greedy little urchin good coin for the favor. No doubt she would still try to blackmail him into buying her silence. Well, he would deal with Miss Gardner tomorrow. If all went well tonight, he might even want to reward her.

He glanced around, surveying the darkened chamber. He'd landed in the bedroom, as luck would have it. A sea coal fire smoldered amber-gold in the grate. Good. She wouldn't be cold after he'd declared his intentions and taken her to bed.

Through the door that adjoined her suite, he glimpsed her sitting in the next room on a saber-legged rosewood chaise, a book on her lap. Her beautiful, long hair was loose, gathered over one shoulder. Rapunzel. He wanted to twist it around his neck, his arms, his hips. He could almost feel the softly spun strands caressing his back, his belly.

His beautiful Renaissance angel.

He moved quietly toward her. She hadn't noticed him yet. In his day he could have sneaked aboard a ship of pirates and slit their snoring throats before he disturbed their dreams. Surely he could sneak up on the woman he desired and—drop to his knees beside her.

He walked straight into one of the potted plants on a marble pedestal that flanked the door. She leapt to her feet, her luminous eyes widening in shock.

"You!"

"Damn it, Emma." He caught the pot of English ivy before it could crash to the ground, then rebalanced it carefully on the pedestal. "Please, whatever you do, don't scream."

"I have absolutely no intention of indulging in such a useless act." She looked up slowly into his face. "If your appearance here is in regard to those lessons in deportment again, which you desperately need, I shall refer you to a certain French count who is an acquaintance of Devon's. I understand he is more than happy to instruct Englishmen in the re-fined arts."

He walked her back into the chaise. "Darling, I don't give a damn about my manners. I never did."

Her breath caught, a tiny hitch of sound that be-lied her composure. "Obviously."

He lifted his hands to her shoulders. "I came here for one purpose only."

Her mouth dropped open. "Adrian Ruxley, if you do not leave this instant, I shall—"

"I adore you," he said, lowering his mouth to hers. "And I want you to be my wife. Emma, please, put me out of this torture. Do you feel as I do? No, don't answer. I already know."

He kissed her before she could utter a word. Sol-dier of fortune, he took advantage of her shocked immobility to brush his mouth across hers. He drew her against him and held her so there was no ques-tion of escape. Sensual pleasure pulsed throughout his body as he felt her lips, then her body soften against his.

Knowing Emma, he'd have little time to weaken her defenses before she rallied her guard. But he waited for her answer, anyway, his heart beating, wild and hopeful. He combed his hand through her hair, untangling a knot, cradling her nape, stroking her warm skin.

She moved slightly so that his mouth rested upon her cheek. "Are you proposing to me?" she asked in a soft, precise voice.

"Yes." He laughed, disbelieving, happier than he'd ever been in his life. "Yes."

Her eyes searched his face for deceit. He must look, sound, like a fool. He didn't care about that, either, if she accepted his proposal. "And this is what you wished to discuss with me?" she asked, his skeptical little schoolmistress, the taskmaster he could not survive without. "Why didn't you say so in the first place?"

"When did I have the chance?" he demanded incredulously. "I followed you to a lacemaker's stall, fully prepared to pop the question, only to find Heath picking out a pretty handkerchief for himself. It was *not* a moment conducive to a proposal."

She shook her head in chagrin. "They do know. And they'll kill us if we're caught."

"Let's elope."

"Elope? Tonight?"

He traced his gloved thumb over her lush mouth, then trailed it down her chin into the cleft of her bodice. "Why not?" he asked, his gaze darkly tempting.

She shivered. "And have my brothers chasing us across England? What a honeymoon made in hell. And what an example to the academy. We shall have a proper wedding, or none at all."

He grinned, his thumb rubbing the plump curve of her breast. Her nipple beaded against his large warm palm. "Then you've accepted."

"Did I?" she asked, gazing up at his face as he

boldly caressed her senses into a state of dazed pleasure.

His eyes crinkled at the corners, warm, teasing her. Slowly he lifted his hand away to untie the laces of her bodice and free her firm white breasts. "You did."

She crossed her hands over her swollen pink nipples. Adrian felt his breathing quicken.

"But my brothers—"

"Kiss me, Emma." He swept her over his knee to the chaise. "Put your arms around my neck," he said in a thick voice. "I need your kisses."

She caught a handful of his coat. His body clenched in disappointment until he realized she wasn't pushing him away. No, bless her. She was pulling him closer, right down on top of her, fanning the inferno that boiled inside him.

They stole kisses from each other. Starved, ungentle, greedy kisses. Neither of them were innocent. Adrian understood desire, how to arouse, to satisfy. And to prolong pleasure until one's lover begged prettily for release.

She dropped her head back on the chaise, his sultry schoolmistress, her limbs relaxed, her curves inviting. He stared down at her in helpless desperation. His groin tightened as she laid her hand on his knee.

Suddenly his entire body felt so heavy with sexuality that even the weight of his coat became unbearable.

He began to wrench it off only to stop as he felt her hands at his shoulders, assisting him. He closed his eyes, drew a ragged breath. "It was a fumble that first night. I took advantage of you, although not on purpose."

"And you admit it?" she asked steadily.

"To my disgrace."

"I accept your apology." She twisted her hips. It seemed vulgar to voice her wants. Her body observed no such restrictions.

"It wasn't so much of an apology," he murmured. "It was more of a warning."

Her deepest muscles contracted, quivered. "A warning?"

He inhaled, his voice deep pitched with pleasure. "It won't be a fumble this time—"

"Adrian—"

"—and you aren't going to convince me this is an improper act between a man and a woman who are now to be wed—"

"—for the love of heaven, I do not wish for an apology. I want *action*."

His eyes darkened in pleasure. "Then I shall act."

"And if you don't touch me soon, Lord Wolf," she whispered low, drawing his coat from his broad shoulders, "I will embarrass the very name of etiquette."

He groaned. "As your husband-to-be, I would like nothing more than to oblige your wishes." He angled his head and caught her hand. "But it's ladies first, isn't it? You see, I do take instruction . . ."

He slid his gloved hand beneath her robe. Then, with taunting deliberation, he stroked his way up her ankle to her bare knee to her belly. Her breathing deepened. She turned her face into the cushion, murmuring, "Gloves, my lord," with a spellbinding laugh that stirred his predator's instincts. "A gentleman *must* remove his gloves when touching a woman intimately."

"Is that an unbreakable rule in your manual?" he asked, idly easing his leather-clad fingers between her folds. "Or are you inventing new rules as we go along?"

"Adrian," she breathed in shocked delight as his gloved forefinger slipped inside her. "This—"

He leaned closer, inserted another finger into her tight passage. "I've never gone by the book myself. I seem to be an animal of instinct. Forgive me."

"This"—she shifted, her gaze widening in anticipation; her shoulders arched—"isn't civilized. This is, well, I don't know what it is."

"I don't either, but I like it very much and suggest you wait before deciding."

She laid her hand on his strong wrist, her inner muscles gripping his leather-gloved fingers. It was decadent. It was desire. And she felt the purity and power of it to her soul. "How long must I wait?" she whispered.

He drew the rest of her robe up to her midriff.

His heavy hand lay possessively between her sleek thighs and the gold-tinged curls that daintily concealed her cleft from his ravenous stare.

To be her lover he would have gone down on his knees and begged. He was besotted. Bewitched. He whose skills for fighting had made men plead for mercy would forever lay down his sword and dedicate his life to pleasing her if she would allow him.

"There hasn't been a moment since we were first together," he said hoarsely, "that I haven't thought of you."

Her quiet sigh of pleasure encouraged him. Slowly he finished untying the ribbons that lay against her shoulders. She made no attempt to dissuade him. His hands eased the thin muslin down her graceful back. Her breasts hovered above the sheer fabric, her nipples silky pink and luscious. "Oh, Emma." With her aristocratic features and flowing hair, she looked like an elegant concubine. He felt his erection bulging against his trousers, straining the tight seams to the bursting point.

Slowly, he told himself. She deserved his time, the best he could give her after their initial awkward indiscretion. "I am trying to control myself," he explained. "I'm afraid I feel a little wild at times."

"My wild wolf."

"Tame me, Emma."

"Why?" she whispered. "Sometimes a lady knows when to appreciate what nature has unleashed. A storm over the mountains. Rain at a summer picnic. A duke who does not follow the rules of his realm . . ."

His heartbeat raced so that it hurt to draw a breath into his lungs. Sexual tension gripped his muscles, thickened the very air he shared with her. His cock ached heavily in his trousers. How he craved this woman.

She pressed herself into his hand.

With a low growl at this unexpected enticement, he pulled off his damp glove and sought the sweet tenderness of her flesh. Her submission. He had waited for her capitulation, knowing that he was hers from the first time he'd seen her.

"You must think me a devil," he said in a raw voice. "I have deliberately enticed you to abandon those principles you esteem."

"And what," she asked in a voice even deeper than his own, "if I admit to you, my devil, that it is you I esteem most dearly? That I would give up everything to be yours?"

He rubbed his free hand over his face. "Then I am yours to do with as you wish. Polish me. Instruct me. Turn me into one of those mincing Englishmen you admire. I care not. Just don't refuse me, Emma. Make me into whatever you wish, but I beg you with all my heart, make me yours."

The Boscastles, Heath reflected in annoyance, had never exactly been known for their patience. Drake had practically drummed a hole in the library desktop. Gabriel had gone through three of Heath's best cigars. Devon kept wandering back and forth to the window until at length he had settled in his chair to nod off.

It was, therefore, a relief when the eldest Boscastle brother, Grayson, graced them with his domineering presence. "Did you hear a suspicious noise when you entered the house?" Heath asked, not one to waste words.

Grayson shrugged out of his cloak. "It was probably me slamming the door. Am I too late?"

"That depends," Heath said, sitting back in his chair. "Does Jane know you are here?"

"Of course not," Grayson said. "Have I not always been the soul of discretion? Jane is preoccupied with some new Italian shoemaker. At least that's what she said."

Devon started to laugh. "She knows."

"Precisely what does she know that I have not been apprised of?" Grayson inquired with a dark look around the room.

"Sit down," Heath said. "And I shall tell you the facts as I understand them. It started less than a fortnight ago at a wedding . . ."

Grayson frowned. "It always starts at a wedding."

Heath paused. "On second thought, I would feel better if one of you walked around the house to investigate the noise we just heard. I'm willing to stake my name that it was *not* a door slamming."

*   *   *

Harriet stood in vigil in the garden beneath Lady Lyons's bedchamber as she had countless times for her brothers during the course of one of their Mayfair robberies. This was an easier lay, though, even if less exciting. She couldn't see a bleeding thing from her hiding place and while she wouldn't go to gaol if she got caught, she wouldn't win a purse of sparklers, either.

Nothing had happened.

Not a glimpse of his nibs playing at rantum scantum with Lady L, an event that, by Harriet's estimation, should be under way at this moment.

She sank down on the summerhouse steps. She'd been half hoping to hear her ladyship screaming off her garret, her with her grand manners and all.

"Her silence tells the true story, don't it?" Harriet whispered to the skinny gray cat who'd wandered up to sniff at her shoes. "You and I have our share of secrets, eh, Puss?"

Harriet had seen enough of life in Seven Dials to gather that men and women took an inordinate pleasure in joining giblets. But while Harriet might be a liar and a thief, she cherished her own virtue. Not that it mattered much to a girl destined for Newgate. Still, Harriet—

The cat turned its head. Harriet blinked, hearing footsteps from the direction of the kitchen. Someone muttering in annoyance about the bench she'd dragged across the door in the event a busybody decided to snoop about the garden. Lord Wolf hadn't paid her for that particular act of precaution.

She'd collect it from him later, with interest, if he had a good night.

The door rattled harder. A disembodied voice from an upstairs window called down to her.

"Psst. *Harriet.*" That Butterfield pipsqueak's reedy voice wafted down. "Miss Boscastle is looking for you."

She shot to her feet. "Hell's bloody bells."

There was nothing to do for it. She had to hide Romeo's ladder from yon idiot banging at the door, not to mention hiding her own sorrowful self from Charlotte Boscastle's patrol.

It wasn't the first time she'd hefted a ladder over her scrawny little back in the name of impropriety; it probably wouldn't be the last. Still, at this rate she could go into retirement on what his lordship owed her for doing her duty.

Chapter Fifteen

Sir Gabriel Boscastle swore to himself and vaulted over the bench he'd dislodged from the doorway. God knew it was a crude tactic to delay one from entering the garden. Still, it was effective. He hadn't wanted to break down the door. And if he'd known the lay of the house a little better, he would have found another point of exit. Well, he was the one who'd wanted to be included in all the London Boscastle family intrigues. It was time to prove he could connive with the best of his cousins. His own family had given him more heartbreak than happiness. Who'd have thought, as bad as he'd been, that he would be embraced by the London fold?

The garden looked innocent and undisturbed in the moonlight. For all he knew two of the servants had been stealing a few moments alone and he'd ruined their plans. He almost felt guilty.

He strolled about a few moments, spotted a gray cat sitting on the wall. Nothing to arouse suspicion until—

He narrowed his eyes, came to a standstill. A pale-haired figure had just emerged from the house, her movements denoting some furtive purpose. What the devil—

"Charlotte?" Disbelieving, he stepped toward her, laughing at the tiny shriek she emitted. "What are you doing out in the cold?"

She took a startled breath. "I should ask you the same thing."

"I came out to smoke a cigar," he replied, then patted his vest pocket as if to verify the fib.

"Well, I was looking for . . . for Harriet." She sniffed the air. "Odd. I don't smell any smoke."

He glanced around. "I don't see Harriet, either—"

But he did, all of a sudden, spy the ladder that lay precariously balanced against the side of the summerhouse. And almost at the same moment as did Charlotte, judging by her audible intake of breath.

Neither of them said a word. Gabriel had no idea what Charlotte made of the discovery. Or exactly what a ladder against the wall meant, although he had a good idea that this was something Heath would want to know. It was not Gabriel's job to judge, only to report back to the Boscastle brothers as soon as possible.

He could not imagine Wolf eloping with Emma. Or anyone being brave enough to elope with her for that matter. He did think it was rather a shame she was such a prude. With that apricot gold hair and creamy alabaster complexion, she was a beautiful woman and would make some poor man absolutely besotted and miserable one day, he was sure.

Was that man Wolf?

"Well, I suppose we should go back inside before we're missed," he said casually.

Charlotte practically pushed him in her hurry to reach the door first. "Splendid idea. Now—"

A thin voice floated down to them from the dormer window. Her white face overshadowed by a frilly nightcap, Harriet sat perched across the sill. "Would the pair of you mind taking the chitchat inside?"

Gabriel scowled up at her. "You wouldn't be talking to me, would you, Miss Sauce-Box?"

"Yeah. What if I am?" Harriet peered down at him for several moments. "Hey, I know that 'andsome face, don't I?"

Gabriel snorted. "If you're referring to me, I doubt it."

"I've seen you in the slums," Harriet insisted. "Sneakin' about, you were."

"Not me," Gabriel said in annoyance. At least not in recent years.

"Maybe you have an evil twin," Charlotte whispered amusedly.

"Maybe I'm evil enough to be triplets," he retorted. "Which reminds me. How are those brothers of yours?"

"I don't ask." She gave him a suspicious look. "How are yours?"

He shrugged. "I don't know."

"Ah."

Harriet pounded her fist on the sill. "Some of us do need our beauty sleep, you know. If you keep that blether up, you'll wake up the whole house in a minute."

Gabriel raised his brow. He had a hunch the whole house, if not all of Mayfair, would be in an uproar before morning.

Emma moaned, sinking into the mattress. "Please draw the bedcurtains," she whispered. As if darkness could veil their indecent desire for each other.

He loomed over her, his shirt hanging halfway off his shoulders. He looked raw, sexual, and he acted it, too. "What if it pleases me to look at you?"

"You shouldn't—"

"Ssh, love," he said, unfastening his trousers.

"My head is swimming," she said in a quiet voice. "I think I'm going to faint."

Her eyes fluttered shut as he lowered himself onto the bed. His large hands glided in gentle possession across her face, her throat, then her breasts. His erection pressed hard against her bare hip. His clean scent, mint and male spice, stole enticingly into her senses.

"You're not going to faint." He kissed the engorged tips of her breasts, his voice a seductive whisper on her skin. "At least not until after I've f—"

"Adrian," she gasped, opening her eyes. "Not that word."

He laughed, locking his leg over hers. "Fine," he murmured. "I won't say it, but I'm going to do it to you good, Lady Emma. Shall I suck on your breasts first? Or may I stroke your lovely quim?"

She caught her upper lip in her teeth. "Must you describe every detail of the acts we are to experience?"

His sharp white teeth closed around a delicate nipple. Her spine bowed in pleasure. "It's all in the details, isn't it?" he murmured, echoing the words she had spoken to him at the wedding. "The little touches."

Her breath caught on a broken laugh. "I shall take you to task . . . later."

His thumb spread through the dewy curls that crowned her cleft. He inhaled raggedly, then began to rotate the stiff pearl of her sex. "You're silky wet," he said, his voice deepening to a soft growl. "Temptress."

Temptress. Her. Of all the names used to describe her, this was the most unlikely, the most lovely— Oh, *heaven*. He wedged another finger into her secret place until she could feel herself stretching, weeping against his hand in supplication.

"Not yet," he whispered.

She thrashed her head, lifted her hand to his thigh. Her body trembled with irrepressible need. His thumb teased her clitoris, light flicks that drew a deep moan of frustration from her throat. She felt his heavy shaft thicken against her thigh. She moistened her lower lip with her tongue, imagining his organ in her mouth, between her legs.

"You feel like cream, Emma," he said, his face intense. "I'd like to taste you—"

She was dying, lost, desperate. So desperate. "Don't say—"

"I'd like to rub my face in you. All that cream."

Her hips bucked. She spread her legs shamelessly, riding his knuckles when what she really wanted, needed, was his thick member inside her, assuaging her hunger. "I can't—"

"May I have a lick, please?"

"—breathe. I can't think or breathe."

He withdrew his hand, waited a heartbeat before plunging his fingers back inside her snug passage. Her back stiffened; her quim gripped him so tightly that he groaned, then worked her faster. Her sensitive muscles shivered.

"That's it, love," he whispered, low and wicked. "That's how a proper lady shows her lord what she wants."

She sobbed as her body convulsed. Then, as if the pleasure, the relief, did not completely undo her, he bent his head without warning and burrowed his face between her thighs. Warmth burst through her veins as his tongue replaced his fingers and thrust into her swollen folds.

A proper lady.

Oh, yes. Yes. She was squeezing his shoulders with

her legs, hugging his hard body. And he seemed to like it, even when she undulated against his mouth. He made a growling sound, and his big hands clasped the cheeks of her bottom to draw her closer.

The pulsations were still echoing all over her body when he pulled himself off her. He slid off the bed, his face carnal and beautiful in the grainy shadows. He stood studying her bare form, undressed with hurried grace as if he guessed how she ached to behold his nude body. Indeed, Emma could not take her eyes from him.

Lustful, that's what she was. As badly behaved as Hermia pursuing male aristocrats to sketch for art. But Adrian was a masterpiece of nature. His bare chest might have been sculpted from marble, the striated muscle and faint scars bearing witness to strength tested.

In fact, she was so impressed by what she beheld that her appreciative gaze drifted downward over his hard belly to the heavy organ that stood like polished steel between his thighs. A sigh of unadulterated desire escaped her. He was a man to make any woman weep.

She closed her eyes to mask her thoughts. And heard him laugh as he lowered his beautiful body to the bed. "It's all right to look at me, you know," he said, walking his fingers across her breasts, giving each nipple a pinch before he parted her juicy pink folds.

"I want to look at you," she whispered. "You're ever so lovely."

"You're better than cream and cherries, yourself. You liked what I did, didn't you?"

She writhed against his gentle stroking, still unbearably sensitive. "I would think my present position speaks for itself."

He slipped his free hand under her bottom and moved her onto her side. "Then let's try another position."

He lifted his hand from the throbbing flesh he had recently stimulated, inhaling deeply. And then, as if she were a delicacy, he licked the essence of her from his fingers. She was too shocked, too aroused to react. She had never—the satiny knob of his penis pressed between the cheeks of her bottom and slowly penetrated her cleft. The sensation, the silken pleasure of his huge shaft as it pressed toward her feminine core, stole her breath.

She arched her shoulders in anticipation. He brought his large hand up to her breasts and tugged her tender nipples between his glistening fingers.

"Now," he whispered, biting the back of her neck, "I want you to forget everything you know about being a lady."

He chuckled at her outraged gasp, but a moment later, after she'd wound up on her stomach, he was too engrossed in sinking his cock inside her to even think, let alone speak. The damp walls of her sheath squeezed him in welcome. He drew a breath between his teeth and teased the head of his erection into her passage. With every inch of him she drew inside, he could feel her flesh resist, then moistly stretch, making a home for his pulsing shaft.

He felt the shiver that quivered down her spine. And sent him over the edge. His proper Emma had the graceful back, the sexual allure, and shapely arse of a courtesan. *His.* He was almost all the way inside her. His teeth ached.

His alone.

He lifted his arms above his head, releasing a soft growl of sexual possession, and surged. She bucked, groaning into her pillow, and lifted herself onto her knees.

He turned his head, afraid that if he watched her delicious body taking him inside her he would spill his seed upon her thigh.

"Does it hurt?" he whispered in a raw voice, not certain he could stop at this point, anyway.

She gave a small shake of her head. "Only a little."

He thrust. She arched her pelvis and rotated her hips with exquisite slowness, gloving him to the hilt. He withdrew, struggling for breath. His spine flexed, he pumped into her, harder now. A little faster until his cock felt ready to burst in its skin. She moaned softly; her body tautened, and he kept telling himself she was no virgin, but a woman experienced. A woman who had not made love in years; yet she'd aroused him to the point he could not even speak.

For a moment he was afraid. His phallus was exceptionally thick, and he was on the verge of losing complete control. He heard her breath quicken, felt her soft hands grip his arse. Then she swiveled her rosy bottom against him, bouncing, encouraging him to continue. "Don't stop," she whispered in a low voice that excited him. "Whatever you do . . ."

She need say nothing else to unleash his instincts. He threw his head back and gave her what her body had begged for. Mindless, he drove in and out, his stones tight, cradled in the crevasse below her slit. Her sheath absorbed every hot, aching inch of him. A growl of pleasure rose in his throat.

"Too good," he muttered. She undid him, gave the meaning of desire a depth that frightened him. He had to possess her. He was consumed with need.

His voice broke. His chest heaved. He jerked his hips, and lifted her against him, his body straining in spasms of the most potent release he had ever known. He moved until he could not breathe, gave himself to her and took even as his senses fragmented and his heart thundered in his chest and head.

She shook beneath him as if she, too, would shatter, secured by his strong arms around her waist. He held her. Pray God, he would hold and love her every night for the rest of his life, anchored, at peace, with the only woman who understood him and beckoned him back into the light.

At length she twisted against his arm, kissing his neck. In reluctance he withdrew from the warmth of her body to lie beside her. Her fine gold hair caught between their flesh like a veil. He regretted again his brash attempt at seducing her that first time. He wished he had waited to give her the attention she deserved.

He was a man who'd learned to mark the passage of time only by monumental events. The death of his mother. The first Christmas his father admitted that he did not believe Adrian was his son. The October day he'd left home with the caw of ravens rising in the distant woodsmoke.

The day he'd met Emma.

It was a blessing he hadn't lost her, that her brothers had not sent him away. And since he could not find the words to express what he felt, he rolled onto his side and kissed her, hoping that somehow she would understand.

She twined her arms around his neck and pressed her fragrantly damp body against his. A surge of desire swept through his noble intentions. He would have happily continued debauching her had his own conscience not stopped him. "Emma." He slid his hand down the seam of her backside. "I have to tell your brother. Your brothers."

"Now?"

Her delicate body slipped out from his grasp. Before he knew it, they were both sitting up in bed with a coverlet pulled over their legs. She looked so disheveled, so desirable that he wished he'd had the sense to keep his mouth shut.

But the time had come. This was not a little indiscretion to be laughed off in a few months. What he'd done, broken into her room and ravished her, had incurred a debt of honor. Happily he was more than willing to pay it, even if he might have gone about his courtship with more finesse.

"Surely you don't mean to go downstairs and announce your intentions at *this* hour?" she asked in a voice that not only made him straighten his shoulders but reach for a sheet to cover his privates. "After what we've just done?"

"It's better than having them find us here, isn't it?"

She regarded him in horror. "I would sooner drown myself in the Thames."

He grimaced. Her anxiety was infectious. "I will take on your entire family—the Prince Regent and every power in Europe—to claim you as mine."

She stared at him, then started to giggle.

He raised his brow. "Is that meant to be helpful?"

"No, it's just—every power in Europe—"

He kissed her on the nose as she burst into another fit of giggles. "What happened to your propriety, madam?"

"You."

He rose and strode toward the window, not a stitch covering his sculpted body.

"Guarding my honor is all very well and good," Emma said to his receding back, the pragmatic lady of protocol again. "However, you must wait until morning."

"Are you sure? Somehow one senses the matter will not wait."

Emma recovered her garments from beneath the disarrayed bedclothes and quickly redressed. Nothing brought out the best in the Boscastle siblings like a crisis. She absolutely shone when others were forced to depend on her. "I think you ought to leave as quietly as—"

"Too late," he muttered from the window by which he'd entered her room.

Her blood went cold as she came up behind him. "What is it?"

He shook his head in disbelief. "The ladder is gone. That little guttersnipe must have moved it. She's double-crossed me."

She peered around his imposing shoulder. "Guttersnipe?" She had just realized what he'd said. Even fully dressed, his manly proximity disconcerted her processes of logic. "Oh, *no*, Adrian. Please do not tell me you engaged *Harriet's* help in this scheme. Of all the wretched ideas—"

"I wanted to see you. I had no other neutral parties in the house to ask." He shrugged sheepishly; then he raked his hand through his hair in a gesture that awakened Emma's deep-seated nurturing instincts. She had wiped her brothers' bloody noses, bandaged their cuts, and mended their broken toy swords on more occasions than she could recount. It came naturally to her to boost the male ego when it flagged, even though she remained unconvinced that her siblings had learned much from their youthful misdeeds.

She, on the other hand, had gained an invaluable insight into the male psyche. It seemed a man was made of equal parts pride and vulnerability, of unspeakable crudeness and violence at his worst, of valor and self-sacrifice at his best.

She had always insisted her own brothers stand up for themselves, even if she was hiding in the wings to defend them when necessary. She had encouraged them to try to think their way out of dangerous scrapes.

Now, as unbelievable as it was, she found herself pitted against the very men she had trained to be guardians.

Adrian laughed. "It looks as if I will have to find another way of escape."

"Do you think you could climb that tree outside my window?" she asked anxiously.

"I could climb that tree in my sleep," he retorted. "However, it won't do me any good while Drake is sitting on the garden bench beneath it, smoking a cigar."

"Drake? Are you sure?"

"Not unless you have a gnome in your garden who smokes cigars."

"I don't think I've *ever* seen Drake sitting under my window before. What am I supposed to do with you now?"

He pulled on his shirt and trousers, covering his distracting nudity. "I'll sneak downstairs and if anyone catches me, I suppose I'll have to claim I had just let myself into the house."

She shook her head. "It's rude to have entered without being invited. No one will believe you."

He kissed the top of her head. "It's not as rude as what we were doing, trust me. Hand me my boots, sweetheart. Whatever happens to me was well worth it."

Blushing, she reached under the bed. A moment later she was pulled back between his legs, and they were kissing again, his tongue stroking hers as if they had all the time in the world to indulge their passion.

"I'm going now," he muttered, releasing her with reluctance. "But I'll have you know it's killing me. Expect me back after I've put everything right with your family. Oh, Emma, how I need to be with you. We need each other."

She glanced toward the window. "Perhaps Drake has left the garden. Shall I check?"

"I'll check outside your door," he said, sighing again as they disengaged.

They met back in the middle of the room fifteen seconds later.

"He's still there!" she exclaimed.

Adrian frowned. "Hamm is lying across the landing of the staircase in a rather strategical position. By the look of him he's encamped for the night."

"It's a trap." She backed up against the wall. "Adrian, we have been caught in a Boscastle trap."

He looked around appraisingly. "I don't suppose there are any secret doors or hiding-holes at my disposal?"

"Sorry," she muttered.

"Your brothers did a bit of sneaking around in their day, didn't they?"

She scowled up at him. "That regrettable truth is not in dispute."

He stared past her. "Where does this door lead?" he asked, motioning to her dressing closet.

"That is where my maid sleeps, and do not walk in there unannounced. She's forty-two years old and has never entertained a man in her room."

He knelt and peered through the brass keyhole. "Well, there are two men in there now. No sign of the maid, though."

"What?" Disbelieving, she bent her head to look for herself. "Heaven help us. It's Grayson and Weed."

He straightened with a soft laugh of resignation. "Then it is an ambush. I suppose there's nothing to do but face them together. Every possible means of escape is blocked. Devon must be at the front of the house."

Emma rose, backing away from him. "I would rather stay in my room for the rest of my life than face my brothers in a situation like this. They will make my life miserable and relish every moment."

"There will not be any blame laid at your door," he assured her. "I'm the one who's going to get thrashed. Make sure I have a proper burial, won't you?"

She blanched at the mere thought of a confrontation in her bedchamber between Adrian and her brothers. She could only pray that they would control their outrage and remember her students, whom Emma had failed. The scandal of her affair would be emblazoned across the broadsheets by morning for all of London to behold. She could just imagine Alice Clipstone cackling with vengeful glee upon learning how her rival had been caught in an affair of passion.

She smiled suddenly. Adrian was right, though. Caught or not, their stolen night together had been worth it. His love meant more to her than her reputation, which still mattered, for she did not want to taint others by association. But—bliss, passion, the love of her life.

He was worth it.

And he did need her.

He moved back toward the bedroom. She trailed after him. "You're wrong," she murmured. "It's me they'll wish to thrash. I have been anything but humble in pursuing their best interests."

"I beg your pardon?" he asked, swinging around to stare at her. "Your brothers would *hurt* you?"

She shook her head impatiently. "Not in a physical manner. But I shall be forced to listen to their mockery for the rest of our lives. The rogues would love nothing better than to catch me in a lapse after all the lectures I have delivered. Moral compass of the family, I called myself."

"It's my fault, though." He grasped her hands in his. "I led you into this, Emma. Would you have ever had a liaison with another man?"

"Of course not." She drew a breath and forced a wobbly smile. "Fine. Then we'll face it together. We shall be brave—"

Someone knocked softly on the main door of her bedchamber suite. She gasped, suddenly not feeling brave at all.

"Do you want me to answer that?" he offered.

"Hide in the closet until I tell you to come out," she whispered. "Perhaps I can convince whoever it is to go away."

He laughed ruefully. "Do you think there's a chance?"

She swallowed. "I think Napoleon has a better chance of escaping from Elba than you do of leaving this room undetected."

Adrian allowed her to take two valiant steps toward the door before deciding he would have to intervene. He strode past her, not giving her time to stop him. He'd meant what he said about being together for the rest of their lives, and he might as well prove himself a man of his word.

His gaze met Emma's. She looked so poised and self-possessed that for an instant he reconsidered. He wasn't a skilled diplomat or a master of manners. But then male pride won out.

And he opened the door.

Chapter Sixteen

❧ ❧

Heath entered the maid's antechamber that adjoined Emma's small suite. His brother Grayson was prowling restlessly in the confined space. "Anything of interest to report?"

"Yes. There is a squeaky floorboard in front of the window."

Heath chuckled quietly. "No sign of the two lovers?"

"Not a peep." Grayson stretched his arms over his head. "What about the other women?"

"As far as I can tell they are still in the drawing room gossiping away. Jane is here, by the way."

"Jane?" Grayson appeared surprised for only a moment. "I see. Ah, well. Perhaps she's hoping for some advice on her new shoes."

Heath hesitated. "Let's hope so."

"What do you mean?"

"Nothing. Just a feeling. With all those women gathered together—"

"All routes of escape are guarded, aren't they?"

Grayson smiled in satisfaction. "There is absolutely no way on earth that Adrian can leave this house without encountering at least one of us."

Adrian had prepared himself both physically and mentally to defend his position to Emma's brothers. He was more concerned, in truth, with defending her and was ready to take the entire blame for the situation. However, he did not have a clue how to react when he cracked open the door and saw two women standing in the hall.

The younger of the pair, whom he recognized as Emma's sister-in-law Jane, the Marchioness of Sedgecroft, took immediate advantage of his surprise and barreled through the narrow opening. He cringed when he realized who had accompanied her—hell's bells. Jane's companion was none other than Hermia, the large-boned Lady Dalrymple of artistic mischief.

Jane closed and bolted the door with urgency.

He stared at her. "Is Hamm still on the stairs?"

"Yes," she replied, pressing her ear to the door. "And Devon is patrolling the entry hall. The entire house is surrounded by the enemies of true love."

Emma covered her face in mortification.

"There's a perfectly good explanation for why I'm hiding here," Adrian began, only to hesitate at the direct look Jane gave him. "There is," he insisted. "Isn't there, Emma?"

Jane's dark green eyes sparkled with mirth. "Well,

I doubt it will appease four overly protective Boscastle brothers."

"How did *you* know he was here?" Emma asked quietly, lowering her hands.

"Charlotte put Harriet to the Boscastle torture," Jane replied.

Adrian opened his mouth to curse, then reconsidered. "Were you sent to take me prisoner?" he asked Jane with a frown.

"No," she said. "I've come with a plan for your escape."

"A plan?" He gave her a skeptical smile. "I don't think it is possible, but I do appreciate your efforts to intercede on my behalf."

Emma suddenly abandoned her forlorn air and stepped in front of him. "What is it, Jane? Are Julia and Charlotte in on this?"

Jane nodded. "All the female forces, including Chloe, are mobilized and ready to provide the necessary distractions."

"Then proceed," Emma said, drawing a breath. "And, Jane, I do not know how to thank you."

Jane smiled affectionately at her. "When I married into this family, it was with an understanding of how much Grayson cared for each and every one of you—as I do myself. However, my husband and I are not of one mind when it comes to the execution of his duty toward those he loves."

Adrian cleared his throat. "I beg your pardon, but—"

"Yes, do come on with it, Jane," Hermia said, unfastening her heavy gold-velvet cloak. "We don't have all night, and the darkness is our ally."

Jane's mouth firmed. "You're absolutely right. Adrian, sit down and—you will have to remove those boots."

"My boots?" he said with a blank look as he sat obediently on the chaise.

"Your wig, Hermia." Jane held out her hand.

Adrian turned white as he fully comprehended what Jane's scheme entailed. "Her wig? You cannot suggest—Now wait a minute, when I said I would do anything to—"

Hermia tugged off her lacquered gray-blond ringlets and approached the chaise with a critical frown. "Our hair was not of a dissimilar color in my youth. I do not, however, remember ever once sporting a shadow of beard upon my jaw. Nor a cleft in my chin."

"Well, we do not have time to shave him," Jane said.

Emma shook her head at him in embarrassed sympathy. "I'm so sorry, Adrian. It truly hurts me to witness your humiliation."

"Not as much as it hurts me," he muttered.

"If you do not wish to watch, Emma," Jane said, unfastening Hermia's necklace from the older woman's neck, "you'd be better served by standing in the closet and making sure Grayson does not enter."

Emma retreated a step.

"Is there no other way to sneak me out of the house?" Adrian asked as if not truly expecting an answer.

Jane frowned as she positioned the wig over his head. "Do you have a better suggestion? If so, speak up now. The Earl of Odham is waiting outside in his coach to collect Hermia. He has agreed to help you escape."

"Who the blazes is the Earl of Odham?" Adrian demanded, feeling as if he were an actor in a theatrical improvisation.

"He is an older nobleman who once courted Hermia's favor," Jane replied.

"And betrayed me," Hermia added.

Adrian frowned. "I'm sorry to hear it."

"Don't be," Hermia said with a ruthless smile. "I have been making the poor fellow pay ever since. You can trust him. He has never betrayed me again."

"Do you have another idea, Emma?" Adrian asked hopefully.

"I have my entire life," she replied with great deliberation, "attempted to represent and obey the graces as I understand them."

"It is deception or discovery," Hermia said in a straightforward voice. "Make up your mind now, Wolverton."

"Emma?" Adrian gazed up at the hovering wig as if it were guillotine.

She nodded decisively at Jane. "I think he needs a

spot of rouge if he is to resemble Hermia. And, for heaven's sake, let us at least roll up his trousers."

Adrian followed Jane down the stairs, past Hamm's dutiful scrutiny. Apparently the footman harbored a fond regard for the robust Lady Dalrymple, for although he lurched to his feet and bowed deeply to Jane, his gaze lingered on what he presumably took to be Hermia's stalwart figure. "May I escort your ladyship to the carriage?"

"No, you may not, Hamm," Jane said firmly. "Lady Dalrymple is feeling a bit under the weather and does not wish to be fussed."

Hamm appeared stricken. "I am sorry to hear this. I trust it is nothing serious."

"It is—" Jane hesitated, "a hoarse throat, I believe. She must go home without delay and rest her voice."

"She certainly must," Hamm said in concern. "Shall I bring a coal brazier to the carriage so she may warm her feet?"

Adrian swore to himself and resisted the urge to push Hamm down the stairs. It was humiliating enough that he was practically leaning on Jane in order to keep his balance. He could barely walk in Hermia's black buckled pumps, whose seams she had unstitched to squeeze onto his big feet.

"Her ladyship does not need to be cosseted," Jane said with a tight smile. "If you are distressed for her welfare, you may open the door so that the earl can take her home."

Adrian nodded vigorously.

"Yes, of course," Hamm said, hastening to obey. "And if there is anything else—"

"Is that you, Hermia? And Jane?" Lord Devon Boscastle, Emma's younger brother, strolled into sight, halting at the bottom of the stairs. "Are you going home?"

Adrian scowled in the shadows of the hood drawn around his face. He debated whether he should make a quick escape through the hall or run back upstairs like a coward. He vowed that if Jane got him out of this coil without causing Emma further embarrassment, he would name his firstborn after her and employ every shoemaker in Europe to keep her delicate feet in fashion.

"Hermia does not feel well, Devon." Jane grasped Adrian's hand and dragged him down the remaining stairs. "It is a throat ailment and she must not breathe the damp evening air. Would you be a darling and fetch my gloves from the drawing room?"

Devon straightened, his face pensive. "Well, actually, I'm supposed to stay in—"

"Devon!" His sister Chloe came flying through the hall and launched herself at him. "You wicked boy! I haven't seen you in an eternity. I was telling Dominic how much I've missed you."

He gazed over her shoulder at Adrian and Jane,

resisting as Chloe tried to pull him the other way. "Didn't we just have dinner three days ago?"

"This," Adrian muttered to Jane, pulling Hermia's cloak around his shoulders, "is an indignity from which I shall not recover."

Jane strode forward, her voice low and steady. "Kindly walk, Hermia, and do not strain your voice in iddle prattle. Ah, there's your faithful Odham now."

Adrian caught his buckled shoe on the pavement and would have pitched into the street had Jane not quick-wittedly lent him the weight of her shoulder. The earl, a spry white-haired man in his sixties who had been in love with Lady Dalrymple for years, dashed across the street from his carriage.

"Does Odham know why this masquerade has been enacted?" Adrian asked through his teeth.

Jane shrugged. "Julia was supposed to tell him, but I'm not sure whether she made it past Heath's guard."

He frowned at her. "Isn't Odham in love with Hermia? How am I supposed to explain—"

"Into your carriage, my little flower of mischief," Odham said, slipping his arm conspiratorially into Adrian's. "Wonderful performance, Wolverton. It does remind me of my rakehell days. A little disguise only enhances desire, eh?"

Adrian suddenly found himself spirited across the street and into the earl's waiting carriage. He barely managed to wrench off his pumps before Odham pushed him onto the seat, rapped his knuckles against the roof, and the driver urged his two grays into a smart trot.

Odham stamped his foot in glee. "We've done it! This is the most fun I've had in decades. Hermia has always been known for her daring. Heaven help me, Wolverton, the woman drives me mad, I tell you. And now I've tipped the scales in my favor."

Adrian pulled the cloaked hood from his head, his expression morose. "I don't wish to appear rude. Obviously I am indebted to you for life. However, I must ask—have we ever met before?"

The earl's dark brown eyes lit up. "Speaking as one scoundrel to another—does it really matter?"

Adrian grunted and glanced out the carriage window. Jane stood on the sidewalk, a satisfied smile on her face. A tall man emerged from the house. He could not tell which of the Boscastle brothers it was. But one thing was certain, the devious Jane would undoubtedly keep him at bay.

And tomorrow there would be the devil to pay.

Heath stood behind his sister-in-law Jane, both of them watching the carriage bowl away into the night. A horrible suspicion entered his mind. What had he just witnessed? An escape? It wasn't possible. At length, Jane turned to him, sighing deeply. "It's late, isn't it? I should be putting my son to bed. Is Grayson with Drake?"

Heath stared at the receding carriage. A reluctant smile flitted across his face. "As far as I know he is still upstairs."

Jane glanced up at him, a remarkably convincing actress. "Upstairs? Doing what? I thought you held your male cabals in your study."

An amused female voice called out behind them. "What have I missed that you two are whispering together?"

Heath pivoted. His heart never failed to lift at his wife's presence. Even if, as he was beginning to suspect, Julia and the other ladies of the family had outfoxed him.

He shook his head. No. It couldn't be, but— "Where is Aunt Hermia?"

Julia came down the steps and laid her head on his shoulder. "She's still upstairs with Emma, I think."

"But Devon said—who just left in Odham's coach?"

Jane sailed past him back to the house. "Odham, of course. I shouldn't think you would need to ask."

Heath's mouth tightened. "But I thought that Hermia—"

Julia drew away from him with a frown. "Hermia is with Emma, Heath. If you are worried about her, I'm sure she would not mind reassuring you that she is in good health, although I understand that her throat hurt earlier in the evening."

"I see," Heath murmured.

He walked slowly back into his house, then up the stairs to the hall to come to stand at the closed door of Emma's suite. It was there, a minute or so later, that his brother Grayson found him.

"I say we storm her room," Grayson said, his fist raised to the door. "This has gone on long enough. Wolverton cannot hide in there forever."

Heath shook his head. A wise man knew when to lay down his hand. "Be my guest, Grayson. I would prefer, however, that you not break the door."

Grayson pounded on the door.

It was Emma who answered, her brow furrowed in agitation. "Grayson," she said in annoyance, "whatever is the matter that you are making such an ungodly noise? Is someone ill?"

He pushed around her into the room. "Why doesn't Adrian come out of hiding and answer that question himself? Is he in your closet?"

She looked affronted. "Grayson Boscastle. I absolutely *forbid* you to take another step."

He froze, such was the power of her command. "I do not blame you, Emma," he said after a moment. "Wolverton is an alluring man. Duke's heir or not, however, he will be made to—"

He paused, took a breath, and opened the closet door only to rear back in alarm at the indignant shriek that met his assault.

"Oh, my heavens. Oh, God almighty, Hermia—I had no idea. I had no—"

Lady Dalrymple stood before him, unwigged, her hands on her hips, her ample bosom quivering in its multitude of wrinkles. "I do hope you have an explanation for this violation, Sedgecroft."

Grayson stood in stone-faced shock, unable to utter a word in his own defense, until Heath, laughing, pulled him aside. "It's over."

"What the devil do you mean?" Grayson demanded, stumbling back out into the hall.

"We have been trounced," Heath said with a rueful grin. "It is time to beat a retreat."

"Did you find him?" Devon called up from the entrance hall below.

Hamm's gravelly voice resounded behind him. "Lord Wolverton has not passed through the front doors, my lords. I have stayed at my post as you requested. There is no possible way that he has escaped our guard."

Grayson turned to Heath with an irate expression. "Are you absolutely certain that Wolf was here in the first place?"

Heath shook his head. "I should have known," he muttered in admiration. "I *did* know."

Grayson looked at him in disgust. "Then why didn't you take appropriate action?"

Heath smiled.

Emma had stayed awake all night, or what remained of it, whispering about her secret engagement to Adrian with her conspirators Chloe, Julia, Charlotte, and Aunt Hermia. Now that she had accepted Adrian's proposal, and had admitted to herself what was in her heart, she saw no reason not to share her delight.

In a decorous manner befitting a future duchess, it was to be hoped, and if her dignity had slipped—then so be it. She and Adrian had a life ahead of them during which to make amends.

"The girls will have to learn to address you as 'your grace,'" Charlotte said, stretched across Emma's bed with a dreamy expression and a glass of champagne in her hand.

Jane's footman, Weed, had delivered four bottles of Grayson's prized Dom Pérignon less than an hour after the marchioness returned home from her successful escapade in the name of amour. Chloe had expertly unpopped the cork barks to toast her older sister with the sparkling wine made famous by a humble Benedictine monk, whose profits he donated to the poor.

"It gives being in one's cups a charitable aspect," Chloe announced with glee.

Emma's eyes brightened. "Then drink up, all!"

"To the Boscastles and their friends!" Hermia said stoutly.

"How do we tell the girls about your engagement, Emma?" Charlotte asked softly.

Emma stared down into her glass. "I'm not quite

sure. I do know that I cannot simply abandon the academy without a backward glance."

"Why the devil not?" Hermia wondered aloud, her voice faintly slurred. "I never knew as much contentment in my life as when I gave in to impulse. There. I have said it. My secret is revealed. The world beware. I am a dangerous woman."

"Only to handsome young men who resemble Greek gods," Charlotte said unthinkingly.

Her niece Julia burst into laughter, and it was not long before the other ladies followed suit. Emma slid off the chaise in alarm. "Ladies, please. We must—we must—"

"—drink more champagne," said Chloe, lifting the bulbous-necked bottle into the air. "Oh, Emma, Emma, who would have guessed you were capable of honoring our ancestry? I swear I shall go to my grave with a smile on my face. Adrian is the most adorable rogue, and now he shall be my brother-in-law. Our family infamy lives on, and I am not at all ashamed."

Soon they subsided into weary silence. Charlotte picked up her shoes, kissed Emma, and left to check on the other girls and seek her bed. Hermia fell asleep on the chaise. Julia covered her with a warm counterpane and tiptoed through the house to join her husband for what remained of the night. Emma and her little sister Chloe snuggled in bed together as they had often done in childhood. In joyful times, and in sad, Emma had gladly mothered her wild siblings. And now they would have to manage without her. But could she let go of them?

Chloe rested her head on Emma's shoulder. "If *I* gave in to my wicked impulses, I would cast up all those occasions during which you lectured us on—"

"Do not turn wicked," Emma said sternly, then softened the effect of this admonishment with a sigh. "Not when I am so thoroughly chastising myself and—bubbling over with happiness."

"Then nothing shall spoil it," Chloe whispered. "Live, Emma, enjoy life."

Emma sighed again, smiling at the memory of Adrian escaping her room in Hermia's wig and cloak. What if her brothers had caught him? What if one of her students had awakened in the midst of his gamble? It was sobering enough to consider what would become of the academy once her betrothal was announced.

But if Emma understood the hypocrisy of the Polite World, the scandal of her secret affair would fade away in forgotten notoriety once it was realized that she would one day become a duchess. And be with the man she loved into the bargain.

Chapter Seventeen

❧ ❧

Adrian arrived at Grayson Boscastle's Park Lane mansion at nine o'clock the following morning and formally asked for Emma's hand in marriage.

Grayson graciously accepted the offer with an appropriate display of surprise and pleasure, as did his wife Jane. In truth, Jane's astonished exclamations of delight almost convinced Adrian that he had dreamed the events of the previous evening. All was well that ended in holy wedlock, apparently.

"I say this calls for a celebration supper," Grayson announced, rubbing his hands together with a self-satisfaction that hinted he might have plotted this romance himself. "Could we manage it, Jane?"

She smiled at him. "It should pose no inconvenience at all, dear husband. The staff is now accustomed to throwing lavish affairs at the last moment."

"Nothing lavish," Adrian said quickly, thinking of Emma's preference for the subtle. "I do believe that for all concerned we should marry as quietly as possible."

And so it was that Jane excused herself to leave the two men to discuss widow's settlements and jointures while she hastened about the happy duty of planning a family wedding. Which meant, of course, that she and the bride would require a new wardrobe and footwear to match and that the Italian shoemaker would need an army of elves to assist him. Jane decided that she would simply have to treat herself to a dozen new shoes to celebrate her sister-in-law's engagement.

Another Boscastle fallen victim to the family heritage of passion. It was Jane's role, as she perceived it, to ensure that the path of matrimony followed as smooth a course as possible. One conveniently forgot whatever mischief preceded the wedding march.

As the daughter of an earl, as well as wife to a marquess, she understood intuitively that the addition of a duke and duchess to the family line was a connection to be ardently embraced, if not exploited.

Jane's son Rowan, her husband's heir, would grow up with a duke's son as his cousin and playmate. It was the proper order of life in the English aristocracy. In another decade, indeed within a year, few in the haut ton would remark upon or even remember that any impropriety had preceded the union of Emma and Adrian. No one outside the family dared to mention the scandal of Jane's own marriage.

For the time being at least, all was well in the world of the Boscastles.

That same evening the Marquess of Sedgecroft hosted a supper party to announce the engagement of his sister, the Viscountess Lyons, to Adrian Ruxley, Viscount Wolverton, heir to the Duke of Scarfield.

Only a few select members of Society, outside the Boscastle family, received an invitation to this affair. The Earl of Odham brought his beloved Hermia, both of them expressing disbelief at the announcement. Two members of Parliament and their wives attended. Still, all in all, it was a private affair.

The wedding two days later, in the private chapel of Grayson's Park Lane home, proved to be another exclusive event. Emma felt so calm before the ceremony that Julia asked her in private whether she required a vinaigrette to prevent a faint.

"If I lived my entire life in this family without fainting," Emma replied, "I doubt I shall do so today."

Yet when she saw Adrian in the chapel, she came as close to a swoon as she imagined possible. He was dressed in a formal deep-blue frock coat and black broadcloth pantaloons. At his side hung a ceremonial sword which she prayed to all the saints in heaven, he would not be tempted to use until after they had exchanged vows. Indeed, he looked so grand that Emma, in an unadorned dress of silver tissue, felt herself pale in comparison.

It was her second marriage, however. She could

not in good conscience wear virginal orange blossoms in her wreath. A semi-veil would suffice to hide her blissful smile from the small assembly of guests. This wolf was hers to tame.

Grayson gave her away, and afterward the wedding party enjoyed a breakfast of coddled eggs, prawns, and lamb cutlets followed by apple pudding, raspberry jelly, and lemon cream. As expected, there was a three-tiered wedding cake with heavy white icing.

Adrian toasted his bride with a glass of champagne and the three comfits he had stolen off their cake. "I'm sorry." He squeezed her hand in his. "But it appears I shall never change."

She smiled up at him, her heart in her eyes. "I should never forgive myself if you did."

It rained on their short drive to the London hotel where Adrian had resided off and on for the last year. His choice of impersonal lodgings had stemmed less from convenience than his reluctance to put down roots again in England. Belatedly he wished he had a proper home in which to be alone with his bride.

It was his wedding night.

He tried not to think of Emma's late husband. It seemed so petty and unfair to confess jealousy of a man who in death could not defend himself. But Adrian was a practical man, one who had learned to survive.

And he required Emma to survive. If that was a

weakness, he did not deny it. She was the warmth of a candle in winter darkness. He did not need anyone, or anything else, but her.

He shrugged out of his jacket while she went behind the screen to wash. He then opened the wardrobe door and peered inside. He went to the window to check the street below for carriages.

Emma stuck her head around the screen, her face amused. "If you are going to confess on our wedding night that you are a spy—"

"I'm looking for your brothers."

"They aren't there, are they?" she asked in horror. He laughed. "No."

"Thank heavens. Do you mind helping me with this last hook?" She emerged from the screen, her sun gold hair unbound, one hand at her back.

"Please," he said. "Let me help." His heart beat fiercely as they met in the center of the room. Then he pretended to struggle with the hook when his every impulse told him to tear the damn thing from its flimsy mooring.

"Be careful." She angled her head to smile up at him. "The dress is delicate and—"

He placed both hands on her shoulders and ripped the silver tissue gown from her with a decisive tug. Her underapparel followed, the sound of rending silk punctuated by her indignant protests.

"That was my wedding gown, Adrian!"

"It's not as if you're going to wear it again," he murmured, the excuse weak even to his own ears.

"What about our children?" she protested. "What if I had wished to pass that dress down to our future generations? Did you ever think that we might have a daughter one day?"

He smoothed his hands over her bare shoulders. "I have thought of nothing else." He bent his head to hers. "And if we have a daughter, I hope she will be everything like you."

"Adrian," she whispered, bowing her head as his hands drifted down her sides to stroke her back. "I have always wanted children."

He gave her a smile of understanding—far more understanding than she had anticipated. For before she realized what he was about, he'd lifted her into his arms and carried her to their bed.

"Give me dainty daughters who look just like their mother," he said. "Give me sons. Give me you, Emma."

She watched him strip off his clothing, unable to control the moisture seeping from her sex. When at last he leaned over her, she did not attempt to hide her approval of his nudity.

Disconcerted, she realized that not only was she staring at his impressive appendage, but that he understood exactly what had captured her interest. If her late husband had caught her peeping at his privates, he would have pulled off his neckcloth and promptly shielded his manly mysteries.

But Adrian, shameless adventurer and uninhibited devil that he was, merely stretched his muscular arms in languid satisfaction and arched his back, thereby thrusting himself out another few inches for her approval.

"My God, but those trousers were tight," he murmured, one half-closed eye affixed on her face.

She moistened the corners of her mouth with her tongue. "I can understand why.

"Would you—" Her belly fluttered in pleasant confusion. "Would you like a neckcloth?" she asked innocently.

With a deep rumble of laughter, he pulled her against his hard, warm body. "To tie around my tadge?" he teased, leaning in for a slow, promising kiss. "Is there a protocol for such a thing?"

Her heart missed a beat. "I do not believe so."

"That is a relief because"—he rubbed his turgid penis across her belly—"when it comes to certain issues of impoliteness—"

She turned her face into the pillow to smother a whimper, but any attempt to hide her rising excitement from her husband was futile. Her womb tightened in pleasure as he scattered kisses across her breasts. Heaven forgive her, but she was possessed to behave like a voluptuary of Venus. "If I am to tutor you in the ways of a gentleman," she said with a heartfelt sigh, "then we shall have to start with an observation of your worst conduct."

He grinned at the challenge. "Which, in my humble opinion, is when I am at my best."

She struggled up onto one elbow, her breasts

swollen from his ardent kisses. "Show me, so that we may begin to instruct you."

He lifted his head to kiss her, swirling his tongue against hers. He ate delicately at her mouth until she was raking her fingers down the ridges of his back to his lean buttocks. "Your touch inflames me, Emma."

"Then may I please—"

She did not finish, but it was evident he more than understood. His face darkened; he reared back to fulfill her need, his huge organ overflowing her small hand. A drop of pearlescent fluid bedewed her fingertips. An instinct she could not resist bade her to caress the thick head of his shaft.

He threw back his shoulders as if her delicate exploration had caused him pain, then demonstrated openly how he welcomed her touch by thrusting against her hand. Magnificent in his arousal, he arched his spine; in response she rose onto her knees to lay her face against his chest. "I have never craved a woman's touch as I do yours, wife," he said in a raw voice.

"Nor have I ever wished to touch a man in this way," she whispered back. "But I tell you truly, if you do not proceed to make love to me this very moment, I—"

He gently grasped the soft hills of her bottom and contrived to force her back down beneath him, a position she eagerly assumed. Her sex throbbed unbearably. Her thighs opened in invitation to draw him inside her.

His hooded gaze traveled over her with a burning pleasure that acknowledged her offering. His muscular body hardened, hovering above hers. The sweet mystery of all that was male. Pure sexual power. Yet in submission she recognized strength.

And when at last she felt his rod nudge at the petals of her woman's place, when he thrust upward to penetrate her, she thought how very wonderful it was to be a wife and lady of some experience who knew that even decorum had a proper time and place.

As did desire.

The newlyweds would have slept the entire morning had Adrian's valet, Bones, not brought a hearty breakfast to their door, along with an array of gifts and cards from those in the bon ton who wished to congratulate them on their marriage and be recognized in return.

Adrian answered the door, grumbling at the intrusion until Emma gently chided him for his show of ingratitude.

She had taken breakfast in bed only three times previously that she could recall. Most certainly she was not, as her great wolf of a husband, so disengaged from all propriety that she wished this forbidden activity to become a habit.

"I cannot say I feel completely comfortable breakfasting in bed without clothing," she admitted at his pleased grin.

He fed her a slice of imported Spanish orange

from the tray on the bedside table. "You're a shocking young lady. That must be why I fell in love with you."

"Well, do not admit that to your father when you introduce me," she said, her blue eyes dancing.

"I do *not* look forward to that reunion."

"So I have gathered," she said lightly. "But it is inevitable and your mind will know no rest until you have done with it."

His gaze wandered over her in a heated promise. "The only thing inevitable"—he slid his arms around her bare hips and drew her beneath him onto the tangle of bedclothes—"is—"

Another knock came at the door, Bones once again, but this time speaking in such an urgent voice that even Adrian did not hesitate to heed. "It is your brother, my lord. I took the liberty of admitting him to the anteroom. He assures me that he will not leave until you have met with him."

"My brother?" Adrian asked in disbelief. "Are you quite certain of this, Bones?"

Emma sat up indignantly. "He must be mistaken. Only *my* brothers would have the effrontery to interrupt our honeymoon breakfast. Which of the rogues is it, and what is his excuse this time?"

Bones cleared his throat. "It is Lord Cedric, madam. His lordship's brother."

Adrian looked up at the door, smiling incredulously. "Cedric is here?"

"Yes, my lord," Bones answered, "and he is quite adamant about seeing you."

Emma dressed with care and drank two cups of unsweetened tea. She was determined to give Adrian and his younger brother the privacy of a reunion. She had to agree that Cedric's timing was rather off, but then again there may have been some emergency at Scarfield to prompt his inopportune visit. Although Adrian asserted that his father's illness was a ploy, perhaps there had been more truth to it than he allowed. It seemed unlikely that Lord Cedric had interrupted his brother's honeymoon morning out of malice. Indeed, as Adrian had not been in communication with the duke, one could only attribute Cedric's appearance to coincidence. Emma had certainly not dared to insist he invite his father to their wedding, considering the ill feelings Adrian bore him.

Only twenty minutes later she was summoned by her husband to the anteroom to be introduced to his brother. Lord Cedric was a well-built man of average height, who seemed understandably embarrassed at having come at such an awkward time. In fact, he gave Emma the distinct impression how relieved he was that his older brother had married a lady of quality. She dared not speculate on the sort of bride he had expected.

As the sister of the most notorious aristocratic family in London, she appreciated his relief. Indeed, their meeting went pleasantly enough. Lord Cedric stressed the importance of Adrian's return to Scarfield. On this point Emma could not disagree, even if she was content to leave the decision on when this would take place to Adrian himself.

All in all, her first introduction to his family went well. It was only as Cedric was making his leave, congratulating husband and wife once again on their marriage, that his parting comment to his brother hit an unpleasant note.

"Serena will be surprised to learn of your marriage, Adrian. She asks about you often."

Even then Emma might have merely taken note of the female name for future use. Its owner could have been an old family housekeeper, a local spinster, or even Adrian's aunt.

But then Adrian asked, "Serena? Is she still there? She has not married?"

His inflection caught her ear, a combination of fondness, curiosity, and family history.

"No," Cedric said, his gloves in hand. "She isn't married yet. By the way, be careful when you travel home. The roads that surround the village have been haunted by robbers in recent years."

"At Scarfield?" Adrian asked. "I don't remember a single crime in the past."

Cedric grasped his hand. "Times have changed. Perhaps your return will help, Adrian. I do believe we need a man of your experience."

Chapter Eighteen

Emma dreaded bidding her academy adieu and had anticipated tears of regret as that moment arrived. Adrian promised her repeatedly that they would either return to London or would remove her school to a Berkshire location before spring ended. In the meantime, Charlotte, Miss Peppertree, and her sister-in-law Eloise had taken command. She reassured herself that she had left her girls in capable hands.

What she had not foreseen was the impact her whirlwind romance would have upon the academy's reputation. She had forgotten the basic motivation of the parents who sent their daughters to her in the first place—a marriage of merit.

She descended from her husband's carriage the day after her wedding to discover the street entirely clogged with unfamiliar vehicles, a congestion that one would typically expect at one of her brother Grayson's elaborate soirées. "Something must be wrong," she called back to Adrian, who stood looking up and down the street in confusion.

"I hope no one's died during the night," he said unhelpfully.

The possibility sent her flying up the steps of Heath's town house and straight into the arms of her brother himself. "What has happened?" she said in alarm.

He shook his head. Voices drifted from the drawing room; servants marched back and forth with silver trays of tea and fresh muffins. To her great relief she could not see anyone, Heath included, wearing a black armband, nor were there any ominous hangings from the windows to indicate a relative had passed away.

Indeed, there seemed to be some inexplicable excitement in the air—an excitement that apparently prompted her brother to make an escape. Heath kissed her on the cheek, then said, "Congratulations, Duchess. See that they're all gone when I come back. I'll be at the club if Adrian wishes to see me."

Emma stared after him in perplexity. "I'm not a duchess yet. I'm—"

"Oh, Emma, thank goodness you have come. I cannot endure this for another minute. My nerves are frayed. This is fun, but so unnerving."

She turned to behold her bedraggled cousin Charlotte leaning against one of the hallway columns. Or was she hiding behind it?

She peeled off her gloves. "What on earth is going on?"

"I've been fending them off since seven o'clock this morning," Charlotte said in an exhausted voice. "How was your wedding night, by the way?"

"None of your affair, my dear, but thank you for asking. Who have you been fending off?"

Charlotte gave her a dazed look. "All I know is that since your wedding, every debutante's mother and father appears to be consumed with the hope of marrying off their daughter to a duke. It seems you have set a standard, Emma. The haut ton is determined to learn your secrets."

Her secrets.

She stared back through the hall, laughter bubbling inside her. There he stood, her duke's son, her husband, if you please, looking handsomely perplexed at being separated from her. Bless the man. He truly possessed no sense of his own importance, and even if he had, Emma suspected he would neither care nor use it to advantage.

Mine, she thought.

He's mine.

"Oh, Emma, thank heavens," Eloise exclaimed behind her. "Close the door, would you? The girls have not been able to absorb one passage of Italian poetry what with the knocker tatting at every second. Did you have a nice . . . er, evening?"

Emma smiled at her sensible sister-in-law. "Very

nice, thank you. Have you managed to introduce Dante?"

"Barely," Eloise replied. "I do wish you'd warned me that your marriage would cause such a stir. I'd have spirited the girls off to the country for a day. All this excitement does rattle the nerves."

Emma stumbled over a hillock of boxes and traveling trunks that had not been in the hall a few minutes ago. "To whom does this excessive amount of luggage belong?" she asked in consternation.

The deadly quiet that met this question gripped her heart with dread. She peered down for a closer look at the gilt monogram embossed upon one worn leather trunk, whispering "Oh, no—"

The owner herself descended the stairs just as Emma straightened. "I'm ready, darlings. Hasn't Odham got my luggage loaded yet?"

Emma and Adrian shared a look of horrified amusement. "Are you going on a journey, Lady Dalrymple?" he inquired politely. "If so, I shall be happy to have my footmen—"

"—load my baggage onto your carriage?" Hermia breezed past him, blowing him a distracted kiss. "You are such a sweet young man. Odham and I shall settle ourselves in while you and Emma make your farewells. You do not mind if I claim one of the windows for myself? Traveling over country roads does give these ancient bones a shock."

She glided toward the door on a carpet of oblivion, pausing to send a distracted wave in the direction of her niece, Julia, who had ventured forth from the drawing room to investigate the commotion.

Emma turned to Julia. "Is Hermia returning to her country estate?" she asked hopefully.

Julia hesitated. "Didn't she tell you? She's decided that she and Odham should accompany you to the duke's estate."

"Why?" Adrian asked.

Julia exhaled quietly. "It appears that she feels a certain responsibility toward you and Emma, Adrian. Because she . . . brought you together, one might say."

"She won't keep us together by accompanying us on our honeymoon," he said bluntly.

Emma shook her head. "She isn't coming with us?"

"I'm afraid so," Julia replied. "At least she'll have Odham to keep her company."

"Odham?" Adrian said, almost dropping his black silk hat. "Anyone else?"

Julia shook her head in sympathy. "Hamm offered to go, but it was decided he wouldn't fit in the carriage."

"But we're married," Adrian said with a forced smile. "We don't need a chaperone." He looked at Emma. "Do we?"

"We do owe her an enormous debt," she whispered in resignation.

"I realize that," he said, "but couldn't our repayment have waited until a later time?"

Julia lowered her gaze. "It seems she is doing this as a favor to *you*, Adrian. She believes she can act as a peacemaker between you and your father. They were friends once."

"What a kindly thought," Emma murmured as Adrian took her arm and guided her to the door. "How generous of her."

A crowd of spectators had collected on the pavement to witness the duke's heir bear his Boscastle bride off to the countryside. One herring-vendor remarked that their leave-taking reminded her of the legend of Pluto bearing Proserpina to his internal realm. A young male sprat-seller retorted that she was old enough to remember Roman times.

Harriet ran out of the house and tossed a beribboned laurel wreath at the carriage. Hamm the footman shouted a warning to the coachman to beware of highwaymen on country roads. The coachman tipped his low-crowned hat to the crowd and cracked his whip at the six muscular horses straining in their polished harnesses.

The horses charged forward with Hermia waving from her window to the throng in the street. Emma's gaze was drawn to a cloaked woman who stood alone on the corner.

Lady Clipstone. She sniffed, pretending not to notice. It would be spiteful and quite beneath her station to acknowledge her rival's interest. But then Hermia poked her head out the window and chortled:

"Do move out of the way, Alice, dear. The duchess is coming through!"

Emma pulled down the curtains with a gasp of embarrassment. "That's entirely vulgar of you." She settled back in her seat. Soon the peeling of church bells and the rumble of city traffic fell away. "Even if she did deserve it."

On the second day of their journey, they took the Windsor Road for another five miles past Camberly, then veered toward a windswept downs. Soon afterward a subtle fog enveloped them. By late afternoon, the coachman had slowed their progress to a crawl, and he could be heard muttering dire warnings through his heavy wool muffler about the dangers of traveling in the mist.

Adrian had felt his mood darken with every mile they ventured closer to Scarfield. He thought he had forgotten all the old insults. He'd tried to forget.

But the familiar landmarks stood in the fog like old ghosts waiting to greet him.

They had mocked him when he had left. They would probably still be standing when he died and turned to dust.

An abandoned abbey.

The ancient beechwoods where he used to hide for days at a time until his father's estate manager would find him.

The mysterious burial mounds of his prehistoric ancestors.

He sat forward without warning and thumped his fist on the roof. "Make a detour at the next bridge," he instructed the coachman. "Go left around the oak grove, or we shall be wandering in the mist forever."

Emma slept through his decision as did Odham. Only Hermia roused to question his judgment, drawing her cloak around her sturdy shoulders. "A detour, Adrian?" she asked with a frown. "In this fog? I hope you don't lead us into a lake."

He sank back against the seat, thinking of Scarfield and all it represented. His fond gaze slid to his sleeping wife. "I hope I don't lead us into something worse."

Adrian's voice awakened Emma from an enjoyable dream. "We've a choice of continuing and arriving before nightfall, or going back to Ye Olde Bed of Fleas until your English weather improves."

She glanced up, lost in the wicked warmth of his eyes. "You're as born to the clime as I am. Why does it have to be *my* weather?"

"I don't know. Perhaps it's because you're a woman and subject to the same unpredictable moods as the weather."

She gathered her blanket around her shoulders. "Perhaps *you* might have predicted a more direct route. Perhaps you might even have consulted a map."

"We aren't lost," he said with a dour smile.

She gazed past him to what little she could see through the window. Twisted trees wrapped in mist. Gray drifts of shadows like a congregation of spirits.

"We're approaching Buxton Bridge as we speak," he said, taking her hand. "It has five stone arches, and every spring, a village maiden is chosen—"

The carriage ground to a sudden halt. Emma looked up, feeling Adrian's hand tighten over hers. It was deadly quiet outside except for the whickering of the six horses and the rhythmic flow of the river through the stony bed below. The coach's undersprings creaked as the men on the box jumped to the roadside.

"We've stopped," she said, sitting up.

The Earl of Odham opened his eyes. "What's wrong?"

"Queer place to take a rest," Hermia said quietly. "One always remembers the myths about monsters who reside under these old bridges."

Adrian looked up slowly. He frowned at Odham. "Keep them inside."

Emma met Adrian's gaze. She had seen him slide his hand inside his coat. "Do be careful," she said in an anxious voice. "Not all monsters are myths."

He smiled, then turned to the door. Emma gave a start as it opened unexpectedly. Bones, Adrian's valet, stood against the fog. He was unsuccessfully trying to hide his master's sword behind his back. Emma understood the message behind her husband's faint nod of acknowledgment. He meant to confront whoever had stopped the coach in this isolated place should he need to.

"They've taken the coachman and footman onto the bridge, my lord," Bones whispered hastily. "They did not notice me on the back. They were waiting at the other side."

"How many?" Adrian asked, stepping down onto the road.

"Three, I saw."

"Then they are outnumbered." His calm voice seemed unnatural to Emma. Did the man not understand the danger? Oh, fool she was. Of course he understood, and he almost looked as if he relished what would come.

"Stay behind the carriage, Bones, unless I call you. By no means leave my wife unprotected."

"Yes, my lord." In the blink of an eye Bones looked less a London valet than a soldier who had witnessed the brutalities of life. "The coachman and his man were disarmed before they could cry for help," he added in an undertone.

Adrian walked several paces from the carriage, pausing to take his bearings. He knew this place, this bridge. Even in a thick fog he remembered the bridle path that cut through the trees, the myriad places a person could hide.

As far as he could tell, there were only two mounted men on the bridge. Which meant the third whom Bones had mentioned was—his blood boiled over. Where was the bastard hiding?

He swiveled around and stared at the coach. It sat like a tempting jewel on the secluded track. Damn his impatience. Damn his insistence on a detour. Damn him for not taking Cedric's warning about the perils of Scarfield's roads to heart.

If anyone so much as approached Emma and her companions, he would not live to see the following day. And his dainty-mannered wife would know without a doubt that her efforts to civilize Adrian had been in vain.

So be it.

England was no more civilized than the most heathen land he had defended. Men were men, subject to the same temptations and greed the world over no matter how one disguised it.

In the damp haze, he unharnessed one of the coach's six horses and vaulted onto her back. The mare sensed his urgency, pricked her ears, and quickened her pace. He raised his sword, the artfully crafted Persian scimitar that he had been given for protecting a harem. A wolf's head had been engraved upon the enameled silver hilt. He had accepted the gift, thinking he would never use it in England. Or anywhere for that matter.

The report of a pistol echoed through the mist from the direction of the bridge. He thought he heard someone—something—fall into the water below. He resisted the urge to turn around. Instead, he charged full-tilt at the masked horseman who had just emerged from the trees.

It felt odd and yet he recognized what it was, death in the air, the pulsing of blood through his veins. The fog might have been a sandstorm. The masked assailant could have been one of his faceless enemies. Suddenly the weight of the scimitar felt reassuring in his hand instead of unfamiliar. He grasped the pistol in the other and charged.

The rider who approached the carriage looked startled by his appearance. Adrian felt a grim moment of humor. Obviously the normal highwayman did not expect to encounter a victim wielding a deadly scimitar in defense of a ducal carriage.

It was the hardest thing in the world to sit by helplessly while one's husband confronted a band of brigands. Emma scooted across the seat to the window, her reticule beneath her traveling cloak. Whom exactly *was* Adrian confronting? Her throat tightened. She had lost sight of his powerful frame in the fog. The muffled echo of hoofbeats pounding in the mist usettled her.

Odham laid a comforting hand on her shoulder. "Best not to look, my dear."

"Of course she has to look," Hermia said, squeezing in front of him. "How do we know what we are up against if we sit here shivering like spinsters?"

He sat back, busying himself with the leather case he had pulled upon his lap. "Never fear, my dear. I shall put my life on the line to protect you, both of you, and consider it an honor."

Hermia slowly turned her head to regard him. "If anyone thinks that I shall sit by idly while *you* are assaulted—"

He looked up, his eyes bright with emotion. "You are a stouthearted lady, Hermia. I am honored to have known you."

"We're not dead yet, Odham, for heaven's sake. Do you need a phial of vinegar to restore you, Emma?" she asked in concern.

Emma reached into her reticule, her voice even. "Ask me when this is over and I shall surely say yes."

Adrian took advantage of his adversary's surprise and kicked his sturdy mount into a cavalry charge. The horse responded with a hesitant but satisfying burst of speed. The highwayman glanced around in obvious disconcertment, then raised his flintlock to fire.

Adrian swiveled at the waist, his reflexes guiding his horse in a zigzag course toward the other rider. A pistol ball soared over his head. With unnerving focus he watched the other man draw short to reload. "Now," he said softly to the animal beneath him. "Do not be afraid. Keep going. You will be fine."

He dug in his heels, his sword arm tensed in anticipation, and cantered in a semicircle. The highwayman glanced up with a cry of panic. His gaze seemed transfixed by the scimitar that flashed like quicksilver in the twilight mist. Perhaps he thought it an illusion.

The curved blade sang in the air. It had taken many a life and had never failed to protect its owner, or so Adrian had been told. He lowered his arm and watched the man sway on his saddle before pitching backward. His bloodied chest glowed a bright splotch of red in the gray shadows.

With another glance over his shoulder at the coach, he wheeled the horse around and set a steady canter toward the bridge. He could just make out the gaunt outline of Bones sitting sentinel on the box where he had left him. As Adrian could barely see through the smoky mist, he preferred to believe that Emma had not borne witness to what her husband had just done. It seemed too much to hope, however, that she and Hermia had not been tempted to watch through the window, despite his request otherwise.

He dismounted at the bridge and saw two riderless horses tethered to the lower branches of a tree. The criminals to whom the animals belonged had vanished. He tightened his grip on his pistol and detected a weak if angry groan from beneath the bridge. The coachman lay on his side on the riverbank, half-hidden behind a screen of reeds.

"They've gone to the carriage, my lord," he called in a disgruntled voice. "The footman's tied up to a tree, but he's alive. They said they'd gone to look for you."

For him?

He ran past the horse. Another shot echoed in the mist. He kicked a fallen branch from his path and cursed. His heart pounded in panic. Why had he left the coach? That damned ostentatious coach, a lure for brigands on a lonely road.

The bridge was not far from the estate. Several miles at the most. Who had been shot? Not his wife. Not Emma. He had told her to stay with the others.

Two figures on foot materialized from the drizzling gloom and fled into the trees. He raised his gun, thought better of wasting his time, and circled around the coach. Another man sprang from beneath the underbelly of the vehicle.

"Lord Jesus, it's you!" Bones exclaimed, lowering his own gun abruptly. "One of them took a shot at me and missed. Stupid bastards."

Adrian stepped over the cloaked body that lay slumped against the rear wheel. Bones had made a decent attempt to cover the body of the man Adrian had felled. One shot meant for Bones that had missed. That was what Adrian had heard. And yet he had to ask, needing reassurance, "My wife, and Lady Dalrymple?"

Before Bones could manage an answer, Adrian practically unhinged the carriage door to check for himself. Three pistols rose in unison from the dark interior. He lifted his free hand in feigned surrender, at the mercy of an amateur infantry comprised of his wife, Lady Dalrymple, and Odham.

He would have laughed if he'd been able to breathe properly. His relief at finding Emma unharmed had made him feel embarrassingly faint-headed.

As an irregular soldier, he had witnessed the horrific acts that unprincipled men could inflict upon the innocent. In truth, he'd defended a village of women from such abuses. But if anyone had dared to defile his elegant wife—he shook his head then and did laugh. His elegant wife who had just leveled a pistol between his eyes as skillfully as she wielded a lace fan.

"Oh, Adrian," she whispered, her regard dark with relief. She launched herself upon him in a belated release of emotion that matched his own. "We were all sick with worry."

He held the bloodied scimitar behind his back until Bones, recovering his own wits, covertly removed it from his master's possession and restored it safely amid the luggage.

His hand thus freed, Adrian slid it around Emma's waist and contented himself with holding her closely, all the while noticing that Hermia had not lowered her weapon.

He buried his face in his wife's warm neck. "A pistol—in your hands, Emma?" He carefully lifted the gun from her grasp. "A very nice pistol, too. It's a Manton flintlock." He glanced up at her in surprise. "I hope Heath didn't ask you to use it against me."

She hesitated, smiling. "No. It came from Julia, with no specific instructions as to whom I should shoot, only that I should use it if needed. I don't need it, do I?"

"No, Emma."

"What about our footman and driver?" Hermia asked worriedly.

Adrian smoothed his hand down Emma's shoulder, knowing he would do anything to keep her safe. He had hoped she would never understand what kind of man he'd been. That there were some things about him that he couldn't change.

"That's them coming now," he said quietly.

"One of the pair is limping," Hermia exclaimed.

Adrian disengaged himself from Emma with regret. "Stay here just in case."

She released her breath as he hurried through the rain with Bones a few steps ahead. The two men who walked toward her looked bedraggled but not afflicted with any mortal injuries that she could discern. The footman appeared, on closer inspection, to be supporting the coachman against his shoulder.

Odham sent her a puzzled smile. "Why didn't you tell him what you saw?"

"He didn't want me to see," she murmured.

"Ah." He nodded, his mood lifting. "I think that you two valiant ladies could do with a bracing pot of tea."

She turned from the window, color returning to her cheeks. "Oh, to hell with tea, Odham. I think we deserve a bottle of porter each."

Hermia laughed in approval. "Well said, my dear. In fact, I think that is the first piece of advice of yours I am tempted to take."

Chapter Nineteen

※

Adrian's brother Cedric overtook them less than a mile from the bridge. A small band of outriders from the estate accompanied him. He explained that he had been waiting at the main crossroads to escort them to Scarfield and was concerned at their delay. He whitened when Adrian explained what had happened during his detour.

"Thank God none of you were killed," Cedric said in distress. "This is not the homecoming any of us envisioned."

Lady Dalrymple stuck her head out the window. "Two of them escaped into the woods. I shall not sleep for weeks."

Adrian took his brother aside. "My coachman took a pistol ball in his upper leg. It needs attention. There is also a body lying back before the bridge that requires a hasty burial."

"You—you *killed* one of them?"

Adrian frowned. "I hope I wasn't expected to shake his hand and ask him to come meet my father.

I think I killed him, Cedric. That is my wife in the carriage. I would have killed every one of the curs had I caught them."

"I see," Cedric said faintly. He blinked several times. "But you didn't—well, you know—"

Adrian stared at his brother. Was this cowed lordling the result of his father's constant brow-beatings? "I didn't what, man? For God's sake, spit it out."

"You didn't, um"—Cedric loosened his spotless white cravat—"behead this man, did you? The papers were full of reports—I only ask so that I may warn the servants what to expect."

Adrian almost laughed. He realized that his family had kept abreast of his exploits. His father's letters had revealed as much. However, he had not expected that they would *believe* every exaggerated account that had been written about him. "Do not worry," he said in a wry undertone. "We can feed the head to my wolf pack at a later time."

Cedric nodded weakly. "You're teasing me. You always teased me, Adrian. It really isn't fair, you know. Florence and I cried inconsolably when you left. I had no one to stand up for me when you went away."

Adrian clasped his brother's arm. "I'm home for now at least," he said. "And if you allow it, I'll stand up for you whenever necessary."

Cedric dredged up a lukewarm grin. "I'll more than allow it. I am glad to see you again, Adrian.

And life here has not been as tragic as I have made it sound. Sad, perhaps, but let us hope that is all behind us."

It was evening when the ducal coach reached the estate under mounted escort. Emma was grateful to seek refuge in the rooms that she and Adrian had been allotted, even if the duke had made a point of asking to see his son alone.

"I know this will be unpleasant," she whispered to Adrian as they stood together in a vaulted entrance ornamented with stags' heads while their luggage was unloaded. "Do your best to remember his age and the respect you owe him."

He stayed at her side until a servant in formal livery arrived to announce that the upstairs rooms had been warmed and made comfortable for the night. Thereupon he launched into a prepared speech about how heartening it was to have the duke's heir home.

For his part Adrian fought a devilish urge to slap the stuffy fellow on the back and beg him to leave off his long-winded welcome. Emma, on the other hand, nodded as if all this formality were her due and followed the chattering little man across the hall.

And suddenly Adrian felt empty, and on edge.

He watched his wife disappear up the dark Jacobean staircase with Hermia and Odham. He had played on those stairs as a child. He had slid down the balustrade with his wooden sword to terrify the servants and his two younger siblings.

Wild little demon, they'd whispered. Son of a whore and a soldier. No one thought he'd come to a good end.

He had returned to reclaim his past. His birthright. He was a ghost, he thought. The boy who'd frolicked in this house had died years ago.

Hermia leaned lightly on Emma's arm as the pair of them ascended the long staircase, Odham and the loquacious footman leading the way.

"The duke has given us an entire wing," Hermia said in approval.

Emma sighed.

By now Adrian had gone to the duke's private chambers across the courtyard. She knew he'd wished her to accompany him. But she had claimed to be exhausted from the day's ordeal. Poor Adrian, she mused. He would probably have preferred to fight off another band of brigands rather than face his father.

Two chambermaids guided her down a hallway lined with tall Venetian-glass mirrors. "Madam," the eldest maid said, "one of us will sleep on the bench outside your door all night should you require anything."

Emma nodded, not truly listening. Hermia and Odham had been assigned separate rooms at the end of the hall. Hermia was already asking the footman to make certain that any connecting doors were locked.

One of the chambermaids swallowed a yawn. "There'll be a pint drunk to Lord and Lady Wolverton's health in the local house tonight."

Emma hesitated, eyeing Hermia coming toward her. It was perfectly unacceptable to prod a servant into repeating gossip, and yet suddenly she could not resist. "Lord Wolverton must have many relatives, close friends, who have awaited his return."

"We're all relieved to have the young master home, my lady," the woman said. Which was a polite reply but lacking the information Emma had hoped for.

"How convivial of them." She came to a halt outside the door. Hermia had paused to admire her reflection in a mirror. "The girls," she prompted, clearing her throat. "The local ladies will be happy to see him again, I suppose."

For a moment the two maids stared back at her with such an absence of comprehension that she could have shouted. "I suppose they will," was the first's formal, unsatisfactory response.

"Heavens above, Emma," Hermia said as she swept toward them. "Do stop dancing about the issue and ask them outright."

Emma frowned. "As tactful as thunder, aren't we, dear?"

"When one advances in age," Hermia said, "one

is disinclined to waste precious time worrying about what others think."

Emma gave her a wry look. "It seems to me that *some* people did not worry about the polite world even when they were young."

Hermia smiled. "Some of us learned our lessons at a tender age, thank goodness. I could not imagine a life more wasted than one dedicated to pleasing others." She directed her attention to two chambermaids who'd most likely been warned how peculiar London ladies could act at times. "What Lady Wolverton wishes to know is whether her husband has any sweethearts awaiting his return."

"Oh." The older of the chambermaids brightened. "*Oh.*"

"I think I'll go to bed now," Emma said. "Thank you for that humiliation, Hermia. I shall pretend that our experience today caused this unspeakable breach of confidence."

Hermia put her hands on her hips. "Do I need a spoonful of treacle to loose that tongue?" she asked the chambermaid. "Is there, or is there not, a young woman hereabouts who wears her heart on her sleeve for your young master?"

The maid nodded slowly. "You mean, Lady Serena? Why didn't you say so?"

Hermia's mouth hardened. "At last. Is this Lady Serena married?"

"Oh, no, ma'am."

Emma ducked her head, then opened the door to a warm firelit chamber. "Good night, everyone."

"Nah," the maid said. "She hasn't had time to marry what with all the work that fell upon her shoulders when her father took sick. Her day'll come soon, I reckon."

The younger maid chimed in. "There ain't a person within twenty miles what don't worship Lady Serena."

"I see," Hermia said, narrowing her eyes. "A paragon. I don't mean to sound unkind, but this lady sounds to be a bit of a spinster."

"All I know is that she's a beauty, ma'am," the second maid answered. "A spot of sunlight on a cold winter day."

Adrian stood for several moments behind his chair and examined his father's oak-paneled drawing room. This had not been a familiar place in his youth. Children had been forbidden to enter the duke's hallowed sanctuary. Now the entire family, his brother and sister, his medieval aunt, even the stooped estate manager, had assembled to greet the prodigal.

The gratitude on their faces, the affection, all older and more important to him than he'd realized, humbled him.

"The young viscount is home," Bridgewater, the bald secretary, said over and over. "Home after all these years."

"Where's he been, anyway?" his great-aunt asked.

His father stared at him, tall, a stone thinner, but still a man who commanded a room. "It doesn't matter where he's been. He's home."

His sister Florence smiled at him warmly. "And brought a wife. Where is she, Adrian?"

"Is she a foreign woman?" his aunt asked. "I hope the English weather doesn't make her ill."

Adrian chuckled. The only good thing he could say of his family meeting Emma was that she would be able to handle them, and with far more grace than he could muster, too.

"Adrian was set upon by brigands at the bridge," Florence explained gently. "He fought them off, Aunt Thea. Everyone is fine, it seems."

The elderly woman nodded in approval. "Foreign brigands, I suppose. Why did you go away, Adrian? I've missed your company so much. Cedric is boring, and Florence has forgotten how to laugh."

Adrian smiled at her. "I've missed you, too."

"What is your wife's name, dear?"

"Emma. Emma Boscastle."

"That doesn't sound very foreign."

The duke, who had been quietly watching this scene unfold, motioned to his estate manager. "Do you mind taking everyone to the conservatory for wine and cake, Bridgewater? Adrian and I will join you shortly."

And then, moments later, Adrian was alone with the duke, still unable to think of him as his father, but not able to dredge up his former hatred, either. He waited in resignation. There was an old picture mounted on the wall of his mother in a riding habit with her beloved spaniel. A deep ache stirred inside him. She had not deserved to die in condemnation.

"You look well," he said to the duke, "for a man who is suffering a terminal illness."

"I could have been dead ten times over in the time you took coming here," the duke retorted.

"I—"

"Don't lie. I have no wish to fight with you. We have too many issues to pound out concerning the estate."

"Are you and Lady Dalrymple truly old friends?" he asked, seeking a more neutral subject.

"Hermia?" The duke's careworn features seemed to soften. "I sought her favor as a callow youth, and lost. It is to your credit that she befriends you." He put his hand to his breastbone, his eyes suddenly dark. "Indigestion, Adrian," he said with a grimace. "Are you done evading the matter of your responsibilities?"

Adrian hesitated. In his memory his father had always been omnipotent, invulnerable, aloof at his best. At his worst, Scarfield had seemed weak-willed and malicious. And now? He could not deny his father had aged and, unexpectedly, he pitied him.

He shifted. "It's been a long day—"

As if he'd been eavesdropping, Bridgewater entered the room bearing a tray of medicine. "It's time for your evening cordial, your grace."

"Do you have nothing better to do with yourself than interrupt me every five minutes?" the duke asked in more resignation than anger.

Bridgewater smiled. He, too, showed the signs of age and service.

Adrian came to his feet. Bridgewater and his family had been devoted to Scarfield ever since, well, according to Bridgewater, ever since the damned Crusades. And although Adrian could not pretend affection for the duke, he did not wish him ill. He was not sure what, if anything, he felt.

"Aren't you in the least bit curious about your old love?" his father asked.

Adrian managed to grin. "My sheepdog is still alive?"

The duke chuckled as Bridgewater hovered at his side with a glass of cordial. "I meant Serena, the girl you were meant to marry."

Adrian raised his brow. "Do not tell me you've convinced her to wait for me."

His father laughed, and suddenly, to Adrian's surprise, some of the awkwardness between them seemed to ease. "To be honest, Adrian, I think Serena has always been more in love with her horses than with you. Now, when am I to be introduced to your bride?"

Adrian met his father's eyes. "Tomorrow."

"A Boscastle," the duke mused. "How did you manage it?"

He shook his head, unable to hide his pride and happiness. "I don't know. But I will confess she is the best thing that has ever happened to me."

"Married and obviously besotted. I look forward to meeting your wife at breakfast."

Besotted.

Adrian locked the bedchamber door behind him and stared at the alluring figure on the bed. There was a book, still open, in her hand.

The candle on the nightstand had burned low. He blew it out, undressed, and crawled into bed beside his wife.

She sat up with a small shriek of protest. "Adrian, you are absolutely freezing!"

He laughed and pulled her back into his arms. "You're very warm," he whispered, burying his hands in her hair.

"What about your father?"

"I don't know. I'd say he tended toward the cold side, but if you're really curious, you could ask Bridgewater."

She arched her brow. "Since you're smiling, I shall assume all went well."

"Well enough. We didn't argue."

She sighed as if she sensed what he'd left unsaid,

then curled herself around his body. "Still, it must feel good to be home."

The warmth of her presence relaxed him. His wife. "It feels good to be here with you. I wouldn't have come back alone."

Her voice deepened to a drowsy whisper. "It's a beautiful estate, Adrian. The park looked like paradise in the moonlight."

He stroked his hand down her spine. "I'll show you the rest of it tomorrow."

"And I suppose I'll meet everyone then?"

He closed his eyes. It *wasn't* home. Too many painful memories lingered, in every room, in every face. "You've already met my brother. Florence and my father are impatient to see the lady who tamed me."

"No old friends showed up for the prodigal's return?" she asked innocently.

"If you mean Serena," he said mischievously, "then no."

She was quiet for a moment. He wished she understood that there never had been, nor would there be, a woman who could compare to her.

"Do you think," she asked after several moments, "that you might like to stay here?"

"In Berkshire, perhaps. I promised you a country school. But not here. Not now."

"I do feel guilty," she whispered, "that I left my duties in London unfulfilled."

"We can leave whenever you wish," he said idly.

He'd never discussed his foreign investments with her. The typical English aristocrat thought earning money to be a vulgar occupation, but the truth was that he could afford to make their home anywhere she desired.

She sat up unexpectedly, leaving him bereft of her pleasingly warm body. "Are *you* in a particular hurry to make a return journey with Hermia and Odham, my lord?"

"That," he said, pulling her back against him with a laugh, "is a thought to give one pause."

Chapter Twenty

❧ ❧

Emma had anticipated that the next day would challenge the sum total of her social knowledge. She had not expected, however, that Adrian would abandon her before breakfast. She could have cheerfully crowned the devil.

He had gone off riding with his brother to survey the estate, which meant she would sit alone with the duke in the private winter room—a retreat so opulently designed it would have befitted a Roman emperor.

The plasterwork ceiling drew the eye to a fresco of mythic scenes depicted on gilded stucco. Her feet sank into the garden of overblown peonies and peacocks of an Aubusson carpet. She surveyed the sideboard with a sigh of approval. Wedgwood plates of classical design and silver tea urns glistened under the guard of six attentive footmen.

Plate-warmers coddled a golden brown roast turkey, and three mince pies, as well as a beefsteak bursting with savory meat and gravy. She sighed happily at the sight of a tureen of piping-hot porridge nestled between tall pots of coffee, fresh cream, and chocolate.

Heaven, she thought. She had expired in her beloved husband's arms and awakened to discover herself in a paradise of elegant living.

The duke rose from his chair, watching her with the intensity of an eagle atop an aerie. If he had expected his daughter-in-law to be intimidated by either his estate or the grandeur of his presence, he was to be disappointed.

For Emma Boscastle was suddenly hurled into her element, the place amidst the stars reserved for her. In truth, she would have been at ease in any of the world's royal courts. The rituals of aristocracy came as easily to her as breathing. On her mother's death, it had fallen upon her to attend the details of her papa's private life. It was a young Emma who had answered cards of condolences, remembered birthdays, reminded her siblings of their manners. She had worked hard to deserve her parents' faith in her.

She dipped into a perfect curtsy before the duke.

He exhaled in pleasure and lifted his arms to welcome her. "Thank God," he muttered. "Oh, thank you, thank you, God."

And Emma, who had lived with five unruly brothers, understood exactly what he meant. Adrian had *not* married an unmannered woman. Despite the questionable foundation of her romance with his son, she was not about to bring disgrace upon the name of Scarfield.

They embraced like long-lost souls, neither with an excessive display of emotion. That the duke had ever doubted Adrian to be his natural son puzzled Emma. Their resemblance to each other was striking. Both men had the same angular face and long-boned build that lent fluid elegance to their every move.

Still, there was a warmth and wicked spontaneity to Adrian that Emma deduced might have come from his mother. But then perhaps the duke was subdued due to some inscrutable illness. As a wiry balding man detached himself from the wall to assist him, Adrian's father seemed to shrink both in strength and personality.

"This is my nursemaid Bridgewater," he said wryly.

Emma took the chair a footman had drawn for her. "You mean your secretary and estate manager, your grace?"

The duke coughed. "Yes. Go, Bridgewater. Bother my children. I wish to be alone with the enchanting lady who has brought my son home." He looked Emma in the eye. "I assume he came at your encouragement?"

Emma made a show of examining her ivory-handled knife. "I only know that he returned home. And that he has a will of his own."

Perhaps their private breakfast was meant to be a

test of her inner mettle. By the time the footmen brought in an assortment of hothouse peaches, pineapples, and early strawberries, she and her father-in-law were discussing the practical affairs of the estate as casually as they would the country weather.

"Adrian's mother had a talent for tallying my accounts," the duke explained wistfully. "I did not appreciate her intelligence at the time. But the woman could balance our books to the penny."

"A practical lady," Emma said in approval.

He chuckled. "She caught the blacksmith cheating us when Bridgewater missed the offense. Of course, she also chastised me when I neglected to pay a laborer."

"And you, being a man of—"

Emma broke off as the side door opened to admit the duke's attentive secretary. Bridgewater took one look at his master and his mouth thinned in dismay. "You are fatigued, your grace."

Emma stared down at her plate. On one hand she felt that Bridgewater acted in too personal a fashion. On the other, she had to agree that the duke appeared more pale and tired than when he had greeted her. Personal concern for his well-being superceded all other observations. She stood decisively.

"I have overtired you, your grace."

"Bloody stuff and nonsense. Bridgewater is a bothersome old woman."

Bridgewater glanced at Emma as if to beg her support. She said, "I admit I am still overwrought myself from the ordeal at the bridge yesterday."

The duke rose. His steely gaze informed her he was not at all deceived.

"My son has exceeded my expectations in choosing you for his wife. I couldn't have dreamt a lady better suited to becoming the next Duchess of Scarfield than you."

Emma went to his side. Bridgewater was steadying his progress to the door. Perhaps it was prideful of her to enjoy his praise.

But she did.

Only for a moment.

"I'm honored to be your son's wife," she said with her hand at his arm. "I love him."

He shook his head in bemusement. "How the deuce he was able to persuade you to marry him—ah, well. He's inherited his mother's charms and will soon inherit my estate. It's a relief for me to go knowing you will advise him."

They walked arm in arm to the door, Bridgewater trailing. "And where exactly do you plan to go, your grace?" she asked lightly.

"Most likely to Hades."

"Not true," Bridgewater said. "Your grace is going upstairs to rest."

"No, I'm not," the duke said irritably. "I'm playing cards with Hermia and Odham. He and I are both passionate for that woman."

"Well, you must not let your passions get the better of you, your grace," Bridgewater said gracefully.

"Stuff it, you old busybody."

Emma bit her lip as the pair of them, clearly forgetting her presence, began to bicker back and forth. She was certain that the duke would not have permitted such familiarity had he not trusted Bridgewater as one did a cousin or close friend.

By the time the three of them reached the dark vaulted hall, she could see that the duke was indeed struggling for breath. She thought of her own father, how she'd believed him invulnerable before his death.

"He's come back just in time, hasn't he?" a soft voice asked her. Adrian's sister came up the stairs behind Emma. "I think there will be peace now for everyone."

Adrian did not return from his ride with Cedric until late afternoon. Windblown, elegantly commanding his mount, he cantered across the park where Emma was walking with Florence. Both women stopped in their tracks and turned as he dismounted and ran toward them. He was as grand as the estate he would inherit.

Before Emma could greet him in a fashionable manner, he picked her up and spun her in the air. "I missed you."

Florence coughed lightly. "Has it been all of six hours?"

"Nine," he replied, setting Emma back on her feet. "And you'll both be relieved to know that there are no brigands in the area."

"That's where you've been, chasing villains?" Emma asked in chagrin. "You really do love danger, don't you?"

He laughed. "I love you."

Her face grew warm. If they had been alone, she would have had a hard time keeping her hands off her husband. He looked irresistibly handsome in his billowing white muslin shirt, molded leather riding breeches, and—

"You've got mud on your boots."

"So I do."

"We're having a formal supper tonight with the family," she said, biting her bottom lip.

His eyes danced with mischief. "Are you suggesting I'm not decent to dine with?"

Indecent. That's what you are. And that's fine with me.

She glanced away. "A bath would not be remiss."

"Oh, good." He closed his black-gloved hand over hers. "We'll take one together. My father has had a huge Roman bath built."

"Adrian," she whispered, "your *sister.*"

He winked at Florence. "She can take her own bath later."

"You haven't changed at all," Florence exclaimed with a delighted grin.

A groom ran forth to take Adrian's lathered

horse. Cedric trotted past them toward the stables, nodding his head to the ladies. A footman greeted Adrian at the entrance portico with a sweeping bow.

"Shall I draw your bath, my lord?" he inquired, his young voice unsteady.

Adrian glanced down at his mud-besmirched boots with a devil-may-care grin. "Are you all in on my wife's plot to make me a presentable gentleman?"

The footman grinned. "A message arrived for you while you were gone, my lord."

"For me?" Adrian asked in surprise. "What have I done now?"

"What haven't you done?" Emma whispered, covertly nudging him away with her chin.

"I don't know," he said under his breath. "If I've missed something, do let me know. My wife is forever eager to further my education."

She gave a delicate cough. "In private, my lord."

He sighed. "What was this message?"

"Lady Serena says she will be delighted to join you for supper tonight," the footman replied.

Adrian smiled uneasily at Emma. "I swear to you, I had nothing to do with this. Do you wish me to tell her that we are unable to receive her tonight?"

"No," Emma answered him firmly. "If she is an old friend, it would be unforgivable to snub her."

Adrian looked doubtful. "I'm not sure that I ever

explained to you the exact nature of my relationship with Serena. But she and I never were the best of friends."

No matter, Emma was determined to behave decently toward her husband's former sweetheart. As Adrian's wife, a woman of noble birth, she would be compassionate, a gracious winner as it were. She would also, in the most polite manner possible, make it absolutely clear that Adrian was taken for life.

At least this was the advice she repeated to herself hours later as she met Hermia outside her room on the way to supper.

Hermia had dressed in full evening regalia, a crepe turban ornamented with a plume of peacock feathers and a gold evening gown underlaid with layers of cream lace. A spidery gauze shawl dangled over one plump shoulder. "How do I look?" she inquired. "And do be honest."

"You shall catch every eye at the table," Emma answered.

"Hmph. I have just heard from the housekeeper that Serena indeed is a raving beauty. I don't believe it, of course, for housekeepers are seldom truthful."

Emma paused. She was underdressed, as usual, in a long-sleeved bisque-satin evening gown with a silk-flowered hem. "Raving beauty or not," she said. "It would be an insult for us to be late to meet her."

Hermia slowed pace as they approached the dining hall. "She has waited for almost a decade."

"I know," Emma murmured.

"Perhaps because no one else would have her," Hermia added, more from defending Emma than unkindness.

Emma held back a smile. "You are indeed a stouthearted lady, Hermia."

"A woman of a certain age acquires an understanding of human actions," Hermia explained with a dismissive smile. "I will even go so far as to predict that Serena has a malicious nature."

Emma laughed in disbelief. Hermia's predictions were as reliable as a gypsy fair girl's. "Oh, really?"

"Those of us with obvious beauty must strive to develop strength of character."

"Did I hear myself mentioned?" Odham asked behind them, offering each lady an arm. "Strength of—"

"Shallow," Hermia went on. "Vapid. And, most likely, selfish."

Odham blinked. "Well, obviously you were not discussing me."

Adrian emerged from his father's study, somber, lean, and attractive in black evening attire. "Is everyone ready to eat? I'm famished."

Emma examined her husband with unhidden pleasure. "Aren't we waiting for our guest?"

He brushed her cheek with a kiss. "Serena? I believe she sent word she'd be late."

"I told you." Hermia nodded her turban-adorned head in satisfaction. "That is a sign of thoughtlessness if ever there was one."

The meal of oxtail soup, roast pheasant, and leg of mutton was once again served to perfection on a pristine white tablecloth. Emma might as well have been eating bits of chalk for all she enjoyed the painstakingly prepared courses. It was too petty of her, she realized, to allow Hermia's predictions to unsettle her.

Lady Serena was almost an hour late.

And when she finally did arrive, everyone in the dining hall—including the six attentive footmen—looked up in silent expectation toward the door.

"A dramatic entrance," Hermia murmured smugly. "Planned to the minute."

A dramatic entrance. Serena managed that and more as she swept into the room. She stood tall and statuesque to Emma's diminutive frame, a brunette, with dark eyes and the enchanting laugh of one who knows she is beautiful. She captivated the attention of everyone in the hall.

"Gollumpus!" she squealed with delight as Adrian rose politely from his chair to acknowledge her.

And then, fortunately before Emma was prompted to say something uncharitable, such as, "Nice of you to join us for dessert," Serena fairly galloped across the room and thumped Adrian on the back with a blow that would have knocked a normal male under the table.

He coughed, raising his brow. "I suppose I deserved that."

"And about ten more," she said gleefully before she glanced around the table. "So sorry we're late. Lady Hellfire needed a good worming, and then the vicar had to change his shirt." She stared past Adrian at Emma in surprise. "Don't tell me *that's* your wife—"

He grinned. "I won't. But she is."

Hermia nearly dropped her wine goblet.

Emma managed to set her glass down beside her plate. Where in the etiquette manual was *this* sort of thing covered? "Yes, I am his wife and I'm so very pleased to make your—"

"Well, blow me over with a feather," Serena said with a guffaw. "I can see straight off that she's too good for you, Adrian. For one thing she's dainty as a dewdrop, and she's got manners. Did you take her captive in one of your harems?"

He folded his arms across his chest. "How did you guess? I brought back a few pirates for you to play with, too."

Serena poked him in the arm. "I don't need a pirate. I've got the vicar now."

"Who's the vicar?" he asked with a derisive smile. "Another horsey?"

"He's my fiancé," she replied. "In fact, if your wife doesn't mind me stealing her thunder, he and I thought we might announce our engagement here tonight. And discuss plans for the charity assembly to raise funds for the village school." She made a belated curtsy in Emma's direction. "All jesting aside, Lady Wolverton, I welcome you on behalf of the parish. I do hope you and I can become friends and work together for the good of Scarfield."

Emma's eyes misted over with an emotional if unseemly response of tears. To be loved by a man of good heart, to be helpful to the disheartened was everything she could ask of life. And she had no rival for Adrian's affection.

Her obligation to the academy must still be met, and the move to the country would benefit everyone. She would never stop worrying about her infamous Boscastle family in London.

But—she was needed here, too. The duke needed his son. Florence needed a husband. And Cedric surely needed a wife.

There followed a merry evening of nibbling on stewed pears with white cheese, Moselle and Bordeaux wines imbibed in a spirit of celebration. The vicar arrived shortly after Serena and apologized that Lady Hellfire had made him late. Odham expressed his deep concern over her ladyship's health until Hermia gently elbowed him and explained that Hellfire was a horse, not a woman.

And although the duke appeared to weary long before his company, he appeared contented when he excused himself for the night.

Emma walked with him to the staircase.

"I don't deserve this happiness, I know," he said, smiling at her.

"If the gifts we are granted came only by our merit, I think we would all be beggars, your grace."

He nodded. "Perhaps he does deserve you. God willing he will not make the same mistakes that I have when it comes to love."

"Fraud," Emma said the moment she and Adrian stood alone in their bedchamber.

"I beg your pardon."

"Your table manners are impeccable."

"Are you complaining?" he asked in mock astonishment.

"Not about your manners, only about your devious nature. You who pleaded for me to instruct you. You were elegance incarnate from your finger bowl to the filbert pudding."

He unknotted his cravat, smiling at her. "What if I said I was merely watching what you did?"

"I wouldn't believe you. And by the way, Adrian, Serena is one of the most beautiful women I've ever met."

He winced. "And one of the most boisterous. I told you she didn't want to marry me. She knows me too well."

"Or not well enough."

He unhooked the back of her gown with his free

hand. Within moments the bisque-satin dropped to her feet. Her undergarments followed.

"By the way, Emma, *you're* the most beautiful woman I've ever met." He kissed the vulnerable curve between her shoulder and collarbone. "Haven't I made that point clear to you?"

Adrian awoke before dawn and walked to the bluff overlooking the estate. Years ago he had often escaped here during one of his father's tirades. Pretending he was a conqueror who commanded an invincible army, he would plot to storm the house and overthrow the duke. Foolishly he had hoped to liberate not only himself but his mother's ghost.

A strong wind rose from the southeast, fighting his stance. He fought harder. He always had. And now—now he wanted peace. He could still walk away. Emma would fuss and insist he meet his duty, but in the end she would support his decision.

He'd sworn he wouldn't stay.

He'd sworn he didn't care what anyone thought of him. He had come back in part to prove to his father that he'd lived a full life without benefit of family or his aristocratic background.

But suddenly he wondered whether Emma had been right all along. He was the duke's son, heir not only to his father's wealth and position, but also to his obligations.

He was no longer a child playing conqueror. He stared across the estate, at the mist-enshrouded lake, the cattle grazing on the hills, and the village beyond. The golden stone manor house dominated the land as it always had. But it too showed signs of age and neglect.

Home.

It wasn't home.

Home was the warrior angel climbing up the hill to meet him, waving his coat in her hands and shouting that he would catch his death standing out here in his shirtsleeves, and didn't he feel the wind?

He took the coat from her hands and wrapped it around her. She was still fussing about something when he pulled her into his arms.

Scarfield needed a guardian.

The guardian needed Emma Boscastle.

"Is anything wrong?" he asked her, resting his chin on her head.

She wriggled out of his arms. "I'll say. I have just gotten a letter from London."

"From?"

"Charlotte and Heath. 'No need to worry,' they assured me."

"Which of course means—"

"—there's something to worry about."

He guided her down the hill, his body shielding hers from the wind. "I don't know why you would assume that."

"Well, Adrian, Miss Peppertree has threatened to resign."

"But she hasn't?"

"Who knows? I've been warned *not* to believe anything I read in the papers about the academy and Audrey Watson's house."

"Who's Audrey Watson?" he asked curiously. "I think I've heard her name before."

"Well, it's to your credit, believe me, that you are not familiar with her establishment. Oh, Adrian. She owns a School of Venus."

He burst into unrestrained laughter.

"Listen to you," she said in a disparaging voice. "That isn't even all of it."

He sobered. "There's more?"

"Yes, and it's so disturbing. Charlotte has expressed a wish to become a writer."

"That sounds harmless enough." He waited a moment. "Doesn't it?"

"Not when she wishes to chronicle the social history of the Boscastle family," Emma said as if he were supposed to have read her mind. And Charlotte's letter.

He whistled, then said, wisely, or so he thought, "I don't know what to say."

"I'll say it for you," Emma said, her color rising. "There are some social histories that should remain secret. There won't be a single chapter, nary a page—a paragraph—that does not detail some scandal."

He glanced up guardedly at the sky, then back at her. Her delicate ears and nose blushed pink from the wind. Her strawberry blond hair had uncoiled from its chignon. She looked a little wild. How he loved his wife. How glad he was to be done with a life of fighting and fevers and wandering about. His future would be breeding a family, perhaps horses, and he would stuff himself every winter on Christmas pudding with a woman who made him wear his coat to keep him warm.

"Let's have a look at the lodge," he said on impulse, taking her hand. "Cedric mentioned it's in dire need of repair and is being used as a barn."

She wrinkled her nose. "A barn? Oh, I don't—"

"It's going to rain, Emma," he insisted. "Can't you feel it in the air?"

"No." she said, lifting her brow. "And I don't see a cloud in the sky, either."

"That's because you're too short to see as high as I do."

She laughed indignantly. "Toplofty, are we, your grace-to-be?"

Toplofty and a lord of temptation.

Several minutes later he'd lured her into the lodge that overlooked the lake. As she was dutifully taking tally of the bolts and beams that needed to be replaced, he advanced on her from behind and gently jostled her onto a bed of straw. It wasn't a fair fight. The woman was half his size, and his motives were inarguably impure.

"What are you doing?" she said in dismay. "I can't go back to the house with hay in my hair."

"I'm the lord of the manor," he said in a gruff voice. "And you're to do what I say."

"And if I refuse?" she asked breathlessly, sprawled out under his shadow.

He frowned. "I might have to spank your soft white backside."

"As if I'd let you," she said, laughing.

He pinned her beneath him. "As if you could stop me."

He settled down and kissed her, his bare hand slipping under her skirt. "Are you an obedient or disobedient servant? There's a vast difference."

"That depends on whom I have to disobey."

"Obey me."

She laced her arm around his neck, smiling wickedly. "Only if you promise not to tell the master about this."

He cupped one cheek of her tempting backside. "We'll keep it our secret, sweetheart. But you can't let on to your husband, either." He closed his eyes, swallowing a groan. "My God, Emma—"

She went very still, whispering, "It isn't my husband we have to worry about. Adrian, let me go. There's a man standing in the door. We've been found."

"A—who is he?"

"I don't know. Does it matter? We cannot be discovered tumbling in a barn."

They disengaged, Adrian swearing to himself,

Emma looking embarrassed as the intruder strode up to them with a pitchfork in his hands.

"Excuse me," the middle-aged arrival said in a wry voice. "I'm Robin Turner, the lodgekeeper. Can I be of service to the pair of you?"

Adrian whisked Emma to her feet. "As a matter of fact, this is my wife and we're—"

"The new help?" the grizzle-haired keeper guessed. His dark eyes softened with empathy. "Well, 'tis a hell of a way to start service, but I suppose there's no harm done as long as you're presentable when you meet the duke. His heir is come home and we're all to be on our best behavior."

"You're a generous soul, sir." Adrian stood in front of Emma so that she could straighten her skirt and smooth away the pieces of straw that clung to it. "I'll try to repay the favor."

The lodgekeeper shook his hand. "Go on, both of you. Just do the job you're hired to do. I'm not so ancient that I don't remember—oh, hell, get out of here. I'll say nothing of this to the master."

And he didn't.

Not even when, only two hours later, he met with the duke to discuss what repairs were needed on the estate's outbuildings, and was introduced to Lord and Lady Wolverton.

Adrian thought he and his new ally Turner did a convincing job of pretending not to know each other, despite the fact that Emma winked saucily over her shoulder to the lodgekeeper as he turned to exit from the hall. Adrian's mouth dropped. Turner nearly walked into the wall.

The duke gave a puzzled laugh. "Have I missed something?"

"Emma and I made an inspection of the lodge earlier today," Adrian said evasively, his gaze lingering on his wife. "Isn't that what you wished for us to do?"

"Do you know what I wish for before I die?" the duke asked, a canny gleam in his eye. "Come along with me for a minute. I'll share my final request with you, Adrian."

Later that same evening, Adrian laid preoccupied in bed with his wife, she tossing and turning until he finally glanced down at her and asked, "Do you have something on your mind?"

She surfaced from the depths of the Queen Anne pinewood bedstead and asked, "Do you?"

He slid beneath the covers until they were nestled together, his hand curled around her hip. He enjoyed sleeping thus, his body protecting hers. "Explain."

"Your father's dying wish," she said in concern. "Is it something you are honor-bound to keep secret?"

"Actually, no."

He rested his chin against her cheek. Her body tempted him, her spine arching beneath his hand, her skin soft as cream. She waited. So did he, a smile he could not hide surfacing at her question.

It seemed that he'd fought this moment from the day he had run away from Scarfield.

He was stronger now, his only need, his only weakness the woman in his arms.

And finally that woman drew away from him and demanded, "Then are you going to lie here smiling at me all night, or give me my answer?"

"He would like us to present him with a grandchild before he dies. He's stubborn enough to see his request fulfilled, too."

"I see," Emma said, her voice reflective. "And what did you tell him?"

He cleared his throat. "I assured him that we were doing our part to perform that ducal duty."

"You didn't," she whispered, laughter in her voice.

"Yes, I did. But not in detail."

She ran her hands down his lean, muscular flanks. "A duke always keeps his promises."

His mouth captured hers. "I'm only a duke's son. Do you suggest an interim form of etiquette to satisfy the situation?"

She closed her hands around the thick column of his manhood, climbing atop him. He lay back on the bed, staring up at her, his breathing suddenly uneven.

"Practice," she said with a taunting smile. "Hours and hours—no, days and nights of diligent practice."

He laid his hands upon her thighs, his manhood swelling in her fine-boned fingers. With a soft moan of pleasure, she balanced on her knees and guided his engorged penis into her moist cleft.

And sank slowly downward, impaling herself to the hilt. "My diligent wife," he murmured, his hips surging so that she gasped and would have fallen back had he not wrapped his arms around her arse to steady her.

She groaned in slow-rising pleasure. "Adrian—"

"You'll have to forgive me," he muttered as he pumped his hips harder, "but there's really no polite way to do this."

Thus the future Duke and Duchess of Scarfield applied themselves to fulfilling their most important ducal obligation. In Adrian's wicked estimation, the fulfillment could not be drawn out long enough. As his wife had said, details meant everything, and one must practice to do a decent job.

A little duke's heir would need brothers and sisters to keep him company. After all, Emma enjoyed nothing more than taking care of others. She'd grown up with six siblings. Even if Adrian had played a sneaky trick on her brothers to win her, a trick that might easily have backfired, he was grateful that her guardian demons had kept the predators at bay until he had found her. Or she had found him.

Leaning forward, her rosy nipples teasing his

chest, she took his mouth in a sweet, sensual kiss. He rocked harder into her body. She rose with each thrust and rode him until he exhaled in an agony of pleasure.

"If this is a duty"—He closed his eyes, groaning as her buttocks slapped down against his groin. Pearly moisture seeped from her cleft to dampen his stones—"may I die fulfilling it."

She straightened her spine, her body undulating, splintering, so beautiful and uninhibited that he could not stave off his own climax for another instant. "I love you," she said. "And I will love our children—"

"I love you, Emma," he whispered as he fastened his hands around her bottom and flooded her with his seed. A son. A daughter. Duty or desire. It did not matter to him as long as he had his dainty dictator to keep all of them in line.

A minute or so later they broke apart. Untangling limbs and bedclothes, they kissed once or twice before settling back into bed.

"In the end," she whispered, wrapped tightly in his arms, "it all comes down to family. And you've certainly married into one of the most—"

"—loyal and loving families in England?" he finished for her.

She smiled. "I was actually going to say infamous."

He looked down at her, his eyes brimming with

love. "In that case, I'd say there is little reason to expect propriety from the next generation."

"I think we'll manage," she said, smiling in contentment.

He laughed. "I can manage anything as long as I have you."